The Sixth Floor

To Camrie
Just Because

The Sixth Floor

a novel by

Gary DeSantis

ACKNOWLEDGMENTS

My most sincere and grateful thanks to my wife, Kathy, who encouraged, advised, and listened patiently. To my daughter Shannon whose deft editing and perfect ears and eyes for dialog, brought reality to sometimes disjointed and poorly articulated thought. Her extensive work should qualify her as a co-writer. To my daughter Morgan for giving sound advice, counsel and technological skills, where they were needed the most. To Michele Carlotti, who introduced sound grammar and punctuation and labored mightily to instruct me on the use of a comma and semi-colon. Thank you also to Keith MacMurray who provided valuable final proofing and expert advice on content and sound expression. My gratitude is also extended to all the unfortunate "first readers," for their opinions, time, and encouragement. Finally, a hearty "thank you" to the Rinella family for the use of their grandfathers beautiful name.

PROLOGUE

Paris, July 1990

Attorney Bertrand Matisse opened the manila envelope carefully. His silver letter opener glided easily through the flap. Four neatly typed pages fell onto his mahogany desk.

He read,

November 15, 1962

Monsieur Matisse,

If you are reading this, there are two possibilities. The first is that I have "mysteriously disappeared" and suffered a premature death. The second, and most desirable of course, is that I have died of natural causes, hopefully at an advanced age. If the former is the case, please take these contents to the Police. If the latter is the case, do whatever you wish with what is enclosed. Please accept the enclosed payment as my gratitude for keeping this in your able care, and please be assured that I swear on my eternal soul to the veracity of the contents. It all began......

Sincerely,

Luc Lavalle

CHAPTER ONE

Chicago, 1962

He laughed as he considered the cherubic-faced Sister Rita Grace, her voice droning as her wooden pointer tapped the blackboard, "Remember students, all good essays must have the following elements......."

Peter Rinella smiled because, despite her angelic appearance, Sister Rita Grace wouldn't hesitate to turn that pointer on a student if he veered slightly out of line and she didn't give a damn about leaving marks on the poor kid's body. Her rosy cheeks looked like two red apples. When those apples changed to dark crimson it was a sure sign that something bad was about to happen.

"Want another cup of coffee?" Peter vaguely heard over his thoughts.

"Yeah, I guess maybe a half cup, thanks."

The waitress looked interesting, but was not interested. Her breasts were full and her face attractive. He smiled to himself again because he realized that the older he got, the harder it was for a woman to be unattractive.

His thoughts moved lazily and aimlessly. He was stuck in a little restaurant in Chicago. The only distraction, other than his thoughts, was a two day old newspaper. The headlines announced the visit of the president. The purpose of his visit to Chicago was the dedication of the new Federal Office Building. Everyone knew that the president was in Chicago to curry the favor of the pain in the ass mayor—Richard Daly. Peter Rinella, a 54 years old FBI agent, was assigned to provide security for the president. Legally, protecting the president was the mandate of the Secret Service and not something assigned to the Bureau. J.Edgar Hoover, however, the constant self promoter, grabbed power from any agency he could. Security for the president fell into FBI's mission of anti-espionage, organized crime investigation and "internal security." Peter worked alone to improve his effectiveness in the field but also because the Bureau had no authority for presidential protection. It was difficult to justify large resources for something the F.B.I. wasn't supposed to be doing. However, Peter had priority use of the FBI field offices and could utilize field agents when he needed them.

He was oblivious to the greasy little restaurant, the waitress, Chicago, and November 1, 1962. He looked into the gray-dull mirror opposite the counter and saw an image of himself he recognized, but nonetheless surprised him. His eyes were deeply set in a face that was no longer its clear olive color but now had a strange yellow jaundice. His hair was thinning and even when combed to the side, his scalp peeked through and his nose had become more prominent. *Jesus Christ, even my goddamn ears seem to stick out more. I'm starting to look like an old owl.*

He didn't like looking at his reflection and quickly looked down to the floor. As he rose from the counter, he noticed how even that small movement was difficult. His stomach spilled over the top of his belt and he couldn't see his shoes.

The wind froze his face on the walk back to the Roosevelt Hotel.

"Can you spare a buck?" a street beggar implored as he thrust out a filthy woolen stocking cap.

Peter was startled and angry at the intrusion, but still fished-out a dollar bill and threw it in the cap, making sure not to touch any of the soiled fabric.

"Thanks man," replied the beggar, with no real appreciation as he waited for his next mark.

The pan-handlers hat made him think, *I gotta remember to bring my hat when I'm in this ice-box.*

The front of his skull was getting numb. He thought the hotel was closer and his discomfort slowed perceptual time; it took forever to arrive at the hotel.

The stately Hotel Roosevelt finally appeared with its bronze pillars and smoked glass lobby. Inside the elevator was a Negro female operator in a pressed navy blue uniform. The smell of her baby powder and the elevator's hydraulic fluid enveloped him. The operator asked, "What floor, please...sir... what floor?"

Peter came to with the second question. "Ninth." he replied.

The operator pulled the lever and the car rocketed upward and forced the blood from his barely thawed brain to his stomach and then came to a lurching stop. *How can they stand that for eight hours going up and down? Losing your goddamn stomach every four seconds?*

Room 914's television was connected to "Roosevelt-vision," that brought in two stations from Milwaukee as well as the three Chicago stations. After he flicked the TV on, he reclined on the bed and thought about how difficult presidential security was. As he stretched out his legs, his mind slipped away.

CHAPTER TWO

Meadville, 1940

He was reclining on a small rug outside their bathroom. He heard his wife's gentle voice,

"You are such a good girl to tell mommy you had to go to the potty. Cam you're a big girl, huh?"

He could see his daughter's chubby legs and worn scuffed white shoes. He couldn't make out every word she was saying, but he could catch a few words mixed in with giggles and shrieks. Suddenly, out of nowhere he heard her high pitched voice scream, "Tinks mommy...... it tinks."

He never imagined he would take pleasure in his child's toilet training, but now it was a matter of pride. After all, the kid was barely eighteen months and she could talk, walk, and use the potty. Those were great accomplishments.

He heard his wife laugh loudly, "Yes, honey, it stinks. That's why we use the potty instead of our pants."

His mind returned him to his hotel room. The small insignificant memory reminded him of how much he missed and grieved for his daughter. Three years later and his consciousness was still covered by the dark, lilac of grief and despair. He had lost his daughter, his wife had left him, and he barely had a relationship with his son. Depression and anxiety stalked him and only by strength of will, was he able to stay ahead of them...sometimes. He had to force himself to think of another time and place.

CHAPTER THREE

Meadville, 1914

The temperature was below zero and the morning was illuminated with suspended snow crystals. Peter Rinella, like most six year old boys was oblivious to what was going on in Europe, but Giacomo Rinella, his father, wasn't. January had emerged with a polar fury that Meadville, Pennsylvania had seldom seen.

Giacomo was explaining to his son, "Pietro, when da Italians get into da war, those goddama French and the Ingles are funito."

Peter later realized that the Italians were in the war, had been on both sides and had done no harm to their enemies. As a child, he didn't understand what his father was saying, and he didn't care. He was secure in his father's strong grip as they plowed through the blowing snow. They entered "Rinella's Leather Goods" and smelled the warm, enveloping odor of his father's trade. He was safe in the shop with his father. When he thought about going to school, his stomach tightened and thoughts of the black clad nuns actually brought beads of perspiration to his forehead. Looking back, Peter would realize how odd it was that a six year old could fret so much.

"Pietro, come here. Pietro," his father called to him.

Peter gladly returned to his father's safe world—back from the awful fear of the nuns in their stark black and starched white habits.

"Look, Pietro, at the leather hide. See how nice it feels and how it rolls so nice?" Giacomo did with leather what a great painter or sculptor did with their materials, but Peter didn't really see what his father was talking about. He just agreed. He wanted to stay in his father's wonderful, secure world. A clanging heating pipe brought Peter instantly back to Chicago, 1962. *Let's watch some T.V. and see what's goin' on in Chicago.*

It was a fairly new, white plastic cased model with a golden "Zenith" emblazoned on the front. His mind again, uncontrollably, reverted to his youth.

CHAPTER FOUR

Meadville, 1920

The steps to the funeral home were steep. The front door opened before they even touched the knob. Peter heard a voice come from a short stocky man, with eyebrows that formed one continuous arch.

"Hello, Jack, come in please. Hello Petey," he heard the voice say. No one ever called him 'Petey' or his father 'Jack.' "Your wife is ready. Come in and see how you like what I've done."

As they passed one of the viewing rooms, Peter could see a coffin at one end of the space. The heavy odor of flowers wafted toward them in the hallway. The walls were lined with flowers and surrounded a bronze coffin. Peter's father told him this was how the "Americans" showed their dead. Peter's mother was to be laid out in their home. Her coffin wasn't fancy bronze, but a simple wooden one. His mother's face was drawn tightly across and painted in a perpetual grimace. The cancer initially attacked her liver, spread quickly and, before it killed her, made her suffer. She begged to die and escape the intolerable pain. Giacomo and Peter were helpless in the ugly presence of the cancer, as it destroyed wife and mother inch by agonizing inch. All either could do was pray for her death. At last, she slipped into a deep, painless sleep. Her body convulsed, but she was oblivious to any pain. Her breathing became irregular and every next breath seemed to be in doubt and, finally, she was gone.

Peter's aunt Carmella picked out his mother's finest dress. The undertaker was an Irishman named O'Dell. His face was as red as an over ripe tomato and punctuated by a bulbous, vein lined nose. When he brought the coffin to the house, he and his assistant, a burly Slovak, with one eye, huffed breathlessly getting the pine box up the steps.

"You know, Jack," spoken with a heavy Irish lilt, "I made her look real good. The poor lady suffered, eh? Oh, by the way, I'll need my payment before I leave today. No offense, of course, but you gotta realize that some of you people have beaten me and the Polack here out of our fees."

Giacomo was silent. He reached into his wallet and handed O'Dell the negotiated $375.00. Peter sat silently next to his father. When no one was around, he touched his mother's hand and was struck by its cold, hard feel. This was his first meeting with death and his sorrow mixed with fear.

Hundreds of pounds of food and drink arrived daily with the mourners. His hunger had vanished with his mother's life. His sorrow ebbed, only to overwhelm him in the next instant and squeeze the breath from his chest. Mrs. Cappilinno, one of his mother's friends, appeared dressed in somber clothes, smelling of her kitchen. She paused briefly to exchange something in Italian to Peter's father and rushed to the coffin screaming and praying simultaneously. She turned to Peter and crushed him into her breasts and said something he didn't understand.

The morning of the funeral appeared black like the dark-clad pall bearers. The sun disappeared in a gray sky. The six pall bearers slowly lifted the coffin. Mr. Pelullo, a short, rotund barber who was Giacomo's friend, grunted with exertion. They moved out of the parlor and through the narrow hall leading to the front steps.

"Be careful, don't drop her," O'Dell muttered.

Giacomo cringed as the men barely squeezed through the narrow dark hallway. Peter heard one of the pallbearers utter, "ah fungul" as he tried to maneuver the heavy coffin around the lights. Finally they made their way down the front steps where the black Packard hearse was waiting with its back door open. O'Dell, with his black suit jacket open to accommodate his protruding belly, was at the side of the hearse. His derby hat was cocked to the side and an unlit cigar planted in his mouth and he said,

"Easy now boys—let's slide her in nice and easy. OK, fellas get in the car up there… don't forget to wipe your goddamn feet before you get in."

The procession made its way up the muddy hill to the Irish cemetery, where the Italians were allowed to bury their dead in one of the back dark corners. They made their way to the grave tucked in a mossy clearing of the cemetery. After a few prayers in Italian, the wooden box descended into the soil. Peter wanted to scream in anguish, but was distracted by a guttural moan so deep, he would never forget it. It was his father's, and it was the first and last time Peter saw him cry in sorrow.

CHAPTER FIVE

Meadville, 1920

After his mother death, Peter could hardly bring himself into the parlor where she was laid out.

"Pio", his father snorted, "what are you afraid of? If you stay outa da parlor you shudda stay outa da whole goddama house. You momma wasa everywhere."

Logic finally prevailed and Peter eventually returned to the parlor. Giacomo made arrangements for his niece, Estella, to move in and take care of the household. At first Peter was angered by her presence, but eventually, he accepted her. She cleaned as well as his mother and cooked a little better. Peter felt strange emotions when he was near her. He didn't know what to make of them. He found her large hips attractive and her hair, when not in a bun, and resting on her broad dark shoulders, was beautiful. When he was near her, he felt activity in his groin. He had pangs of guilt for these thoughts, but he couldn't restrain them. He would wait for her to get into the bath tub and try to peek through the door. The door was always locked and a towel placed over the keyhole. One evening, though, she forgot to lock the door, Peter slowly pried it open. Her breasts were full and punctuated by large pink nipples. Her waist flared into hips that resembled half moons. Between her legs, he was surprised to see the thickest, darkest hair he could have ever imagined. He had no idea that women had hair between their legs. He was about to explode in excitement.

He confessed his actions to a priest, once on a first Thursday of the month, and the priest scolded him for spying on Estella and for touching himself. For a short time, Peter restrained himself, but eventually gave in to the remembrance of Estella's luscious naked body. Peter would always find women a powerful attraction and an inscrutable enigma.

CHAPTER SIX

Meadville, 1918

Reading was easy, but math escaped him completely. Any sort of mathematical deduction was impossible and Peter never seemed to improve. He was relegated to the "wren" math group. Wrens were the "dumb kids" who had to get special attention. The longer he was in the wrens, the deeper Peter's despair and anxiety grew, which made the work even more impossible.

Peter also felt a strange undercurrent in the predominately Irish Catholic school. The sisters treated the Italians differently. The fairer Irish kids were able to pay full tuition. Peter and the other Italians were on subsidy because the four dollars per month was more than they could afford. The Italians heard the Irish, German, and Polish talk about the "greasy, dark," Italians. Some were outright abusive. Gerhardt Kunsel was the worst.

"Hey dago, what are you going to do tonight---make some garlic pizza bread?" Or "Wop, you stink like the cat shit cheese you guineas eat---how's come you garlic snappers don't take baths?!!!"

Gerhardt taunted in front of large groups, just out of ear shot of the nuns. None of the Italian kids had the courage to confront him or the others. When things were especially difficult in school, Peter would think of Estella at home and her wonderful breasts and fleshy thighs. Thank God, the days in public high school were blessedly uneventful and totally forgettable.

In the hotel room, forty years later, Peter was still angry about those days at St. Brigid's. Suddenly, he felt his knuckles burning—*god damn it*—as the cigarette stuck to his lips and his fingers raked over the burning end. He hated that more than the cigarette paper peeling his lips. *Christ, I gotta quit these things.*

The pain brought him back to the dingy hotel room but the anger over the days in elementary school hung tenaciously; *they might as well have had two groups for Christ's sake; the ugly ducklings and the swans. At least they wouldn't have been beatin' around the bush about who the chosen ones were.*

CHAPTER SEVEN

Chicago, 1962

Chicago was the center of mob activity in America. The ass-holes in Washington thought Peter's ethnicity would give him some insights into the whole Mafia milieu. *What a joke, because I'm Italian I've got some connections?* He did, however, proceed as though he did, knowing it could advance his career.

The Bureau had compromised a middle level capo who'd hinted at a plot against the president or his brother. Bobby Kennedy raised the ire of some Mafioso's with his attacks on them and their boy, Jimmy Hoffa.

Hoffa had strong ties with the mob in Chicago. It was the mafia dons in Chicago who supported the Kennedy candidacy, and, for all intents and purposes, delivered Chicago and the state of Illinois. The Kennedy's turned their back on the "wise guys" who had done so much for the Kennedy campaign. Pete heard rumors that certain Mafia dons wanted to "whack" Bobby Kennedy, but he was unable to verify anything. The Secret Service might have relevant information, but either was unable or unwilling to share any leads with the FBI, and this reinforced Peter's resentment of the Secret Service.

He inhaled the Pall Mall. And, as the smoke hit his lungs, he considered threats to the president. A clear danger was either organized crime or the Cubans, who were angry about how Kennedy had deserted them at the Bay of Pigs. Everybody had a bitch with the President. Peter's mind was all over the universe. Thoughts and ideas darted in and out and in again. Sometimes the ideas registered on his consciousness, but more often than not, an idea never left a mark on his memory or thinking. He looked out his hotel window and the setting sun nearly blinded him. It reminded him of a blinding sun on a very bright March day in Germany.

CHAPTER EIGHT

Germany, 1945

"Schnell, schnell!!!!"

The little Puerto Rican screamed at the bedraggled German guards with the lightning shaped SS insignias across their shoulders. Looking at Peter, Despuerto muttered,

"This is the master race? They liked it a lot better when they were in charge, didn't they?"

In case they didn't understand what he was screaming, he motioned violently with his carbine toward the gate in the middle of the barbed wire fence. Slowly, the Germans opened the gate doors beneath a sign that read "Arbeit Mach Frei." The eighteen captured Germans and the lead element of Patton's Third Army walked on the camp's brown clay.

"What's the sign mean?" Peter asked out loud.

Someone answered,"Work Makes Free."

The fearful captives and the equally frightened captors, edged toward a long barn-like building.

"What the fuck smells? Holy shit, it stinks in here," whispered Hoyle, a 20 year old Kentuckian.

The smell was a mixture of rotting meat, burned hair, and a sharp acrid acid stench. It hung over the group like a pall. Captain DeLuc, a Cajun from Louisiana, leaned over to Jacob Levinson, the kid from Syracuse, and murmured, "Tell 'em to kick the goddamn door open. If they give you any shit, tell 'em we'll shoot 'em right fuckin' here. I don't know what's on the other side, but if somebody's gonna get shot, it aint gonna be us."

In German, Levinson instructed the captives to open the doors. Without hesitation, one of them opened the black wooden door. No one moved.

DeLuc muttered, "Tell 'em to walk in now, goddamn it—now —what are they waitin for!!!"

Levinson passed the command to the weary, beaten Germans.

"One sideward move and we'll blow their asses back to Berlin. Move in slowly behind 'em. Keep 'em between us and what's inside this shit hole," said the terrified DeLuc.

The group made its way into the long building. It was impossible to see because of the total darkness of the room and the bright sunlight from which they came. Eventually, they made out forms sprawled out on long benches, stacked three-high, and running the entire eighty feet of the building.

"Christ, these are people," Peter heard himself say.

He heard muffled cries. The bodies moved in slow motion as they tried to raise their heads, which were larger than their bodies. Eyes the size of plates, but black as coals, peered at their former captors and their liberators—some were completely naked, genitalia hanging loose. They were black and grimy.

One man got up slowly and was wearing only a pair of striped pants. Every rib was exposed as he walked toward DeLuc. He had only three teeth. He raised his bony arms to the Cajun and one tear coursed down his face. When he got to the American, he collapsed in his arms.

CHAPTER NINE

Port of Calais, 1944

Peter and his comrades hated the army and the war. The desolation of being away from his family was nearly more than he could bear.

Despuerto mused, "What are any of us doing in this goddam place?"

He looked toward Perkins and said, "I don't get why you ended up with the rest of us dumb asses. Couldn't you have got a deferment? Shit, Perkins, you coulda had a cake walk with some blond girl back home, shuffling papers."

Peter didn't fight his draft classification either, even though he might have been able to claim a family hardship. The country was whipped up in a national hysteria over the war effort and, though he resisted an impulse to enlist, he didn't fight getting drafted. Basic training and the miserable red clay of Fort Bragg North Carolina tested his physical and mental endurance. All the recruits hated the red soil, the interminable heat, and the terrible food. Their shared misery united them in a familial bond.

Peter was proud of his performance in the obstacle course and that he survived its live ammunition. All of them performed about the same in the Obstacle Course, all except Randall Perkins. Perkins glided through the barbed wire. He was totally unfazed by the machine gun shells zipping over his head. Perkins had pure athletic skills and a brilliant mind to match. Peter like Despuerto, would often think, "*What's this guy doing here with the rest of us?*"

Randall Perkins could have easily avoided the mess. His father was an executive with the Willy's-Overland Corporation, manufacturers of the "Jeep." Randall could have had a management position in the company that built the military vehicle and gotten an easy deferment. The more he knew Perkins, the more Peter grew to respect him. All the men respected Perkins, but had a hard time understanding him.

His response to the deferment question was simple, "Well, to be honest, I gave it some thought and probably could have gotten one, but I don't know, I think I must've been nuts. I guess I just didn't want to spend the war in South Bend Indiana making Jeeps."

14

"No," said Peter." You couldn't do that, but you sure as hell could have picked a better place than in George Patton's Third Army."

He remembered how he and Perkins were lined up in France with other men of the Third Army. On a small podium, Patton stood wearing a silver helmet, riding-boots, and pearl handled revolvers strapped to his side.

Peter heard himself mutter, "What an asshole," and he heard Perkins laugh and say, "He's an ego maniac—he thinks he's the center of the fuckin' universe."

From the cone-shaped speakers Patton's voice boomed, "You are here today for three reasons: First, because you are here to defend your homes and your loved ones. Second, you are here for your own self respect because you would not want to be anywhere else. Third, you are here because you are real men and all real men like to fight."

At that moment, the man next to Peter blurted, "What's he talking about?! I can think of a lot of goddamn places I'd rather be than in this shit hole with this jackass tellin' me what a REAL man does and don't do."

Peter looked at the tall, thin, blond guy who was probably six foot two and not 190 pounds. He had a day's growth of beard—maybe older... blond guys didn't have to shave every day like the dark Italians did—his sandy hair jutted from the front of his helmet and just grazed his tanned forehead.

"Well, maybe the asshole is right, but I wish ta hell I didn't haf ta listen to his goddamn bullshit when pretty soon some guy will be tryin to plug my ass!!"

This was Peter's introduction to Wendell Forrester. Though not as tall as Randall Perkins, he was more handsome. He regaled his tired comrades about his encounters with the girls back home in West Virginia.

Perkins, Forrester, and Despuerto were the best friends Peter made during this miserable time, and, maybe forever. Peter was with the three of them on the same day, in the same ugly place, and shared the same loathing for General George Patton.

CHAPTER TEN

The Ardennes Forest, 1944

Snow was falling in flakes the size of a man's thumb and Peter knew from his experience back home how this kind of snow would accumulate quickly. They marched all day behind the tanks and artillery carriers and eventually would get a turn for a ride in the back of the troop carriers. There wasn't enough transport for the entire Third Army so some of the dog faces marched while others rode.

Forrester leaned toward his comrades, "In West Virginia we got weather like this—only a lot worse. Yea we do. Sometimes it'll snow for weeks in them mountains and the only thing that'll save the day is the taste of a good lookin' woman. I was with Betsy McCarthy fer three days once. No shit, I did everythin' to that po girl but tie her to the bed. Shit, maybe I done that too. She hollered so much from cumin' her voice was hoarse."

Despuerto replied,"Bullshit! You asshole! You probably held the poor girl prisoner and she screamed to get some help from your ugly ass. They shoulda thrown you in jail fer kidnappin', fer Chris' sake."

Oblivious to Despuerto, Forrester continued, "Ya know ta be honest...I can do it once a night with the same girl but if you could give me three different ones...yea I bet I could take care all three in one night. Yea...I'm sure I could."

Peter and Randall looked at Forrester and didn't say a word as they slogged through the mud and snow of the Belgian woods. After a few minutes Perkins finally asked, "Wen, if you had so much experience with women, why is it you still have a dick between your legs? I mean, how come you haven't worn the damn thing off?"

Forrester seriously replied, "Ya know, Mr. Perkins, a fine musical instrument is made ta play and play. At first, I kinda tuned it myself but decided later ta let some a the ladies get chance at it—if ya know what I mean? After all who'd ever wore out a Stradivari by playin it a lot?"

No one replied to Forrester's ramblings. The only thing they considered was the frigid temperature and their exhaustion. Despuerto finally asked aloud, "Why are we doin this? I mean what is the purpose of this goddam marchin'. Jesus Christ, I think we're goin 50 fuckin' miles a day. "

"How come they gave us these leather boots?" Peter asked. "Have those ass-holes ever walked in goddam mud as thick as shit and as cold as ice with leather boots!!!?"

They looked around and hoped a Sherman tank might be making progress to the lead so that they could hitch a ride and sit close to the exhaust pipes to get some heat. Perkins murmured just loud enough for all to hear—almost a whisper above a pant—"Patton has to get us to a place where the 101st is holed up and circled by the Germans. Rumor has it, the Germans are trying to break out and get to Antwerp. Of course, Patton will take the challenge as long as he is in a jeep and we are busting our asses marching 30 miles a day."

Forrester countered, "Well ya got to give it up to him, he sure got balls. He ain't 'fraid of a goddamn thing, the fuckin' jack ass."

"What bothers me most about Patton," Perkins panted again, "is that he is one of those people who never considers the possibility of being on the wrong side of judgment. They're dangerous. They are so sure of being right, they'll pay any price. That kind of person scares me."

Despuerto spoke, "Guys, I am so tired. I thought I was cold, but I'm actually more tired and hungry than cold. Are the assholes goin to feed us or are we gonna have to eat those shitty K-rations again?"

"Yeah, I could really go for a warm meal," Peter offered. "Do you think we'll ever get one?"

"No. Not as long as Patton has us moving this fast. They don't have time to set up mess tents and get supplies to them," Perkins answered.

Lester Peterson, a 2nd lieutenant just out of college, moved back toward his charges. "Men, as soon as the sun goes down, we're going to set up camp. Maybe set up a few salamanders to get warm and get something to eat."

Salamanders were fifty-five gallon drums of diesel fuel as a starting source with wood and scraps. They stunk, but were a quick, portable source of heat. All of them were happy at the thought of some heat, but happier with the prospect of getting a few hours sleep.

CHAPTER ELEVEN

Chicago, 1962

Peter's mind came back to his dull room in Chicago. He had to make some calls and see what the locals had on the capos. Peter knew "la familigia" had some issues with the President. He also knew the strife between the mob and the Kennedys had escalated, but to the exact degree he was uncertain. The local cops arranged a meeting with Tony Manzini. Manzini and Peter met in the same greasy spoon that had become Peter's "headquarters." At a booth, they rested their elbows on an oily table top. Peter raised his cup to his lips and smelled the restaurant in it. Manzini's appearance was no surprise to Peter. He looked Italian. Peter judged him to be about 5'7" or 5'8" and 230 or 240 pounds. Manzini carried most of his weight in his stomach. His skin was olive and illuminated by light green eyes. His hair was thinning and combed over to hide the baldness. His fish- like lips were a light pink and hung just below a broad nose. He had three chins that vibrated with his voice. He was an almost completely stereotypical Italian."So how'd you get in the Mafia?"

Not looking up, Tony replied,"My uncle was a soldier forever. He helped me with the connections. I would hang around the social club and fetch beers for guys and, little by little, they gave me more shit to do. I would pick up numbers money and little shit like that. I got put in charge of prostitution and then they let me run some dope. I was honest and turned in every dime I got, and never sampled what we were hawkin', except for the girls, sometimes. They don't care much about that. I got made when I was 25. I don't care what anybody says, these guys are my family."

Peter had to ask, "So how come you're talkin' to me now?"

"I'm here because your cop buddy, Flavio, asked me to meet you."

Peter responded,"Appreciate it. My name's Peter Rinella; I'm assigned as a special agent in the Internal Security Section of the FBI. Part of my job is the safety of the president and he's going to be visiting with Daly in about two months, and I have to make sure he gets out of here with his balls between his legs. We know some big guys are ticked off at him and his brother and I'm trying to find out if they're a danger to President Kennedy. That's it in a nutshell."

18

Manzini sipped his coffee and was silent. He looked Peter in the eyes, still not speaking, only sipping his coffee. Finally after a few minutes Manzini said, "I don't know nothin' about that shit except that there might be some hurt feelings here or there. I can tell you John Kennedy has been sleepin' with Sam Giancana's girlfriend for almost a year."

Giancana was "il capo de tuti," the boss of bosses, and rumor had Kennedy in bed with Judith Exner—Gianacana's former girlfriend.

"So Sam is pissed that Kennedy is bangin' his girlfriend?" Peter offered.

"Fuck no," Manzini whispered in his cup. "He couldn't give two shits about that cunt. I think Sam wants her in D.C. with Kennedy. I think she might be tippin' him off on what the president and his brother are up to. I don't know shit about whether anybody is going to knock off the Kennedy's and frankly, I don't give a fuck if they do. If I did know somethin' there is no way I would tell you or anybody else. I don't give a damn what your name is. I don't know a goddamn thing. Have a nice day Rinella."

With that, Manzini squeezed himself out of the booth and slowly began to depart and then, after a second, moved back toward Peter and said, "Let me tell you this, jack-off, if and when he gets it, it will be where nobody expects. It would be perfect, if both of 'em got whacked at the same time. Good luck, asshole, and don't get stuck in the middle."

CHAPTER TWELVE

Chicago, 1962

Peter was amazed at the tortuous path his life had taken that ultimately delivered him to Chicago in 1962.

He could have been a better student, but he was constantly distracted by his own nervousness. If it wasn't the nuns who were attacking him, it was the Irish and German kids with their "hey dago— time to eat some pasta" shit. If it wasn't them, it was his own feelings of inadequacy and insecurity trying to fit in with groups who either ignored or hated him.

His only solace was his daydreams of Estella and her fleshy thighs. Even that aroused some anxiety. She or his father might catch him trying to sneak a glimpse of her nakedness. Worse yet, they might discover him in the midst of his self-gratification. Estella never said a word indicating she knew how Peter thought. Once while she was doing the laundry and he was helping pull the clothes out, she accidentally brushed against him with her hand. Peter had to immediately leave the room and satisfy himself. Estella was Peter's first "lust." Unfortunately, Estella found a boyfriend, got married, and left the Rinellas. Thoughts of Estella and her husband in bed doing what Peter wanted to do with her aroused passion and jealousy. The months after Estella left were terrible.

Looking around his hotel room, drawing deeply on the Pall Mall, Peter was   contemplating his next move. It was important to assess the danger facing Kennedy in Chicago, and he remembered what Manzini had told him. He mulled over the scanty facts. *If they hit him, it won't be here, too many boys here to do it in Chicago. No, if they try to get him—and that's a big if—it will be in a place where they aren't headquartered and with some talent they bring in from outside. Maybe they bring some guys from Sicily or who knows where, to do the job. I wonder if Washington has any idea of how pissed these guys are? Has anybody tightened protection around the President? Well, I should probably make note of this in my daily log and notify H.Z. in DC about the risk.*

Herbert Zaun was the Harvard grad, ex OSS agent who drifted into the CIA after the war. He was too abrasive and arrogant to make it in Allen Dulles' CIA, and, after nine long years of conflict and strife and was assigned a back desk in Langley, Virginia. When Ike was elected in '52, H.Z got a friend to get him a position in the FBI. He held a middle management post and was assigned agents in the advance teams. He developed a very strong taste for Cutty Sark. His drinking only seldom interfered with his job, but it resulted in him coming in late occasionally. H.Z.'s eyes weren't blood shot, at least not the eyes themselves, but the area around the eyes was a deep almost, scarlet- red. Peter found HZ brilliant but distracted. H.Z. met Peter at the Chicago field office.

"You know, Pete," H.Z. mused "Washington is full of a lot of bull-shitters. Sometimes I wonder how so much shit can come from these people. The CIA is a good example of how to mismanage money and skill. Dulles has his own agenda, and no one knows what it is and if it squares with country's best interest."

Peter listened to HZ's ramblings and realized that both of their careers were irrevocably mired in place. They both were marking time by walking on a professional treadmill. He told HZ of his incomplete investigations. Peter knew only half of what he was saying registered on his boss' mind.

"Well, Pete, what are you going to do next? Do you think you can make out exactly what's going on here?" Peter thought, *No, I can't and if I could, I would have already told you what was going on.*

"Pete, see if you can get some more definite information and answer the particulars and get back to me. Ok?"

"Yeah, HZ, will do."

His meeting with HZ was worthless as were most of their encounters.

Peter's sauntered back to the Roosevelt to contemplate his next move. It was clear something was going on with the Mafia and the president. When, where and how were the issues. He was certain nothing would happen in Chicago. Whacking Kennedy in Giancana's hometown would be insane. Mayor Daly would be embarrassed if the President of the United States got knocked off in Chicago. No, if it was going to happen, Chicago was not going to be the place. He was also sure that if the mob was going to hit Kennedy, it would use a sharpshooter. No bombs or anything messy and complicated. It would be delivered surgically, quickly, and of course, without any connection to the Mafia. Peter had a good idea where it *wasn't* going to happen, but that was it. He stretched out on the bed, lit up another cigarette, and thought about 1944.

CHAPTER THIRTEEN

Ardennes Forest, 1944

After another brutal and freezing day of marching, Peter and his comrades surrounded a salamander and choked down K-rations. Despuerto mumbled, "You think Patton is eatin' this shit? I'll bet he is sittin' down at some table eatin' a hot meal and drinkin' some goddam French wine."

No one replied, but they knew he was probably right. They followed Patton because they had no alternatives. Peter turned to Perkins and asked, "Ran, you're a smart guy, can you figure out what the fuck we're doin' here? I mean is this crap part of some kinda plan? What the fuck is the meaning of this shit?"

Perkins was silent for a long time, but then quietly replied, "What are you asking? 'what the meaning of life is?' for Christ's sake. Who the hell knows? I can't tell you how it works day to day, but I guess I have an idea how things operate in general. I figure we have a soul that gives our brains some kind of guidance and personality. When we die, the soul leaves and eventually comes back and begins another life. Of course, we suffer here so I guess we're here for atonement, forgiveness and maybe... perfection."

Everybody was silent as they kept their attention on their K-rations and cold coffee. After a minute, Peter asked, "That's Hindu or Buddhist or something, right?"

Perkins just nodded. Forrester was confused and asked, "Ya' mean we lived before and will live again?"

"Yeah," responded Perkins, "but we don't have a conscious memory of any past lives or experiences—like amnesia." He was quiet for some time then continued, "After we die, we go somewhere surrounded by other souls to spend time, who knows for how long, to then be united with another identity."

Peter didn't want to dispute Perkins, but he didn't buy the mumbo jumbo of soul transportation and soul cleansing. Forrester uttered reflexively, "Ran, you are the smartest guy I ever knew, but you're so full a shit...ya really are."

A smile creased Perkins' face as he looked at the West Virginian and he said quietly, "You might be right my friend, I might just be full of shit."

They spent the rest of the time in silence and forced down their frigid food.

CHAPTER FOURTEEN

Chicago 1962

Peter sat in his room and tried to plan his next move when the memory of his daughters beautiful brown eyes emerged. Cam was an intensely intelligent woman but dogged by an equally intense shyness and self doubt. Her intelligence was so different that she somehow alienated herself from those around her. She attempted vainly to fit in but to no avail. She became a non-judgmental person who was quick to smile and accept even though she didn't necessarily agree. She was a smart, kind, and articulate woman but few people got to know that. An amazingly maternal soul, she would never have the pleasure of delivering and caring for a life she produced. Peter's mind could not stop the agonizing thoughts of his child.

Her image on the cold gurney seared his consciousness. He saw her arms dangling, palms up, next to her body. Her eyes were closed as though she was sleeping. Her lips, full and beautiful in life, joined easily in death. He couldn't forget the cold hard feel of her body as he draped her in agony, crying bitter, burning tears of sorrow and anger. He could not, would not, forget that image, or ever be the same person again.

CHAPTER FIFTEEN

Bastogne, 1944

As the Third Army approached Bastogne, the temperature dropped almost instantly to single digits. No one knew how cold it was and they were afraid to ask, as if knowing would make their discomfort more real. The narrow paths were frozen and that actually made movement easier. The tanks and trucks also picked up speed and made following them more of a challenge. Snow was falling and Forrester, with a Chesterfield dangling from his lips, twanged, "I thought someone said if it's real cold it never snows?! What the hell would they be thinkin?! Its god awful cold and this white shit keeps fallin."

Perkins replied, "You know that is a myth. It has more to do with the amount of water in the clouds and will fall regardless of the temperature. Wen, now that I think about it though, the polar ice caps don't get as much snow as you'd think. "

The noise of artillery grew in intensity. No one said it, but they were getting nervous about the impending danger. Peter looked over at his comrades and knew that some of them might not be going home. *I might be spending eternity in the Ardennes for Christ's sake.* He huffed and panted trying to maintain the quick pace and croaked, "Guys, I gotta quit smoking. Christ, I can hardly breathe. Shit, it's only getting worse."

Peter heard someone murmur, "I don't think the government would be giving us these free cigarettes if it knew the godamn things slowed us down."

Despuerto immediately responded, "Don't worry about cigarettes bein bad for you. Bein with Patton is a helluva lot worse. That sonofabitch is goin to get us all killed."

All of them laughed hysterically at Despuerto's wisdom. Peter, through his laughter snorted, "No shit, Pancho, if we don't freeze or starve to death first…."

Perkins replied, "You fuckin' guys don't get it, do you? We're proxies. We're here in place of Roosevelt, Eisenhower, Patton, all of em. We're going to kill or be killed by the poor bastard proxies on the other side, who are there for Hitler, Goebbels, and that fuckin' crew."

CHAPTER SIXTEEN

Chicago, 1962

Peter sat in the arm chair with his shoes propped on the bed and mulled over his options. He was sure any attempts on the President's life would be at another venue and that he would have to expand his investigations to other sites. He turned over options and calculated a plan and mumbled to himself, as though speaking his thoughts made them more organized and reasoned, *Where else would the president be going? Would someone try to pop him in D.C.? No. How could they get him there? Security is way too tight. All of this might be bullshit, or it might be real. Maybe I'll call HZ and see if he can connect me with some F.B.I. field guys, and, maybe, someone in the President's Secret Service detail.*

Peter smiled to himself as he thought of the poor communication between the F.B.I. and the Secret Service. Information was a valuable currency and sharing it with one or the other group was like giving money away. Hopefully, he could get some information from the Secret Service, and, by some miracle, get direction from H.Z.

The hotel room grew smaller and Peter felt the cold sweat of anxiety. His heart began to beat wildly, and he couldn't catch his breath. *God damn it, here we go again?*

The emotional storms would descend and the intensity would build until he was literally ready to scream. He wanted to rip his clothes off and run forever.

As a child, Peter had difficulty controlling his emotions, but the physical nature of his fears and nerves was magnified after the war. Sometimes, he would be sound asleep and be wakened with a vise grip around his chest and breathing as though he had run five miles. He had to draw himself inward and ride out the storm. After the one of these dark episodes, he would be totally spent. In the recovery periods, his mind operated with incredible clarity and memories would gently waft through his brain. Pleasant thought escaped him as he was ripped back to December 23, 1944.

CHAPTER SEVENTEEN

Ardennes Forest, 1944

They had just passed an arrow sign indicating Bastogne was 17 kilometers away. Forrester asked, "Anybody know how many kilometers it takes to make a mile?"

No one answered. Forrester shrugged and pushed his feet over the frozen mire and deepening snow. The wind increased and made 5 degrees feel like 20 below zero. The wool helmet liners were pulled tightly over their ears but offered no protection for their faces.

"Goddamn it," Peter heard himself murmur, "it's so cold everything on my body is numb!!! Christ, my balls are going to fall off and I'm not going to feel a thing. Hey Despuerto, those balls back there are mine."

No one laughed at Peter's comment. He looked around to see if his comrades had heard his repartee and noticed Lt. Peterson stride toward them

"Men, we have to send some trucks back to bring some artillery and other supplies up here. Perkins, Rinella, Forrester, Despuerto, get on the back of one of these trucks coming up and help load up the stuff."

The men just smiled and looked at each other as though they found ten thousand bucks. To get out of the weather and sit on their asses for an indeterminate amount of time was a gift from God.

Just as Peterson finished his order, a green dual axle straight truck with canopy sides was making its way in the opposite direction. They sat on the wooden benches in the back of the truck. Rinella and Perkins raised their feet on the benches and sprawled out while Forrester and Despuerto lowered themselves to the floor and rested with their backs against the sides of the benches.

"These trucks are made to carry a hell of a lot more weight than four grunts," opined Forester.

"No shit," offered Despuerto, "this is a lot better 'n pushin' snow up to our asses."

They were confident that their bad luck had finally taken a turn for the good.

CHAPTER EIGHTEEN

Meadville, 1933

The memory of the truck made Peter's blood rush to his head. He had to stop the memory or the demon would appear with full fury. To stop the unpleasant thoughts, he forced himself to think of the first time he met Millie.

He knew Ambrosio Prutto had sisters because he always complained what "pains in the ass" they were. He assumed they resembled Ambrosio, and that was not a good thing because he had a short forehead, broad nose, and puffy lips. When Ambrosio asked Peter to meet his family and have some spaghetti, he quickly agreed. Ambrosio owed the slender dark paisano a favor and this was a way to pay him back. Peter had gotten him the job at the diner when jobs in 1933 were hard to find. All of the Prutto kids, except the youngest, were trying to find any kind of work. The Depression had dug in and no one could get work anywhere. Ambrosio got a job that paid real money and his benefactor was Peter Rinella.

They arrived at Ambrosio's house. It was on the other side of the tracks and bordered by a dirt alley. Peter was surprised at the condition of the Prutto house. His house was no mansion but was posh by comparison.

Two of Ambrosio's sisters were on the front porch. Peter guessed them to be fourteen and seventeen. Their dresses were hardly fashionable and looked as though they spent their best time in the 1920's, but they were clean. The girls had well brushed hair and were attractive. They shared Ambrosio's dark hair and dark eyes, but not his dark olive skin, or quirky facial features. Peter wondered where the light almost reddish complexion came from.

The younger one, Katrina, giggled when her brother introduced them. Her eyes and hair matched as though only one brown color was available. Her teeth were as white as ivory but the two front teeth were exceptionally large. She giggled at every opportunity.

The older sister, Jenny, was not as attractive as her sister, but appeared much more serious. Her teeth were thinner and not nearly as white as her sister's. She did, though, have the beginning of a very interesting body. Her breasts were ample and her legs smooth and well proportioned. Her eyes bore directly through him.

He was embarrassed to feel his heart rate quicken and his blood flow increase. He told himself how Jenny was too young and any exploration of the young body was not possible. In that moment, he heard Katrina utter, again with the interminable giggle, "Hey Mr. Peter, how about you teachin' Jenny how to drive? Papa won't teach her or let her drive his truck and Ambrosio is too lazy. Can you drive?"

Without interruption or waiting for an answer, the young girl continued, this time without a giggle, "Do you have a car? What make is it? How come you didn't bring it?"

Peter owned a 1923 Packard but as usual the car was in Budasky's garage for repair and he didn't have the money to get it "out of hock." He had to wait for at least one more pay and a few bucks from the Texas Lunch's register to retrieve his ride. He replied, "I let my father have it today. He had to go outta town."

The thought of giving the older sister a driving lesson was a pleasant thought but not appropriate given the age complications. From inside the house, Peter heard a screeching thin bellow, "Ambrosio, Jenny, Katrina, vena ca. Es la hora para mangana."

Peter could smell the tomato, seasonings and boiling pasta. The odors literally made his mouth water. As Ambrosio opened the screen door and escorted him into the parlor, Peter felt a squeeze on his ass. He realized his rear-end was being felt up. He turned to see Jenny looking at him with a coy smile. Flattered, he said nothing and followed Ambrosio into the house. The parlor was dark with a large amount of furniture perfectly placed around a floor model Motorola radio. The Prutto furniture was well worn. The massive chair next to the radio, Peter guessed, belonged to Mr. Prutto. Right in front of the radio, on a little stool, Peter made out the form of a little elfin character. Ambrosio beckoned, "Daniello, this is my buddy, Pete Rinella."

The radio volume was on full bore with music and static intermixed. Ambrosio almost raised his voice to a scream, "Daniello, this here's my pal—his name's Pete" and then in lower tone toward Peter, "the kid don't hear too good. When he was a baby he got scarlet fever and it messed up his hearing. You gotta yell everything to the kid. It drives me crazy but that's the way it is. He has a helluva time in school. He don't hear nothin, so he can't learn nothin."

The little form just revolved on the stool and muttered something unintelligible to Peter. Ambrosio spoke again, "Oh, he don't talk too good either. I spose if you don't hear so good you can't learn to talk too good. We know what he says though. In school he don't say nothin' and that gets the other kids to callin' him names like 'dummy' and shit like that. It's a damn shame."

CHAPTER NINETEEN

Chicago, 1962

Peter fiddled with the Roosevelt's television. It was 6:30 and his day had been a total wash. He had stopped at the Secret Services field office on Michigan Boulevard and met with chief officer, Howard Percivale.

"So, Ragnella, what brings you here to our beautiful city?"

Peter, pointing to the card he had given Percivale, "It's Rinella, sir —and I'm here investigating organized crime's possible attempts on the President's life."

Glancing from the card to Peter's face Percivale quickly apologized for his name gaffe and added "Well, if the young man wouldn't cat around so much and keep his pretty wife and family in DC we could more easily keep an eye on him. He's always traveling here or there looking to bed some strange ass—we just can't do enough security stuff to feel totally confident about his safety. Well, as far as I can say, he is good when it comes to any threats in Chicago or the whole Midwest for that matter."

Peter probed, "Do you have any information about the Kennedys pissing off the mob enough for any of them to want to do something to him?"

Percivale responded, almost in a whisper, "No, but we don't run in the circles some of you people run in, so I don't have anything concrete. There is no question Jimmy Hoffa is upset with the President's brother and we all know the involvement of the mob in the Teamsters Union. There are millions and millions of dollars in Teamster retirement funds, and the Guin—er, excuse me—Italian American mobsters have had clear and open access to the Hoffa administration and those funds. If Bobby can nail Hoffa, there's a good chance the Teamster bank will be closed."

Peter tried to interrupt with a question but Percivale kept rambling, "Really, they would like to get Bobby more than John. JFK, however, would be completely uncontrollable with Bobbie's elimination. I guess it would be more efficient to eliminate the President and that neutralizes his brother. The next President would appoint a new Attorney

General because no one outside his family can deal with Bobby—especially, Lyndon Johnson. You know all this, right?"

Peter nodded and asked, "Do you know how or where any attempts might be made?"

Pericivale was silent, almost as though he hadn't heard the question. He just tapped his fingers together making a loose knit tent and, after a minute, finally offered, "No, of course not—don't have a clue. You guys at the FBI have a good list I'm sure of who the actors are and probably could finger any one of them in an hour of any attempt. Right?"

Peter wasn't sure if the question was rhetorical or Percivale was really looking for an answer. Peter ignored the question. The accidental slur about Italians bothered Peter and made him dislike Percivale. Looking down at his watch, Pericivale said, "Well I gotta be going—we've been on the trail of a counterfeiting ring operating just outside Skokie. I can't follow up on every crack case who threatens the president's life and track down the artists and engravers who think they can make a better ten or twenty. Just can't do it all with a staff of seven guys to cover the entire Midwest."

Peter thanked the agent for his time and made his way back to the hotel and its television. He turned on the T.V. and recognized the familiar heads of Chet Huntley and David Brinkley. He noticed wisps of smoke, from Huntley's cigarette breeze past the broadcaster's slightly graying hair. *What a classy guy.*

Brinkley was ok, but his fair complexion and well groomed appearance, and the way he hardly opened his lips when he spoke, really annoyed Peter. *Brinkley went to the ventriloquist's school of broadcast journalism. The department chair had to be Edgar Bergen!*

Lying on the bed, Peter watched the newscast and lit up a Pall Mall and tried to plan his next day's work. He decided to get something to eat and looked down at his expanding stomach. *Maybe I should try to get in a little better shape. My physical and shooting exams will be coming soon. I won't have a problem with shooting, but Christ, I don't know if I can run a mile under twelve minutes and I sure as hell can't do one pull-up let alone ten. I need to start getting ready. After the news, I can get a cab and go down to Cicero and grab some pasta. Man, could I go for fresh Italian bread, spaghetti, meat balls, and short ribs.*

The thoughts of dinner made him think of his first meal with the Pruttos and the first time he saw Millie. It seemed like both yesterday and a century ago.

CHAPTER TWENTY

Meadville, 1930

Ambrosio led Peter into a darkly lit dining room. The room had only a few pole lamps around it and no central lighting or chandelier. The dinner table was rectangular and easily accommodated twenty people. The Pruttos used only a portion of the table. Ambrosio led a caravan into the dining room with Peter, the two girls, and the hapless Daniello. Mrs. Prutto stood at the head of the table behind Mr. Prutto. She was perfectly round. She was five feet tall and with her dress hanging well below her knees, she appeared shorter. Her salt and peppered hair was pulled back in a tightly arranged bun.

She motioned for everyone to be seated and for Peter to sit next to Mr. Prutto. Mr. Prutto was stoically seated with his back firmly anchored to a high backed chair. He stared at Peter with the clearest blue eyes ever placed in an Italian. Mr. Prutto ignored Peter's attempt at introducing himself and left Peter's hand hanging in the air.

Mr. and Mrs. Prutto exchanged words which Peter couldn't understand. Dialects from region to region were as dissimilar as completely different foreign languages. After he heard them speak in their Northern dialect, it was easy to understand where the Prutto's blue eyes and relatively light skin originated. Mrs. Prutto brought the spaghetti with a light tomato sauce on top, not the usual dark red sauce Peter knew. He heard a commotion at the front door and a female voice bellow, "See you guys later and make sure you get to the club on time, ok!! I'm tired of hangin' around, lookin' like some floozie hopin' some guy will pick her up!!"

He heard a quick female reply, "What's the problem? That what you was doin wasn't it!!!??"

Then he heard the original voice screech, "I gotta get inside....my father is gonna beat my ass if I make him wait for his dinner—see you later."

Like a whirlwind, she arrived panting and looking about the room until her eyes settled on Peter. "Sorry Pa, but Emelina was foolin' around and before you knew it," Looking at Peter, "Who are you? I spose another one of Ambrosio's dead beat friends. Ambrosio, where do you find these guys?"

Peter felt foolish. He was sitting at the table and this girl had just called him a "dead beat, another one of Ambrosio's worthless friends." She immediately smiled at Peter and winked at him with her left eye.

He realized instantly how beautiful she was. Her hair was short with broad waves through it. Her eyes were not brown or blue, but the most radiant hazel he had ever seen. Her breasts pushed against her one piece dress and were accentuated by a tightly drawn thick cloth belt. Her waist was perfectly proportional to her breasts and hips. Her nose was short and her lips full. Peter was able to barely croak, "Ah, ah, my name's Peter Rinella and I manage the Texas Lunch. I gave your brother a job there as a dishwasher and janitor and he asked me to have dinner with your family."

Peter's heart was pounding and his face was beet red. He wasn't able to say another thing.

"Fancy that—aint that something-- you gave my brother a job. You gotta be nuts!"

The elder Pruttos shot her a killing glance. He heard Mr. Prutto start a lecture to the girl, Peter only picked out a few words. The discourse lasted a few minutes. Peter leaned over to Ambrosio and whispered,"What'd your father say?"

Ambrosio quietly replied, "He told her to watch what she said in front of strangers about her older brother. He said I got a job and she should have the energy to keep hers too instead of hanging around clubs and bars looking for who knows what. He told her to quit putting the rouge and lipstick on like some goddamn whore and, if he found out she was smoking, he was going to tie her up in the house and never let her out, except to go to work.

Peter glanced over at Aemilia and realized how much he wanted to know her.

CHAPTER TWENTY-ONE

Chicago, 1962

The cab ride to the hotel was uncomfortable. The Rigatoni he just had for dinner burned at the back of his throat. *Acida again. No one makes sauce like my aunt Carmella. Restaurant cooks are barbarians.*

Another rift brought more of the acrid taste into his mouth. He arrived at the Roosevelt and made it quickly to the elevator. Unfortunately, the elevator operator was the female Negro who propelled the elevator like a rocket. Peter got to his room with the acid indigestion burning a hole in his chest. Rummaging through his bag, he retrieved three Rolaids and jammed them into his mouth. Peter knew from past experience the fire had to be completely quelled before he attempted to lay down. Too soon, and the whole miserable process would begin again. *What a mess I am. If it's not the nervous attacks, it's the goddamn acida!*

After pacing thirty minutes, Peter was able to recline on his bed with his head elevated on two pillows. He resisted with all his effort thinking of the night in Belgium. As a diversion, he thought of every woman he had ever been with, the smiles of his children, and the complexities of trying to keep John F. Kennedy in one piece. None of it worked and his mind was dragged back to the dual axle truck.

Like someone unable to avoid looking at another vomiting, Peter was transfixed on that brutal night in Belgium.

CHAPTER TWENTY-TWO

Belgium, 1944

Merlin Jones was proud of the fact that he was able to get his GI license. He finished the ninth grade in Lexington, Kentucky. Like everyone else in his family, he got a job to help support the family. It was always back breaking work. Sometimes he worked in construction, mixing cement, or hustling bricks and cement blocks. During the winter, he worked in a foundry pouring boiling iron. He was always bone tired. When he got his draft notice in early 1943, he welcomed it.

After basic training, he was assigned to an artillery regiment and became a loader for the howitzers. He still had to do backbreaking labor. He saw a posted notice listing two positions for truck drivers with a G.I. license. In Kentucky, his uncle let him drive his moving van and Merlin was able to drive that truck better than most men drove a car.

The driving test for the GI license was no problem. He had a difficult time with the reading necessary for the written part of the test. For two weeks, he labored over the manual and was able to pass the written test. With pride and confidence, he sat behind the wheel of a dual-axle Ford diesel hauling four guys and supplies from a supply depot in Le-Harve to front lines near Bastogne. He heard the men talking in the back, and, while he drove, eaves-dropped on their conversation.

There was barely enough room for the four men and the supplies. Despuerto and Forrester squeezed themselves between the cases, while Peter and Perkins sat on the floor. The truck slid and lurched on the well worn road bed. The narrow Ardennes roads were not designed for the amount and type of traffic that assaulted them. On either side of the road were pine trees or hedge rows that made driving on the road like driving in an unlit tunnel. The men in the back of the truck were oblivious to the scenery.

Out of nowhere, Forrester ventured, "You know, my pappy told me never to go to a whorehouse until you jack off first. That way you can get yer money's worth."

No one said a word.

CHAPTER TWENTY-THREE

Meadville, 1924

Peter smiled at the thought of his first visit to a brothel back home in Meadville. It was owned by a Negro woman—Flossie Jane Simmons. It had fourteen working girls—most of them Negroes. The house was located in the worst part of the little town, but was an island of opulence in a sea of despair. Immaculately maintained, the house's windows were transparently clean and nothing was out of place in the small front yard. Flower beds encircled the front porch and the clapboard siding glowed in a crisp, bright yellow with dark green trim. Inside, the house smelled of pine oil cleaner and floral bouquet.

Peter was sixteen when his uncle brought him to the house. Flossie had perfectly coiffed

jet black hair arranged in tight curls. Her lips were large and bulbous and coated with dark red lipstick. She was short and compact.

"So," she queried, "yo Giacomo Rinella's boy, huh? Well I guess so since yo here with your uncle Guidano."

Immediately, she turned to Guidano and asked, "how old is dis boy? Yo think he is old enough ta be here?"

Peter's uncle responded, "Missa Flos I spenda mya first tima in a woman when I wasa thirteena years old. Disa boy isa almosta eighteen. Maybe you canna fix hima up wit a younga one, huh?" A second later, Guidano added, "remember I only pay tree dollars and not a goddama penny more."

Flossie shook her head, pulled Peter by his shoulder, and led him to one of the bed rooms. In the room, reclining on the bed was a young light skinned Negro. She was wearing nothing but a white silk slip. She had the same curls as Miss Flossie.

"Ok, boy, dis is Mae. She aint much older n' yo. The difference is she been around a little mo. Mae, dis is Giacomo Rinella's boy and as far as I can figure, dis is his first time."

Miss Flossie left the room and Peter was left standing staring at Mae. Her features were "white." Her nose and lips were thinner than Flossie's.

Peter had no idea what to do, so he simply stood next to the bed and said nothing. Mae also was silent. She lifted her slip slowly up her legs until she got to the top of her thighs and then stopped.

"Ok, boy, why don't you join me on the bed" tapping a position next to her.

Peter obeyed, again not saying a word.

"Let me help you get out of your clothes," she offered.

Slowly she unbuttoned his shirt and pants and laid them gently on the floor next to her.   His excitement was clearly apparent and Mae smiled. She brought her lips to his and kissed him fully and then inserted her tongue into his mouth. This was a new experience for him.

They kissed for a few minutes and then she brought her mouth down to his chest and licked his nipples. Slowly, very slowly, she trailed her lips down his abdomen and eventually enveloped him. Quickly, Peter reached a back breaking orgasm. With that Mae promptly announced, "Well, that's it for today. Hope you enjoyed yourself."

Without a word again, Peter dressed and exited the room and heard Mae call out, "You have a very nice day and hope to see you again."

Peter was too embarrassed to tell his uncle that he never got to "know" Mae. He reported what a great experience it was and how he hoped to have it again.

"Ok, Pio, buta the nexta timea you gotta paya da money youselfa," his uncle added quickly.

Peter's memories of Mae were jarred by Despuerto's laughter who bellowed, "I gotta tell you guys this! Every time I go to a whore house I jack off first too." They roared, knowing that they all shared the same secret.

CHAPTER TWENTY-FOUR

Ardennes Forrest, 1944

Merlin Jones guided the truck as gently as possible through the ruts to avoid capsizing. *This truck will tip over if a dead man farts.*

At the same time, he knew he had to keep a consistent pace or the trucks ahead of him would get out of reach. *Holy shit, Lord, let me keep this thing goin' where I got to go.* He prayed as well as he could pray.

Suddenly, Jones heard a loud cracking noise like fifty baseballs being hit by fifty bats. At the same time, he heard a powerful diesel engine sound and, off to his right, he saw black fumes spewing over the firs and hedgerows. His heart pounded when he saw the front of a gray-green German Tiger tank smash through the foliage and flop across the small narrow road. He heard the engine rev up furiously as the right track stayed stationary and the left turned so the front of the monstrously large tank squared up on the front of his truck. *Oh, my God…oh dear Lord it's facin' us!!!!*

Dirt, snow, and rocks flew behind the left track as it churned the black soil and snow under it. Furiously, Jones slammed on the brakes and threw the vehicle into reverse attempting to escape the massive tank and its lethal 88 millimeter canon.

As he reversed the truck, he heard the men in the back scream. Jones saw a black, leather clad torso peering out of the Tiger's turret. The Waffin-SS tank commander barked something to the tank crew Jones didn't understand. He saw a flash and a puff of smoke but didn't hear anything as the 88 millimeter shell tore into the engine block of his truck, and Merlin Jones was immediately pulverized before the sound arrived.

The truck was thrown ten feet by the explosion and rolled over three times before it came to rest on its side. Inside, the van body was aglow with engine parts, shell shrapnel, and punctuated by Jones' darker body parts. Despuerto was struck above the eye by shrapnel and screamed as blood squirted down his face. Forrester was hit by the supply boxes in the shoulder, shell fragments in the chest and knocked unconscious.

Peter was hit in the left thigh, right calf, and right hand by shrapnel. He felt blood rushing down his face and a massive bump on his head immerged. He heard himself crying, "What the fuck...... is everyone ok, is everyone ok!!!"

The pain was too monumental to process. He pulled himself over to Perkins who was under five or six boxes of supplies. Slowly, Peter slid the boxes from Perkins' body. He rolled him over, and, to his absolute horror, he saw something he would never forget. Between his blue eyes, just above the bridge of his nose, Perkins had a lethal entry-wound the size of a quarter. Randall Perkins died with his eyes wide open.

In anguish and despair, Peter screamed, "Medic, medic, medic—we need.... medic. Please God.... a medic!!!!"

That was the last thing Peter remembered.

CHAPTER TWENTY-FIVE

Luxembourg City, January, 1945

He awoke to a blinding light in his right eye. His mind was disoriented, but he was able to understand that someone had propped his eyelid open and was moving a light from side to side. He found his voice enough to ask, "Wha, wha, is goin' on? Wher, wher, am I?"

A soft and slowly speaking voice replied, "Corporal Rinella, you're in a military hospital in Luxembourg City. You had a serious concussion and a lot of bleeding. We were able to patch up the wounds pretty well. The concussion and brain swelling caused you to pass out and spend 8 days in a coma. That was the most serious injury. Sometimes brain injuries like that can be fatal. You were very lucky, my friend... very lucky."

Peter understood what the tall balding man was saying, but found it difficult to form words to ask questions. He knew that he wanted to ask what happened to his buddies in the truck, but couldn't form the language to ask. He was frustrated.

He heard the man ask, "Do you feel this?"

Peter felt an object being dragged down the length of his left foot. The voice responded without hearing his response, "Very good, we are getting good reflex on both feet."

Peter felt a pin prick to his little finger on his right hand. The voice commented, "Good. I can see you have feeling there. Here, how many fingers.... follow my finger."

A few seconds after the question was posed, Peter managed a response. The man spoke slowly again, because it was difficult for Peter to understand him,

"My name is Major McDermott and I am a neurologist. I treat men like you who have had brain injuries. You are going to be fine but it may take a few weeks for you to gain all the cognitive functions you had before the injury. I'll be stopping by every day to look in on you. In the meantime, some of the nurses and other folks here are going to be getting you up and around and taking care of any of the complications."

Without delay, Major McDermott exited the room and looked over his shoulder to say, "Good... no questions. If you need anything talk to one of the nurses. There are some fine ones here."

Peter's head was pounding. In his haze he didn't realize it was hurting him until after the doctor left. He noticed several beds on either side of him. Most of the men in the ward, like him, had bandaged heads. None of them looked awake and a few moaned. Peter felt overwhelming fatigue. He was unable to stay awake. He slipped back into unconsciousness.

Slowly the fog around Peter's mind had lifted. He was able to form language but sometimes was at a loss for words. He was beginning to remember the night he was nearly killed. He asked the nurse who would check on him what had become of his comrades.

At first, Captain Laura Fitzgerald was evasive, "Corporal, we have had so many casualties and I can hardly keep track of every one in my section. I do all the brain and spinal cord injuries and someone else does gastro, and someone does orthopedics. The doctors and nurses specialize in one thing."

Peter thought, and nearly said, he didn't care about specialization. He just smiled and looked interested because he was talking to a superior officer and knew he would get no information by being a pain in her ass. His mind cleared enough to know how to get around the nurse.

Fitzgerald was a thin faced Irish girl with red hair and freckles to match. She wore army fatigues two sizes too big. She wore a wedding ring covered with gauze.

Peter asked why she used the gauze and she responded humorlessly, "It keeps blood and God knows what else off my ring."

Finally, after a few more days, Peter gave her the names of his friends and that afternoon she returned more somber than usual. "Corporal, I hate to tell you this but your friend Perkins is dead. His remains will be sent back, but I can't tell you when. Unfortunately, bodies are still stacked like cord wood. The bitter cold weather, thank God, has offered some reprieve by freezing the bodies. Despuerto and Forrester have been moved to a hospital in England. They both survived but I heard your friend Forrester may have lost his leg. I am not sure, but that's what I heard. Despuerto apparently had a lot of damage to his arms and face but will recover."

Peter heard the report and was silent. After the nurse left, Peter sobbed just as he did when his mother died. He realized that he might never see any of those men again

His depression deepened as the other patients received mail from home, some almost daily. He hadn't gotten any mail from home for weeks. *I guess the mail hasn't caught up to me yet… maybe it got lost in some mail bag in England or wherever they sort the stuff.*

Thoughts of home became an obsession. One day, a young hospital chaplain, a Catholic priest named Father Getz, came by and Peter asked him to inquire why he hadn't gotten any mail. The priest, without any ability or intention of doing that, smiled agreeably and replied, "Sure, sure, I'll get to the bottom of this."

Every time he thought about the ugly day in December, Peter would break out in a sweat that would drench his clothes. His mind would take him on a path of emotional upheaval. His heart rate and breathing would spiral out of control. He constantly had to try to manage his anxiety.

CHAPTER TWENTY-SIX

Meadville, 1930

He forced himself to think about Millie and his first conversation with her. They were sitting on the Prutto's front porch after the spaghetti dinner. Peter had barely eaten because he was a little embarrassed and somewhat unsure of the circumstance.

Mr. Prutto was intimidating and Peter wanted to make a good impression on him. Making a pig of himself was a sure way to be labeled a "covone," an ill-bred, discourteous slug.

He sat on a porch swing and she on an old wicker chair facing him. When she got up he could see that her garter belt was fastened to her stockings just at her thighs. He tried to hide his glances, but Aemillia quickly noticed and found more reasons to get up for one thing or another. She smiled at Peter's discomfort as he tried to make conversation, "Aemillia, where do you work, er, what do you do?"

"I work at the Malleable in the core room. Do you know what cores are? They go in molds and allow the melted iron to go through to the shapes made in the molds. It's piece-work so the more cores I make, the more money I can bring home to my mother and father. I get up at five in the morning, walk about two miles, bust my ass for eight hours—if I'm lucky and I can bring home twelve bucks a week, of which I see maybe a buck!"

Peter was silent. He just looked at the very attractive woman. Finally, he got up enough courage to ask, "Sometime… maybe we can go to a movie, or maybe go to a dance at the Jeffersonian Club? For a buck or two we can get a good meal and dance for four or five hours, my treat, of course," he added very quickly not wanting her to think he was after the dollar her parents gave her out of her check.

She said nothing and looked at the thin, dark haired guy her brother brought home. After a few moments, which seemed interminable to Peter, she replied, "Sure, not a bad idea, but I need to get some things straight with you before we go anywhere. First, my friends call me Millie. Aemillia drives me nuts, ok? Second, whatever my father thinks, I'm no whore and if you think you're going to get in my pants you better find someone else, got it? Third, I decide if and when we ever go any further than just friends—got that?"

Peter tried to interrupt but only got as far as, "I never" and "I wasn't thinking anything" as she hammered her points home.

After she was finished, Peter allowed her some time to catch her breath when he spoke, "Ok, I understand and if we just get to be good friends that will be ok with me. Honest, I just wanted to spend some time with you and get to know you better."

Millie considered Peter's answer and asked, "So, your name is Peter what again?"

"Rinella, Peter Rinella…my dad's the shoe maker on North Street."

"Ok, Peter Rinella, what are you doing Tuesday night? There's a movie at the Park Theater with Ronald Coleman that I have been dyin' to see."

Peter was pleased to accept the invitation and started to wonder how to get his car out of hock at Budasky's Garage.

Millie was true to her word and did not give herself up easily and was always in charge of their relationship. He managed his sexuality by continuing his regular trips to Mae. He thought wistfully of the years he visited her.

CHAPTER TWENTY-SEVEN

Meadville, 1926

He was able to conventionally consummate his meetings with Mae if he masturbated before getting there. After sex, depending upon how busy she was, they would spend time talking.

He asked Mae, "Why is it you don't talk the way the other Negro ladies here talk? I mean no disrespect Mae; you talk a lot like us."

Mae laughed, "Peter, I speak far better than YOU and YOUR PEOPLE because I am far better educated than all the girls in this house, and most of YOU PEOPLE too. You know, I graduated from high school in Detroit, not some cotton field in Mississippi like the other girls here. Why do you come to see me, there are other white girls here and maybe you could get lucky for free outside. Why are you with me?"

Peter thought for a while, "Mae... I really like you...I feel comfortable with you. You're sexy, smart, and you make me feel good about me."

Appreciating his answer, Mae offered, "Well, Mister Rinella, it's high time for you to go to the college of Mae. I'm gonna show you how to make love to a woman. After some lessons, you and every woman in your future will be grateful. I absolutely guarantee it."

With that she took his head in her hands and said, "Now, kiss me very slowly and take your time. Women appreciate kissing."

Slowly, as though taking a child through a primer, she instructed Peter on the use his hands, fingers, mouth, lips, and tongue. He wasn't sure but it seemed she may have climaxed once or twice. He was sure she was beginning to enjoy their sessions and wasn't acting to get him off. After one of their many "tutorials" Peter asked, "Do I have to leave now? Do you have anyone else comin' to see you?"

She replied, "No, not really, but remember Flossie likes us out in the parlor in case someone comes in and needs to see the 'quality of the offerin.' I have a few minutes, I guess."

"Well, Mae, I was just wondering why... how you ended up here? —you know, based on your education and background."

Agitated, the vein on her forehead betrayed her anger. She responded, "Don't.... do not ever ask me, 'what's a nice girl like you doin in a place like this?!!` If you even get close to saying something like that again I will kick your ass out the door!"

Peter tried to interject, "I...I...Didn't mean to..."

Mae heard nothing and continued. "Do you know how many times I hear that from you white guys looking to 'change their luck with a darkie'? And doin things with me and to me they would never do to another woman and then have the nerve to ask, 'what's a nice girl like you doin workin here?' Not that I owe you or anyone an explanation, I'll give you one because you are young, ignorant and because I kinda like you."

Mae seemed to cool down and continued with her usual composure, "Do you have any idea what's it like for a woman, especially a Negro woman, to get a decent job today? The only work I could get in Detroit was as a maid in some woman's house or some hotel. Hell, if I'm going to clean some lady's mess for nearly nothin', I might as well fuck her husband for a whole lot more."

Peter laid there speechless.

Through nearly his entire relationship with Millie, Peter visited Mae. Despite their growing relationship, Peter always had to pay the going rate. Neither questioned the financial basis for their meetings. After six years and an especially, energetic session, Mae rolled over and looked Peter squarely in the eyes and asked, "You are dating a white girl, huh?"

Peter felt defensive but answered truthfully, "Yea, she's the sister of one of my friends... She seems to like me and it's kinda nice to go out with her sometimes."

After a moment Mae asked, "Have you made love to her yet— used the lessons you've learned?"

Peter was embarrassed but again compelled to the truth, "Well we haven't done everything yet, but almost, and she seems to like it pretty well."

After a longer period of silence, Mae replied,"You know, I think it would be better for both of us if you quit comin' to see me here. It's time for you to move on with your life. It's crazy for you to keep on visitin' with me."

Peter was stunned and aghast at the thought of not visiting Mae. He barely spoke,"Mae I, I......like comin' to see you. I......really like spendin' time with you and talkin' to you. I like you...It's not just sex.

I....don't know if I can stay away from....I, I...have very strong feelings for you."

Tears welled in his eyes, reached the brim and finally rolled down his cheeks to his jaw line. Mae was surprised at his reaction, "Peter, you'll be just fine and after a while you'll get over not comin' to see me and you'll manage."

She cradled his head into her bosom and quietly whispered, "Ok, you have to get dressed and get goin'. Thank you for spendin' time with me. I hope you learned something. Now come on, get goin.... Today's on the house."

Peter walked down the porch steps and he looked back. Tears stung his eyes, and he saw Mae standing at her bedroom window. One hand was holding a cigarette and was held up at the elbow by the other hand. The hand with the cigarette, managed a faint wave.

CHAPTER TWENTY-EIGHT

Chicago, 1962

He awoke to a wailing "all clear" sound coming from the television, and on the screen, a test pattern with a profile of an American Indian in full battle garb. Some hotels had the new device to remotely control the T.V. The Philco "Radar Wave" was an amazing invention, and if you fell asleep with the TV on, you didn't have to get up to turn it off and completely ruin a chance of getting back to sleep. The Roosevelt didn't have the device. *Oh shit, it's three-ten and I'm up and I gotta get back to sleep to feel normal tomorrow.*

The older he got, the more Peter fixated on sleeping. His obsession actually got in the way of getting to sleep. After the nights he couldn't sleep, the next day was agonizing, and reinforced his compulsion and obsession the next evening. *What a fucked up life when your existence depends on a bed.*

His anger and frustration at the 3:10 wake- up call from the TV doomed his getting back to sleep again. Of that, he was certain. If he was able to control his brain and slow it down with pleasant thoughts, he might be able to catch the zephyr of relaxation. He forced himself to think of Millie and the early good times of their uneven relationship. *She was really something.*

He saw her sitting in a booth at the Texas Lunch with a white porcelain coffee cup in her right hand and a Lucky Strike in her left. She took a sip of the coffee in the exact place and left one lipstick mark. After a sip, she took a long, deep drag on the Lucky. Peter smoked Pall Malls because they were longer and he felt he got more for his fifteen cents a pack.

Millie told him, "You know, there's no more tobacco in the Pall Malls than in Lucky's. They just pack the Pall Malls looser. I'll bet you've noticed the Pall Malls burn faster. If we both light up at the same time, we'll be finished at the same time."

Peter looked into her eyes and gave the appearance of understanding and appreciation for her opinion. He was really thinking how frustrated he was without the consummation of their "fooling around." Of course, this was magnified by his forced absence from Mae.

After six years, he was panting for the next sexual level. Millie liked the sense of power the entire dynamic gave her.

"In good time, Peter," she said, "I just have to be sure you're not with me just for sex. I want to be more than a 'piece of ass.'"

Peter got tired of explaining his feelings and said nothing. Between sips and smokes, Millie offered,

"You know Peter we've been going out for a long time and I'm thinkin' if we don't get engaged, you are never gonna marry me. You love me, right? I mean what are you waitin' for? My father is startin' to wonder what's goin' on with us. Do you want to get married or what— don't you love me?"

Peter hated this conversation, as much as Millie hated the pressure for sex, and responded, "Millie you know how I feel about you. Yea I love you and we are gonna get married. Can't we wait until I get a decent job and can afford to get married? Your father makes my ass ache. He has all the goddamn answers except how to get a job for himself. Everybody in the family is workin to support his ass."

Peter had heard this conversation about two hundred times and was able to delay the inevitable for another two years.

Oh shit, Peter thought in the hotel bed, *I need to think of some good stuff, not any shit that will just get me more upset.*

The thought of Millie's wonderful breasts and smooth thighs breezed into his brain. He remembered how she tasted and the first time he entered her body and its wonderful warmth, softness, and moistness. As with the first time with Mae, Peter was a terrible disappointment and lasted only few seconds, but Millie didn't seem too disappointed. After all, they had just gotten engaged.

CHAPTER TWENTY-NINE

Chicago, 1962

The alarm clock showed seven o'clock and Peter euphorically realized he had finally gotten some sleep. Peter was compelled to dispel any good humor with the unpleasant status of his investigation. *Why be happy for at least one goddamn minute, bring your mood down with a shitty thought.*

He had made no progress on assessing the threat to the president. He knew the danger was imminent and was dependent on the mob finding the right time and place, but more importantly, the right person to accomplish the job. He knew nothing more could be done in Chicago and it was time to get back to D.C. He decided to use some vacation time and visit with Randall Perkins' parents in South Bend. He wanted to see where Randall came from and spend some time with his parents.

He called Maggie Johanson at the Bureau's Information Center to find an address and status on Randall's parents. Maggie was an attractive, Nordic looking young woman who, if treated with kindness, was accommodating. If you raised her animus, however, it was impossible to get any information and even J.Edgar Hoover couldn't budge her.

About, ten o'clock, Peter got a call from Maggie, "Peter, I have some stuff for you, but we have to make it quick, the Bureau is upset about long distance charges….. Get a pen and pad…."

Peter wrote down the address for Roger Perkins and quickly got to the train station for the two hour trip to South Bend. *Shit, I forgot to ask Maggie if Randall's mother was still alive and to tell her to memo H.Z. that I was taking a day or two off—goddamn it! When I get to South Bend, I'll call H.Z. and tell him what's goin on.*

He boarded the train and sat by himself. He settled back and tried to prop his feet on the seat in front of him but his belly pushed them down. "I gotta do something about this," he thought and then remembered he hadn't had breakfast yet.

He planned a cup of coffee and wheat toast with marmalade to start his new diet program. He got to the dining car and ordered a cup of coffee and two donuts.

"I'll start watchin' what I eat tomorrow," he swore.

He settled back in his seat finished his breakfast and thoughts coursed through his brain.

CHAPTER THIRTY

Meadville, 1932

His mind settled on his wedding at the Jeffersonian Club. The club had a large room on the second floor of an old downtown-building. Why a club, with ninety eight percent Italian-American membership and no involvement in politics was named for Thomas Jefferson mystified Peter. He asked thirty guys how the club came to be named for Jefferson and no one knew.

The club was started after Prohibition was repealed, and several guys decided to establish a club to take advantage of Meadville's renewed appetite for alcohol. Mr. Caravella, the leader of the group, found it was easier to get a liquor license for a club than a tavern and wrote a charter and by-laws for the Jeffersonian Club. Mr. Caravella had long since passed and no one was ever able to answer the naming choice.

The security door was propped open for the Rinella-Prutto wedding and three hundred guests streamed into the room. Mrs. Prutto made her sauce, as did Peter's Aunt Carmella. Both women were explicit that the different formulas not be combined and be evaluated on their own merits. Both monitored the levels of their respective pasta dishes and would check reviews after someone ate their handiwork. Carmella chose ziti for her pasta while Marie Prutto chose rigatoni for hers. It was easy for them to circulate the large room and see who was eating which pasta and get a quick opinion. Mrs. Prutto asked only those who ate her dish for an evaluation, while Carmella would openly ask the ziti-people and more discretely poll the rigatoni-people. If the Prutto sauce eaters would give a favorable review, Carmella tried to persuade them to try her recipe and assured them, quietly again, how much better her sauce was prepared.

Four musicians played. There was a drummer, a mandolin/guitar player, piano player, and trumpet/saxophone player. The musicians played all Italian weddings but had no name for their group. They were simply called "the guys." They played tarantellas, other Italian folk and wedding dances that everyone recognized. At times, rarely, they ventured into modern "American" tunes but struggled. Guests howled mercilessly either because the music was poorly played or because they didn't want to hear "American" music. In either case, no one was discrete about their comments.

Someone hollered out, "Play another goddamn song!" or "What do you guys think, you're Glenn Miller or Tommy Dorsey!!!!??"

The guys were oblivious to the comments and continued until the song's conclusion. It was the "Italian music" that got all the guests on their feet and ignited the room with stomping feet and twirling bodies. Peter and Millie were seated at the head table in the center of the room surrounded by their attendants. Peter's best man was Ambrosio and his other groomsmen were Joe "Red" Frisina, Alfonso Daddio, and Orlando Macaluso. The men were guys from the neighborhood and Peter met Alfonso at Miss Flossie's.

Millie chose her sister Jenny as her maid of honor and her sister Katrina and Emilena Bosco as attendants. As most Italian weddings went, this wedding party was small--most Italian weddings had twelve or fourteen attendants. The number of invited guests was typical.

Peter was interested in seeing and talking to his maternal cousin, Peter Rubino. Rubino had just been elected to a seat in the U.S. House of Representatives and was a celebrity. He was a family icon and sat at a table in front, with Peter's father.

The money box was placed right next to the newlyweds, and as was Italian custom, only money gifts were given.   In 1938, the gift amount was affected by the economy, but all the gifts, albeit small, were spendable. Unlike American weddings where guests brought dishes, tea sets, and shit no one would use in thirty years, Italian gifts were all green. Peter and Millie decided to spend their wedding money on a trip to Niagara Falls.   Their stay would be limited only by the amount of money they collected. Giacomo encouraged them to save their wedding haul for furniture but they decided to buy what they needed, on credit at Cardinals furniture, and have fun with the wedding cash.

Giovanni, Millie's cousin, stood prominently next to the cash box to safeguard the contents and insure that it got to its rightful owners. Giovanni was five foot six, two hundred forty pounds, and looked like a Buddha. His best black suit covered half of his stomach and exposed his partially unfastened pants. Peter or Millie had never heard of money being stolen from an Italian wedding, or any wedding for that matter, but Italian weddings always had someone similar to Giovanni playing that role. No one in their right mind would have attempted any bad behavior around the money box.

Peter's father provided the liquor, wine, and beer. The wine was from the private stores of Mr. Bergamasco and reportedly the best red available. In lieu of a gift, Bergamasco donated the wine which was the only non-cash gift the newlyweds received. Giacomo purchased three kegs of Iron City and one of Rolling Rock. He bought Rolling Rock for his sister-in-law Carmella who was addicted to it. Since Carmella had spent two weeks preparing the sauce and half of the wedding cookies, Giacomo thought this a small price to pay. It also pacified Lorenzo, Carmella's husband, and made Giacomo's life much easier. To hear Lorenzo say one more time, "I gotta no goddama idea whata you woulda do ifa Carmella hada not adone thisa goddama worka! Whata dida thata goddama Prutto familigia doa?" was more than Giacomo could bear.

Hopefully, Carmella would get a little tipsy and, "Maybea Lorenzo willa geta una pogue" Giacomo winked.

The guests were so hungry that they began eating before the arrival of Father Catalano and his required grace before meal. He did raise a glass of Mr. Bergamasco's red and toasted the couple, "May Jesus Christ bless this young couple with happiness, good fortune, and many healthy children."

Few guests heard the toast because they were dancing to the Italian music of "the guys." Peter made it over to thank his cousin Peter Rubino for making the journey to Meadville from Connecticut. Rubino shook Rinella's hand and congratulated him,

"Peter," Rubino said, "if ever you need anything and I can help— call me. This is no bullshit. I mean it and promise to help you if I can. Nothing in this world is more important than family—nothing."

Peter felt good about his cousin's support, hugged him and kissed him firmly on the cheek. Peter grabbed Millie's hand and they circulated around the room, greeted their guests and took a turn on the dance floor. It was late and time for them to leave for Niagara Falls. The thought of getting Millie in a hotel room convinced Peter to get a room before they got to Niagara Falls. Peter whispered his intentions to Millie and she just winked and stuck her tongue in his ear. Peter's heart began to pump and his mind reeled. *This is going to be a great marriage.*

CHAPTER THIRTY-ONE

South Bend, December, 1962

The train pulled into the South Bend depot. Peter had the good sense to phone ahead from the station in Chicago to make sure the Perkins' would be home. He had to remember to thank Maggie for getting him the phone number. It was amazing how much information the Bureau could access on anybody it wanted.

Mr. Perkins sounded frail but alert. It started to snow and Peter had a bitch of a time getting a cab. After ten minutes, he finally got a yellow Checker that took him to a two story home with white clapboard, black shutters, dark red door, and a nice front yard. He got colder and wetter as he waited for someone to answer the doorbell. He was agitated, *goddamn it, why the hell didn't I bring my heavy coat.*

Slowly, the figure on the other side became more visible and it was a small, almost wispy figure wearing a gray cardigan sweater. He was bent over and the top of his balding head was visible. Slowly, the figure raised his head as though it took a lot of effort and thinking to do it. From his jaundiced, wrinkled face, and thin white lips.

Peter barely heard the greeting, "You're Mr. Rinella? You were in the army with Randall?"

Not waiting for an answer, he showed Peter into the center hall colonial. Looking to his right, he noticed a bed in what once was a library or parlor and now served as a bedroom for someone who had trouble navigating the stairs. Peter followed the man down the hall to one of the sitting rooms to the left and removed his drenched suit jacket.

Peter began the conversation, "Yes, Mr. Perkins, Randall and I were in the same outfit together. We were together from basic training until the day.......he was killed. He was a great guy. I'm sure you know that. He was one of the smartest and nicest guys I've known."

Looking at Peter for a moment, Mr. Perkins whispered, "Oh, yes, we loved Randall, he was a great kid. He was at the top of his class and did his mother and me very proud. You know his mother never really recovered from his death. She was never able to bounce back. He was our only child and our lives centered on him. You know she passed in 1948, but really she died in December, 1944."

Peter said nothing as the older man continued, "He could've done anything he wanted to—he got into Penn, that's Ivy League, you know. He could've been a doctor or lawyer or anything, he was that smart. Instead he decided to........"

Mr. Perkins never finished his thought and Peter was left hanging onto to his explanation,   so Peter asked, "He decided to do what, enlist in the army?"

"Oh no, that came later," responded the old man. He continued finally, "No, no he decided to go into the seminary. He decided to be a priest. We were surprised but pleased with his decision."

Peter was absolutely shocked. In the two years he knew Randall, he didn't even know he was Catholic, let alone someone who was going to be a priest. Peter asked, "What...what happened that he enlisted in the army instead of becoming a priest?"

After what seemed like minutes the old man answered, "Randall and another seminarian fell......... in love."

Peter's jaw dropped and he had to steady himself in his chair. He shared many hours in all sorts of situations and never had any indication. *Jesus Christ, Randall was queer.* Peter was at a complete loss for words as the old man continued, "He felt it was sinful and wrong for a priest to have those feelings so he left the seminary after a year and a half. He enlisted in the army shortly after that. You know, I could have gotten him a deferment. I was an executive with Willy's and we were heavily involved in war work. I had a lot of connections in the army, but Randall wouldn't hear of it. Maybe he put himself at risk to atone for his sins. I guess fate and God made the final decision."

As the old man spoke, it became harder for him to catch his breath and the emotion of the subject made it even harder. Despite his labored breathing, he forced himself to continue, "Elizabeth and I didn't care who Randall loved. We didn't care if he got married or had kids or anything like that. We loved him for who he was. I can tell you the world lost a lot on the day he was killed; he could've done remarkable things with his life."

Peter, still stunned, managed to say, "He was everything you thought he was. I was proud to know him and I'd like you to know he died a hero."

Peter was stretching the truth a bit, but he felt compelled to offer the old man some solace. Mr. Perkins replied, "I thought so...thank you for taking the time to come and visit."

To ease his shock and discomfort Peter timidly asked, "Would you happen to have some Scotch? I sure would like to have a shot to warm me up a bit. The snow gave me a chill."

"I do," replied the old man, "how about some Dewars's?"

Peter replied, "I'll take it over ice with a splash of water."

CHAPTER THIRTY-TWO

South Bend To D.C.,1962

Peter was amazed that he missed knowing the real Randall. He purchased a ticket for the trip back to D.C. The Bureau insisted that any agents traveling distances greater than ten hours by car or train fly instead. The airline ticket was more expensive, however the accountants in Washington figured the wages of the agents against the cost of the ticket and that made the airline ticket a much better deal. Peter enjoyed flying but fellow passengers drove him crazy.

On a flight to Minneapolis once, he was seated next to an older woman with obviously colored hair who was smoking Lucky's and drinking gin and tonics. After her second drink, she became more talkative and tried to strike up a conversation with him about the safety of flying.

"You know," she said, "you are a lot safer flying on an airplane than riding in a car. There are far more deaths on the roads than in the air."

He smiled, nodded, and agreed with her. The third gin and tonic made her even chattier. He pretended to be asleep but she still detailed every bit of her sad family history—alcoholic-abusive husband, alienated children, and demanding-unappreciative siblings. Peter wanted to say, *we all got shit in our lives and nobody wants to hear yours. My stuff's as bad as yours, but I wouldn't tell a perfect stranger everything in my life.*

Instead, he simply nodded and tried to appear interested in her sad tales of woe. After they landed in Minneapolis, he helped her out of her seat and while they waited to disembark, she asked, "What are you doing in Minneapolis?"

As casual and nondescript as possible, Peter replied, "Work... I have to do some work in and around the Twin cities."

To his absolute shock he heard her ask, "Where are you staying tonight? Why not spend the night at my house?"

Peter didn't believe his ears and almost asked her to repeat her question but he was sure he had heard her correctly and politely responded, "Oh, thank you very much for the invitation but I have to meet some of my associates for dinner and a meeting, but thanks anyway. I appreciate the offer."

When he got into the terminal, he thought, *I'll be a sonofabitch. The only chance I get with a woman comes from some old lady. Why wasn't she at least a forty or forty-five year old woman looking for some fun?*

The movement of the train brought him back to the trip to D.C. Peter knew the Bureau didn't give a shit if he spent two and a half days on a train because he used his vacation time for the trip. He almost laughed out loud when he considered his situation, *what kinda life do you have when you don't give a damn if you waste your vacation time on a train? How pathetic.*

The leisurely train trip back to D.C. gave him a lot of time to think uninterruptedly about the million of things he always obsessed about. He knew his sleep and other natural functions were going to be seriously interrupted and as always, they were a major concern. *I wonder how much extra for a sleeping berth...I wonder if the food club has any prunes? Oh hell, who gives a shit,* He laughed out loud at his pun, *maybe this is a good time to rid myself,* Again he marveled at his quick pun, and, Now playing the pun game to the fullest, *put these demons to bed. It's not only pathetic but it's goddamn funny.*

Sitting in the Pullman looking at the scenery pass by, Peter began to think about his first years of marriage. He worked at the Texas Lunch and Millie had her job at the Malleable. They rented an apartment on Market Street with two bedrooms, a small kitchen, dining room, and parlor.

Their first year of marriage consisted of nightly sex, followed by a quick dinner, and a few hours of radio. Peter loved to listen to sports, especially baseball while Millie liked the "Shadow" or "Sherlock Holmes." Both of them liked "Gun Smoke," and "Burns and Allen." All of America, the Rinellas included, was addicted to the "Amateur Hour."

Above all, sex was the constant in their lives. Peter was proud of the techniques schooled to him by Mae. Millie seemed to enjoy it as well but sometimes she had to be adept at faking her orgasms to get the whole thing over and done.

She also discovered, early in their marriage, that his orgasm was the end to their love making. If it was over for her husband, Millie knew, it was over for her as well. Peter never knew any of this because Millie realized his ego would not accept it. A few times, Millie became frustrated with her lack of completion, waited for him to fall asleep, and went into the bathroom to satisfy herself. Most of the time, though,

Millie was quite satisfied with her husband and their marriage seemed ideal.

About five years into their marriage Millie told Peter, "Well, I think I'm pregnant. I haven't had a period for two months and my breasts and nipples are tender as hell. I'll go see Dr. King but I'm pretty sure he'll confirm it."

Peter was shocked and responded, "What... how'd the hell did that happen?!! I thought we decided to wait a little longer to have kids. Jesus Christ, we're doin' ok now with you working but what're we gonna do when you can't anymore! I thought you were makin' sure that wasn't gonna happen!!"

Millie looked directly at him and said, "You know goddamn well how it happened! Why's it up to me all the time to take precautions? Anyway, I won't be off work long. My mom can watch the baby when you and I are at work... the more I think about it, the more I know we can manage it. Aren't you a little happy we're gonna have a baby?"

Her question was plaintive and Peter could see she was near tears waiting for his answer. A couple of minutes passed and he realized he had acted like an asshole.

He wrapped his arms around her shoulders and nudged her head to his chest and said, "Of course I'm happy that we are going to have a baby. I know you are gonna be a great mom....we'll be great parents."

After a few more minutes, he asked, "Hey, Millie do you think we are gonna have a boy? If we do, I'd like to name him for my grandfather, or if it's ok with you, maybe my father?"

Millie wasn't sure what she was carrying, but was sure she didn't like Peter's choice of names. To prop up his feelings, she assured him they were most definitely going to have a son. Eight months later, after a labor that lasted twelve hours, Carmella Marie Rinella entered the world. Her name was a compromised affair of Peter's aunt, Carmella and Millie's mother, Marie. Both families were duly represented, and, though a bit disappointed, Peter immediately fell in love with his pudgy, screaming, beautiful daughter. His life had been changed for the better.

CHAPTER THIRTY-THREE

Meadville, 1939

The Rinellas had to move. Climbing the stairs to the apartment with a child was a pain in the ass for both Peter and Millie. Millie especially pushed for a larger apartment or full house. Peter agreed, but knew a whole house was out of their reach.

"You know, Millie, the only way we can get a house is if we move down on West Street with the shines. I don't know how we can afford a larger apartment, let alone a whole house. Millie you gotta be realistic."

Millie ignored Peter's protestations and every morning scanned the newspaper for apartments and houses for rent. If she was feeling really optimistic, she searched the "Homes for Sale" section. Her task was complicated by the necessity of tending to her Carmella Marie. After the baby was born, her mother convinced Millie that breast feeding was better for Carmella Marie and any problems with getting milk after Millie went back to work could be worked out easily. Millie was glad she decided to breast feed her baby and found it satisfying to maintain the intimate connection with her child. Peter was also glad because when Carmella awoke in the middle of the night he could stay in bed while Milled had to tend to the baby. Millie grew tired of the walk to the bedroom and brought her daughter in bed with them. When the baby awoke, she slipped down her nightgown, exposed a nipple for the baby and went back to sleep.

Peter, who had gotten use to sex on a regular basis, took issue with Millie's position of, "No hanky-panky with Carmella in our bed!! Who knows what she'll remember when she gets older for God's sake?"

Peter had to catch Millie when the baby was napping in her crib. He gradually accepted the situation and helped in changing diapers and, when Carmella got older, he fed her regular food. His greatest contribution was emptying the diaper pail, and washing the diapers. One afternoon, after he got home from the Texas Lunch, Millie had the "Meadville Tribune" in her hand and was waiting for him at the door.

"Here it is Peter. This is the apartment we have to get before anyone else does."

The apartment was on Grove Street, an "uptown" address that would cost them nearly twenty dollars more per month than they were paying on Market St. He was silent for a few minutes while he tried to work the finances in his head. If they made a few cuts here or there, maybe they could do it. He knew if he strongly opposed her idea, Millie would be difficult.

Finally he replied, "Ok, call them so we can take a look at it. You know, honey, you're gonna have to go back to work pretty soon and we're gonna have to take the baby down to your mom's place every day. You understand that, right?"

"Yeah, I understand that," with a touch of anger in her voice, "but I also understand we need another bedroom and a decent place to raise our child."

After they saw the apartment, Millie declared, "It's darling …. We have to take it."

They signed the lease and moved in two weeks later. It was at Grove Street that Carmella took her first halting steps and spoke her first words. It was also there, after she had been to work for about four months, when Millie got pregnant again. Peter's reaction was the same as it was with Carmella's conception and equally irrelevant. After a normal pregnancy and working until her due date, Millie delivered their son, Vincent Marco Rinella. Peter was ok with Millie's grandfather being represented by the "Vincent" as long as his family was mentioned with the "Marco."

The baby was long and lean, a much different body type than Carmella who was a lot shorter and stouter. Although he would never admit it to Millie, he was glad they had moved to Grove Street. He did tell her many times how happy he was to have their children.

CHAPTER THIRTY-FOUR

Cleveland, 1962

The rocking of the train and the clacking of the wheels hypnotized Peter. The slow movements from side to side coupled with the constant movement forward gently rocked him to sleep. He must have fallen asleep at ten or eleven and didn't awaken until six in the morning. He slowly opened his eyes, but quickly realized that he had slept an uninterrupted six or seven hours. He thought, *wow, I gotta get a bed that does this. I feel like a new man. Some water on my face, a cup of coffee and a couple of eggs, and I'll be set for the day.*

He heard the conductor announce, "Cleveland, Ohio," with an emphasis on *land*, "next station, twenty minutes," emphasis on *twen*. "There'll be a forty-five minute layover while we load passengers and freight for the rest of the east bound trip. You can disembark if you wish, but get a boarding pass to get back on for the continuing leg."

Peter decided to get breakfast at the Cleveland depot restaurant. As he was sitting at the counter looking down at his scrambled eggs, bacon, and toast, it reminded him of a breakfast Millie had made and her suggestion, "You know, Peter, Esther at work told me there are a lot of openings at the Ordinance Plant. If you have a heart-beat, you can get a job there. Esther said there are plumber and pipe fitter jobs galore cuz they are adding new buildings for more production."

Peter was interested because he knew the jobs at the Ordinance plant paid an enormous three dollars per hour but as he said, "Millie, what the hell do I know about plumbing or pipe fitting, for Cris sakes!"

"Peter, they will teach you what you need to know. You're a smart guy and it won't take you very long to learn. Jesus Christ, your buddy, Joe Frisina, got a job at the plant as a pipe fitter and makes four dollars an hour and he's as dumb as shit. If he can do it, you can do it with your brain asleep!"

It was pointless to argue with Millie once she decided something, so he agreed, "Ok, ok let me finish my breakfast. Maybe tomorrow I'll go out there and put in my application. Are you satisfied?"

Millie smiled and gave Peter the little wink she gave when she was happy he agreed with her, or, sometimes if she was interested in "hanky-panky." This time, unfortunately, it was because he agreed with her without an argument.

He got a job at the Ordinance Plant and as a pipe fitter. His major job was to wrap all the pipes leading in and around the buildings in asbestos wrapping. He couldn't believe the size of his paychecks and he realized if they continued, he and Millie might be able to buy a house. His life with his family and job were nearly perfect. The kids were able to sleep by themselves and his intimacies with Millie were getting back to pre-baby levels. *Millie's breasts are much fuller than they were before the kids, and even if they sagged a little more, they're more interesting to fondle.*

On Sundays they went to the Pruttos after Mass at St. Mary's and, on one of those Sundays, Peter heard a loud knock on his in-laws' front door. It was his uncle Guidano and Peter assumed that something had happened to his father.

"Uncle Guidano, is my dad ok, what are you doin here!!!"

"You papa esta ben, dida youa hear da newsa?"

Peter was in total mystery as his uncle continued, "Da goddama Japanesa bomba Hawaii. Disa goddama morning theya bomba alla da fuckina boats in Pearl Harbor. F.D.R. isa gonna maka speecha tomorrow morning."

Peter winced because he realized his draft number, based on birthdays and drawn in September, was very low. If a draft was instituted, he might not go immediately because of his marital status and job at the Ordinance Plant, but eventually he'd go.

On December 8, 1941, President Roosevelt asked Congress to declare "war on the Japanese Imperial Government." His request passed by all but one vote. Three days later, Germany declared war on the United States. The United States was in the Second World War. One year later, on December 10, 1942 Peter opened a notice from his Draft Board,

Greetings from the President of the United States You are to report....

Three weeks later, Peter Rinella was in Fort Bragg, somewhere in North Carolina preparing for his participation in the greatest conflict in human history.

CHAPTER THIRTY-FIVE

Luxemburg, December 1945

He re-boarded the train, settled back in a seat, and followed his mind back to the hospital in Luxemburg City. The doctor was supposed to tell him what was to become of him. Peter hoped he might get a ticket back home, but everything depended on the doctor. Sitting on his bed staring into space, he was startled by the unusual arrival of the "mail man."

"You Rinella, Peter Rinella?" he asked.

Peter's heart started to pound with excitement as he was hoping to finally get some mail.

"Yea, that's me—I'm Rinella."

A very large bag stuffed with letters was tossed on his hospital bed. Peter tore open ropes tying the olive green bag with "U.S. Army Mail" stenciled across it. He found fifty or sixty letters inside. He didn't know where to start the pleasant task of reading the letters.

As he could have predicted, more than half came from Millie. He was looking for envelopes with a picture inside them. He finally found one that had a picture, and, when he opened it, he saw a sweet Carmella and an irritated Vincent forced to pose. Millie had both arms tightly wrapped around their shoulders and he saw that she was trying to make the kids look easy and natural. The kids weren't interested in the photo session. *Oh my God, they have changed so much in the past two years. Christ, they're not going to know me if I ever get back.*

His heart ached for his family and tears welled and he dabbed them to be able to read the attached letter:

> *"My dearest love, we miss you so much you have no idea, or, I hope you do. I talk to the kids about their wonderful daddy and show your picture—the one from our wedding. Carmella as you can see is a little chubby but I think when she gets older she will grow into her weight. Vincent is a hellion. The other day he poked my father right in the eye. I pretended to be upset and corrected him but inside I laughed like hell. I pray for you every night. Please, please take care of yourself and come home to us.*

We love you and need you more than anything in the world, with all my love, your wife, Mill."

The note brought more tears to his eyes and he began to sob. He read all letters from Millie. They were *newsy, lovey* and wonderful. Millie also wrote the letters from his father, uncle Guidano, Aunt Carmella, his mother in-law and even his father in-law.

His father had never told him he loved him, and whether Giacomo actually said it, or Millie added that to the letter, Peter was initially unsure. He chose to believe his father actually said,

"Pio, I love you more than my own life. I miss you and can't wait for you to come home and play Pinochle with me and the guys at the Jeffersonian."

Peter loved all the letters and it must have taken at least an hour or two to read the ones from Millie alone. The most interesting of all came from Millie. Inside the letter was a small inner waxed envelope, and, outside the packet in her beautiful handwriting, were the words,

"Miss You—Want You."

Inside the small envelope were clippings of....her pubic hair. Peter instantly felt himself stir, and every part of him ached for his wife.

CHAPTER THIRTY-SIX

Luxemburg, January, 1945

Doctor Paul Renaud walked into the ward with Peter's chart in his hand and looked at it while looking at Peter between entries. He smiled faintly and looked over his shoulder at the nurse who was following him on his rounds. He wore an olive green lab coat with a stethoscope draped around his neck. He graduated from medical school at Johns Hopkins and was headed for what he thought was going to be a fabulous career in surgery, until he got drafted.

"You know corporal; you're actually in pretty good shape for someone who sustained severe injuries. I don't see anywhere in your chart that you are having any side effects from those injuries. No headaches or numbness or anything like that, huh?"

He didn't wait for a response but just kept looking at Peter's chart. "So, what do you think, corporal?"

Peter didn't understand how to reply. Finally, he figured he should comment on his current status and how that related to his future, so he replied, "Well, I feel a little strange sometimes, almost like I'm looking at the world through fog. I was kinda hoping to be sent back home or at least to an assignment back in the states."

Dr. Renaud now looked directly at Peter and answered, "If you were with Hodges or Bradley or even Clark, I could guarantee you a ride home, but General Patton insists all his walking wounded be reassigned back to him as quickly as we can get 'em back. I'm sorry, but you're probably in Europe until this thing is over. What I am able to do is to send you for a period of recovery to Mer d'Iglise. You will be able to further develop your motor skills and deal with any combat fatigue issues. I can probably get you four or five, maybe even six weeks at Mer and, who knows, maybe this thing will be over by then.
How does that sound? "

Renaud took just enough time to catch his breath and continued, "We aren't sure about the long term effects physically and psychologically from your injuries. It's interesting how the symptoms of 'combat fatigue' pop up, long after physical healing have taken place."

Peter was finally able to respond, "I appreciate it doctor. If I'm not going home it's a helluva lot better than going back to Patton...Thank you."

Before he left, Renaud put his hand on Peter's right shoulder and said, "Good luck, corporal, I need to get back home too."

Peter breathed a sigh of relief, and gathered his personal items, especially his mail.

CHAPTER THIRTY-SEVEN

Mer d' Iglise, February, 1945

He was growing tired of the train ride and wanted to get back to his apartment, dreary as it was, and his desk at the Bureau. It felt like he had been gone for months. His mind wandered back to Mer d'Iglise and the Chateau about a quarter of a mile from the village. Peter didn't know much about the small French village except it was near the English Channel, and was the scene of bitter struggle between the defending Germans and the Hundred and First Airborne unit during the invasion of D-Day. One of his friends in the neighborhood, Tony Vardaro, was killed around Mer. *How's that for a coincidence? Tony gets killed there and maybe I can get saved there if the war ends before I leave the place.*

As he departed the troop transport, he was amazed by the size of the Chateau. When he got inside, he noticed little signs just at the top of the doorways. One, in all capital letters "REGISTRATION," and four others in regular lettering: "Counseling," "Physical Rehabilitation," "Chapel," and "Artistic Therapy."

A young orderly met them in the hallway and spoke slowly as though some of them would have trouble understanding normal speech. He explained registration was first, and over the course of the first few days, they were expected to make an appearance at each one of the named rooms for whatever was offered. They could pick one or two areas in which to concentrate, assuming the facilitators in those areas were ok with it, and they could also omit other subjects, after that staff person confirmed their initial participation.

"We recommend you avail yourselves of all the resources in this facility. Please understand we also want you to spend a fair amount of time in some sort of counseling environment. Your stay here has been determined by the doctor who has sponsored your admission but you can join your regiment any time you wish, but again it has to be approved by our professional staff. You cannot extend your stay beyond the time the admitting physician has suggested. This is not a place for malingerers. Meals are served promptly in the dining room down the hall to the right at seven in the morning, twelve noon, and five-thirty in the evening. Meals are served for one and one-half hours. If you miss the time, you miss the meal. You may smoke here but alcohol is strictly prohibited and if brought in will cause you to be either sent back to your outfit or placed in the brig. Are there any questions?" *Great, we are in the Boy Scout's Division of the U.S. Army.*

The meals were far better than he had gotten in the previous hospital and ten thousand times better than K-Rations. The counseling sessions were ok, too.

The counselor assigned to Peter was a six foot five or six, balding man in his late thirties or early forties. Marcus Schmidt told Peter he was very close to getting his PhD in psychology from Rutgers. Peter knew Rutgers was in New Jersey but really couldn't figure out why Schmidt shared his educational status with him. He confided in Peter that he was grateful to have this assignment because it kept him out of harm's way. They discussed Peter's injury and any side effects from his wounds.

Peter reported, "You know, everything's pretty good. I am sleeping well (a lie) and don't even think about it much."

This was a bigger lie because, when Peter wasn't thinking about his family and going home, he was reliving the horror in the back of the truck. Peter didn't believe that Marcus Schmidt could help him and was resigned to the prison his mind had constructed.

"You know, Mr. Schmidt, I am just glad to be able to spend some time here."

Schmidt looked at Peter and said, "That is a statement of a very well adjusted man, and, I think a sign of your definite stability."

Peter's trip to the chapel was interesting, too. When he looked in, he saw a heavy set, dark man facing the door. As Peter got closer, he noticed a prayer shawl over the man's shoulder and a small cap covering the back of his head.

The man spoke before Peter could utter a word and said,

"Are you Jewish, son?" Peter was surprised and took a moment to utter,

"No...No I' m Catholic. Are there Jewish times, Protestant times, and Catholic times? I should have known that, huh? "

The older man replied, "No, not really, there are no specific times, but if you want, I can set up a meeting with Father Coleman. He's a wonderful man who occasionally drinks a bit much but has a fine mind and great soul. My name is Rabbi Lowenstein, if it's ok, I can spend a little time with you."

Peter didn't want to hurt the Rabbi's feelings and really didn't need to talk to a priest so he replied, "No, no… its fine… but I don't have any deep questions or many religious issues to talk about."

The small room which served as a chapel had temporary pews, a Crucifix and Star of David next to each other on a table that served as an altar. The Rabbi noticed the strange juxtaposition and commented to the other clergy how the army united all religions whether or not they wanted to be.

"Most of the guys I talk to don't have many questions, either" began the Rabbi, "but, if they do, the ones that comes up the most are, 'how can God, if there is one, allow such a terrible thing as war to occur? How can that same God allow such horrible things to happen to good and innocent people?"

"Those are great questions. I wish I'd have asked them."

Both grew silent. After a few minutes, Peter asked, "So Rabbi, how do you answer that question—'what kind of God can let those things happen?'"

The Rabbi waited another moment and replied, "A God who probably knows more about what is going to occur in the future and how, in all its evil and depravity, war serves a purpose in the improvement of man —or at least that is one answer…but maybe the bullshit one?

After a few minutes he continued, "My most honest answer is: I just don't know or understand the whole thing either. I choose to defer to a God I know, love, and trust."

Two minutes passed when the Rabbi asked, "Not much help to you, eh corporal? Are there any other questions I probably can't help you with?"

Peter waited a moment and asked, "Rabbi, do the French call the English Channel the French Channel?"

Lowenstein said nothing at first, surprised at the silly question, but when he noticed the small smile on Peter's face and the twinkle in his eye, both of them burst out in loud laughter that sounded much better than the recorded hymns played in the faux chapel.

CHAPTER THRITY-EIGHT

Mer d'Iglise, March 1945

Peter walked into "Artistic Therapy," with no idea what to expect. Chairs and easels were set up in a semi-circle around an easel, with a large drawing pad, and podium in the center. *That figures, lessons in art and drawing.*

There were only three other "students" in the room who looked as though their minds were in another world and not in Chateau d' Mer d'Iglise. Then the goddess appeared.

She marched quickly and purposely to the semi-circle. She had on a light brown frock. It flowed unbuttoned just below her hips. She was wearing tan pants and, underneath the frock, a white blousy top opened just above her cleavage. She had a thin upper lip and a slightly fuller lower one with just a touch of lip stick. Her face was thin with a slim distinct nose. She had short brown hair, beautiful dark skin, and straight white teeth. Her most amazing feature was her emerald green eyes. Peter had never seen eyes so green, and set in her dark face, they were radiant. Trailing her, minutes later, was a smallish younger girl who was lost in the charismatic wake of the instructor.

The instructor began her presentation, "Good morning, my name is Kathryn Dupree. This class is for development of your painting and drawing skills, but more importantly, for improving your hand to eye coordination. I will be your instructor (and nodding to the younger woman) and this is my assistant is Natalie D'Vale."

He judged her age to be between thirty-five and forty-five and he was mesmerized. *Come on, this is ridiculous! You are acting like some teenager with a crush on his English teacher. You're a happily married man for Christ's sake, with two kids, who shouldn't be thinking this shit.*

He got some control over his wayward thoughts and heard the conclusion of her introduction. "Please remember these brushes, and all the materials here, for that matter, have to be used by others so we need to take care of them. Ok, let's start our program with a description of painting media."

He felt guilt, but Peter knew he would attend all of Kathryn's classes. He justified himself with the thought that he would only be looking and never act (or get an opportunity to act) on his thoughts. *A woman like that would never find me attractive—what the hell does Millie even see in me for Christ's sake? It's like buying a dirty magazine at "Mulligan's" and then jerkin' off later, with no one the wiser.*

CHAPTER THIRTY-NINE

Washington D.C., November 1962

The train pulled into Union Station. He had slept really well and even used the bathroom once. The trip gave him a lot of time to spend with his thoughts and that was good and bad. Sometimes he was comforted by his musings and other times distressed. It was an exercise in mind control.

The cab dropped him off and he walked up the five steps to his first floor apartment. When he got in, the smell of spoiled food covered him. He found an onion in the waste can in the kitchen that he had forgotten to empty. He sorted through the mail piled up on the floor under the mail slot. There were the usual bills and a letter from his son, Vincent.

> *Hey, Dad, thought I'd drop you a line to let you know things are going pretty well. As you know I'm going to graduate in December. I really don't have any idea what I'm going to do after that. I'm worried they might reinstate the draft and I don't really want to go into the army. The stuff that happened with the Berlin wall and all the shit in Cuba with the missiles scares the piss out of me. What do you think I should do? If you have some time, call me, I love you, Vin*

He would call Vinnie tomorrow. He unpacked, nibbled on stale saltines, while he watched T.V., and dozed until ten thirty. He dragged himself to bed and tried to sleep. He missed the rocking of the train. His meeting with H.Z. tomorrow would be important since he had to report some kind of investigation progress. His body struggled with the sheets and his mind, searching for some diversion and relief, brought him back to Mer d'Iglise.

CHAPTER FORTY

Mer d'Iglise, February, 1945

Peter couldn't wait to get into the class to see Kathryn. Natalie was setting up chairs and easels with drawing pads perched on them. On a table in front of the class was a bowl with fruit in it. Apples, pears, peaches, a cluster of grapes, and a banana were placed in the bowl, and after everyone was seated, Kathryn addressed them, "We don't expect anybody here to be a grand master or an instant artist. We are hoping you can develop your fine motor skills and hand coordination by *trying* to do some drawing. If you are able to draw something that actually looks like something, that's great. If you can't, don't worry, it's the effort we're after. We want you to try to capture the object, and in the trying, you'll regain some of your lost skills. Any questions?"

Her lips pursed with the statement and she stood straight from the waist up. Her posture looked artificially straight yet she maintained it with her every movement. Her shoulders were always back and her head slightly tilted to the right. It was as though she was looking at a drawing and needed her head tilted to gain perspective. Peter found her persona captivating. Kathryn could have even pissed on the floor and that would have been attractive to him.

She continued her instruction, "You see this bowl of fruit and notice the shapes and colors attached to them. Notice how common shapes are represented by the fruit. Oranges, apples, pears, are circular. The cluster of grapes is a group of circles within a triangle. The banana is an elongated oval. Take your time but don't go crazy trying for perfection."

Peter looked at the other guys in the room and realized there was not a Rembrandt among them. One of the G.I.s could barely hold the pencil he was given and another was rocking front to back like he was in a rocking chair. The others seemed ok, but weren't making better progress than Peter. He was able to focus on the pad in front of him and away from Kathryn long enough to attempt a simple circle. *That will be easy enough. Shit, I was always able to draw simple forms. Nobody draws a cube better than me.*

His brain told him to draw a circle and he was horrified when he was unable to. It looked like an oval tipped on its axis. More distressing, the lines were nowhere near straight. They were squiggly. He looked down at his right hand and noticed a tremor. Natalie stood behind the G.I. who was rocking and held his hand to help him in drawing the shapes.

Kathryn worked with the guy who couldn't hold his pencil and Peter heard her say, "If you have to, hold it between your thumb and index finger. Yes, yes, that's good. Yes, keep going just like that!"

He saw Natalie motion Kathryn over to him with a nod of her head. Kathryn stood behind Peter and he felt his face flush and his heart pick up a beat. Kathryn bent over his right shoulder and rested her breast on it. She put his hand in hers and started to make the circle shapes. After one, she did another and another.

"Ok, Corporal…..Rinella, yes? I want you to try a circle by yourself"

Peter nodded in agreement and made a much better shape than before. The line was still squiggly but not as wavy as the original.

"You see Corporal," she said, "Practice makes everything go a lot better."

He was proud of his effort and got enough courage to croak out, "Ma'am, could you please call me Peter?"

She smiled and had a twinkle in her beautiful emerald eyes,

"On one condition, you must call me Kathryn."

Peter was fixated by the emeralds, and responded with some effort, "I can do that with no problem, Kathryn."

She turned to the other "students" and said "Ok, please let's try to draw some of the other shapes."

Kathryn helped Peter with his advanced shapes, and in the process, Peter again felt her breast nestled on his shoulder. After her tutoring, Peter looked up at Kathryn and asked, "What are we sketching tomorrow?"

"I think we are going to sketch a cat's skull. It has very interesting shapes and the relationship between them is remarkable."

Peter nodded as though he was interested in the forthcoming art lesson but he would have sketched a pile of manure if it meant being next to Kathryn.

CHAPTER FORTY-ONE

Washington D.C., November 1962

Peter awoke at seven to get ready for his appointment with H.Z. Headquarters was a short bus ride away from his apartment. He felt sluggish and foggy. *I need more than four hours of sleep to feel halfway decent. How can I make any sense to anyone when my mind should still be in the bed?*

He got to the Bureau and took the elevator up to H.Z.'s office. His secretary, who Peter had met thirty times, always asked, "It's Special Agent Rinella?"

Peter wanted to say, *you stupid ass, you have met me thirty times and you still don't know my goddamn name.*

Of course, he didn't and only responded, "Yes it is. I have an appointment with Assistant Director Zaun."

It was the exact response he used the other thirty times. Peter sat across from the massive mahogany desk the U.S. taxpayers purchased for H.Z. Looking in Peter's direction, but not looking at him, H.Z. asked,

"How was your trip from Chicago? I heard you took the train. It's quite nice isn't it?"

Peter thought H.Z. was making an attempt at the appropriate small talk before getting into the substance and replied,

"Actually, I took the train from South Bend, Indiana. I was visiting some friends there and decided to take some vacation time to get reacquainted. Thanks for asking."

H.Z. wasn't listening and continued his pleasantries. "How's your boy doing? He graduates from high school, doesn't he?"

Peter, amazed he even remembered he had a son, replied, "College....he is graduating from college this December."

Peter wanted to say more about Vincent but knew H.Z. really wasn't interested in Vin or what he might be doing.

"My son's a sophomore at Dartmouth." H.Z. added, looking off in space.

He got up from his desk and moved to his window and looked over the city with his back to Peter. "He wants to be an attorney like his father and grandfather. He has this idea about the law being a profession where wrongs are righted and truth is codified. Once I wanted to represent the poor, unjustly accused. I quickly disabused myself of that idea when I realized I couldn't make much money defending the 'poor.' I joined my father in his practice which did mostly tax law. I took some undergrad courses in accounting and got my C.P.A. Lo and behold, I got good paying cases defending the rich, unjustly accused. It paid exceptionally well, but I hated every minute of it! The war came along... the C.I.A. and later a job with the Bureau in the tax section tracking down the rich and justly accused....sometimes."

He turned around and faced Pete, "That wasn't very interesting either. I got so damn tired of accounting, fraud, and human greed I couldn't stand it. When this job came open, I went to Mr. Tolson and asked to be given a chance at some criminal investigation. Now I deal with far more interesting human foibles. How often does one discuss plots to assassinate the President of the United States, huh? Ok, Pete, what do we have?"

Peter blinked in surprise at H.Z.'s effusiveness and replied, "Well sir, I believe the Giancana family is very upset with the president and has the capacity to plan and execute any assassination attempt. It's a very large and well connected organization. They have ties in Chicago, of course, but also in Miami, New Orleans, L.A., New York... everywhere. Do I have any evidence of an actual plan? My answer is no. I can tell you with absolute certainty, though, if they want to plan and carry-out an attempt on the president, no one will be the wiser. No one will be able to pin a thing on them. I've also heard Bobby Kennedy has pissed off one of the bosses in New Orleans."

H.Z. was looking out in space again. A minute passed when he said, "There are a lot of people who'd like to assassinate the president. The Cubans hate him, too. The C.I.A. likes to remind everyone, the potential of a 'foreign power' doing something is another possibility, but I think the Russians are too smart to do anything to start a Third World War. No, that's not happening. They know after eight years we put out our trash and make new garbage. I think a more distinct possibility is the racist, anti-Negro fringe. Our president has talked about protecting Negro rights in the south and enforcing the Supreme Court's integration ruling. That, my friend, has angered a lot of very dangerous people."

Peter asked, "Do you want me to assist in that investigation, sir?"

H.Z. finally showed some emotion and looked directly at Peter with a very large smile, "Pete, you would stand out like a sore thumb down there with those crackers. Nothing like an announcement the

'F.B.I. is here.' We have some informants in the K.K.K. and some other crazy groups and they're doing just fine. No, you're going to stay where you are. Try to get something concrete. I want you to look at any planned trips the president will be making and see if the Secret Service will share any information with you. Oh, by the way, watch what you give them. I want any developments to be kept in the Bureau. Assistant Director Tolson and Director Hoover would be very appreciative of our work. Do you understand?"

Peter didn't quite understand how to proceed but had to agree with H.Z. and said, "Yes, sir, I understand fully."

H.Z. stood up and offered his hand to Peter and dismissed him with, "Thanks for your time. Take all the time you need here in D.C. to develop something we can go on, and make sure you run your travel plans through Sarah." *Oh, great, Sarah, who doesn't know my name, has to approve my travel requests.*

As he was leaving, Peter heard H.Z. say, "Pete, my wife left me. She left me for a younger man. Apparently, he's better in bed."

Peter turned around to acknowledge the statement, but didn't know what to say and lamely replied, "I'm sorry to hear that, sir" and continued through the door.

He breezed through the outer office and said, "Have a nice day, Sarah. H.Z. told me to run my travel needs past you. Please, expedite any requests from *Peter Rinella,*" (as pleasantly as possible), emphasizing his name.

CHAPTER FORTY-TWO

Washington D. C., December, 1962

Peter rode the elevator down to the fourth floor to the office he shared with Morgan Morgan. Peter chided his office-mate, "Who names their kid with same first name as his last name? What the hell possessed them to do something that crazy!!??"

Morgan responded, "Pete, my given name is Jasper, after my dad's father, and my middle name, Morgan, was my maternal grandfather's first name. What name would you use? How does Jasper Morgan sound to you? Maybe I should call myself J. Morgan Morgan?"

Peter never got tired of the joshing, however Morgan grew tired of the routine and simply rolled his eyes when the subject came up. They shared an office that was twelve by twelve. Filing cabinets on either side of their desks made it appear both men were in matching caves. The desks were government-issue gray gunmetal with darker gray plastic tops. Morgan, who graduated from Brown University, was old money, the stereotypical Ivy League kid. He was six foot one, athletically built, sandy, blond thick hair, and crystal blue eyes.

Peter razzed him, "Hey, Morgan, why don't you do the cover of the Harvard Catalog—for Christ's sake you look like you just got off the Mayflower."

Morgan smiled broadly and replied, "Pete, you know I graduated from Brown and I wouldn't hold a Harvard Catalog let alone have my picture on it! Oh, by the way, I've had sex with some Harvard girls which convinced me that not all women are created equal. Those from Harvard are far inferior."

Peter respected Morgan's piercing intelligence. He quickly assessed the problem and came up with a plausible plan of action. He was assigned to general crime matters--bank fraud, kidnapping, and all other violations of federal laws.

He made his bones during the Second World War when he worked the espionage desk and tracked down Nazi spies. He was the youngest agent on the desk and was responsible for the filming of the Nazis as they were planning and paying for espionage activity. Twenty years later, that footage was still shown on a P.R. film as proof of the

F.B.I.'s effectiveness during the war. Inexplicably, he was taken off the espionage desk and placed in criminal investigation. He was insulted by the move and thought about leaving, but decided to stay because his career options were limited. He didn't have a law or accounting degree so his activity was confined to "enforcement and incarceration details."

Peter was happy to find the young guy in his chair and waited for him to finish his call, "Morgan, I'm at a complete standstill. I got no idea where to go from here. I know the Mafia would like to whack the president but I got nothin' to go on."

Morgan said nothing for a minute while he mulled the question and replied, "How about calling some field agents in the areas where the mob is a presence. The agents may have not heard anything directly, but maybe they can get you with someone who has. Let's see…... I also have a buddy who is in the president's Secret Service detail. We both went to Brown and he told me the best way to kill the president would be to get him laid four times a night. Maybe he could be fucked to death. He tells me more strange pussy goes in and out of the White House than in the D.C. Animal Shelter."

Peter laughed and decided to take Morgan's advice. He'd start calling field agents in Miami, New York, Detroit, L.A., Buffalo, and New Orleans to start.

Rather than phone each field office, Peter sent a Tel-A-Type to them with the general request,

> *Please send any information relative to potential plots or persons who potentially are a threat to the President. All information, regardless of its seeming inconsequence, is welcomed. Send all information and/ or questions attention Peter Rinella, Special Agent"*

Looking over at Morgan, Peter asked, "What's going on with you?"

Morgan didn't look up but stared intently at an open file and replied, "We grabbed a bank official in Indiana who thought he had the perfect way to "borrow" some money. He was siphoning money from the bank's travelling reserve fund and thought he could get away with it. The bank auditors found the discrepancies and reported the crime to local authorities and us. Pretty cut and dry, this one. This elder in the

Presbyterian Church and pillar of the community is going to a federal pen and his family will be left to live with the disgrace....nice, huh?"

Peter just shook his head and offered casually, "If you need any help on anything, I think H.Z. would be ok with me giving you a hand."

Morgan, deep in thought, said nothing at first and then replied, "Thanks, but so far I'm ok, but if I need a hand, I'll let you know."

Peter hoped Morgan would say that and told him he was going home. When Peter got into the apartment he noticed his reflection in a full length dressing mirror near the front door. He was in terrible condition. He just looked at himself from his tie up. Even his profile surprised him. It was as though some stranger had inhabited his body. He looked again to make sure he was seeing what he was seeing. He looked down and barely saw the tips of his brogues. He bitterly thought to himself, *when I'm naked and don't have a hard-on I can't see my dick. What the hell, even when I have a hard-on, I can't see my dick. How did I get like this?* He started to laugh, almost uncontrollably; *Peter can't see his Peter, hard or soft... I'm losing my goddamn mind.*

He remembered a time when his stomach was much flatter-- when he was able to see his flaccid self and his time at the chateau. Thoughts of Kathryn pleasantly swept over him. They were tinged with passion, longing, and regret, all at the same time.

CHAPTER FORTY-THREE

Mer d'Iglise, March 1945

For nearly two weeks, Peter went to Kathryn's class and actually learned a thing or two about art. That was the farthest thing from his mind. He arrived ten or fifteen minutes early and hoped to see Kathryn and ask a stupid question as an excuse to talk to her.

Before one class, he approached Kathryn and asked one of his inane questions. Natalie stared at him as though he was some silly child. Kathryn took his question seriously and attempted to answer it. Peter stared at her beautiful eyes set so wonderfully in the dark skin. He never heard her response, because he was transfixed by her physicality. Once, he thought he heard Natalie click her tongue over one of his dumb questions. He didn't care. He prayed for Kathryn's attention and assistance. He thoroughly enjoyed the classes and the goddess' presence. He hated to see them end, but took consolation in knowing there would be another class.

Aside from the great art classes, the chateau offered decent food in a large ball room that served as a mess hall. After one of Kathryn's riveting classes, Peter found himself hunched over a plate of roast beef, mashed potatoes, and string beans and realized the guys at the front only dreamed about this kind of food. *Even the officers aren't gettin' this kind of food*, he thought to himself. This was reinforced as he bit into a very warm and soft dinner roll with a generous amount of butter on it.

Suddenly, he felt someone next to him. It was Kathryn, with the omnipresent Natalie beside her. He felt Kathryn's thighs next to his and his heart began to pump crazily. It occurred to him that Kathryn meant for their thighs to touch and that really excited him. His throat tightened but he was able to force out, "Oh, how nice to see you…you too Natalie."

Kathryn adjusted her napkin and arranged her table-ware and replied, "Well, we saw you sitting here by yourself and thought you could use some company. I hope you don't mind sharing your meal with us?"

"Oh, of course not, I am…..happy to have you here," Peter replied sheepishly.

They ate in silence until Peter got the courage to ask, "What nationality are you?"

She swallowed a bite of food before answering, "Oh, I'm French. My father was in the Foreign Service and was stationed in America from the time I was two until I was fourteen. I learned to speak American English there and French from my parents. My father met my mother on his first assignment in Guyana. She was Guyanese, and in those days, it was difficult to have a racially mixed marriage in France."

She started to laugh when she continued, "They thought America would be better! What a joke, of course, it was worse there. People assumed my mother was the household staff so they never traveled to the consulates in the South because of the separate facilities for 'Coloreds' and 'Whites.'" I was light enough 'to pass,' as the Negroes in the States say. I don't know how my mother tolerated that for so many years."

Peter said nothing for a minute and then asked, "You're married, yes? What does your husband do?"

"He's a physician. His mother was Jewish and when the Nazis came in he had to get out quickly. He went to England to join the Free French. He is with them until the war is finished."

Silence again as Peter struggled with what to ask next, "How was it with the Germans? Did you have any trouble?"

She took a moment to form her answer, "Honestly, it wasn't so bad. The average German soldier is no different than any other, really. I wasn't raped on the street if that is what you mean? I wasn't harassed or accosted. Life continued at its own slow pace, like now. Actually, I was able to make some connections in the German command and get some information like troop movements and such to pass on to the Resistance. You know, you have to be sure that such things aren't forgotten because fraternizing, without intelligence, is seen as collaboration. You've seen women walking around with their heads shaved—those are collaborators. All they did was sleep with Germans and not get any military information to give to the Resistance."

Peter felt funny about excluding Natalie and asked her, "What about you Natalie, what's your story?"

He wasn't interested and never heard her reply. Just as they were finished, Natalie moved off to clear her plate, and to "freshen up," when Kathryn leaned over an inch or two from Peter and almost inaudibly said, "How would you like some French cuisine—something different than beef and potatoes? If you like, I will make dinner for you tonight. I live only a half a mile away."

Peter nearly strangled with shock and elation and barely said, "Of course...I would love that!"

She hurriedly gave him instructions to her house and emphasized, "Use the back door off the alley. It's always open and leads directly to my kitchen."

Natalie returned and picked up Kathryn's dishes. Kathryn immediately resumed her ramrod posture. As they departed, she looked over her shoulder and gave him a discrete smile.

Peter sat there for fifteen minutes. His heart pounded and his head buzzed. It wasn't the disoriented injury induced buzzing but the exhilarating blood surge buzzing that made life worthwhile. He went immediately to get a pass and arrange for one of the most improbable events of his life.

CHAPTER FORTY-FOUR

Washington, D.C. December, 1962

Peter's thoughts of Kathryn were interrupted by his ringing telephone. He picked it up and recognized his son's voice. "How'd you know I was home, Vin?"

"I called the office and Morgan said you'd be home."

After some small talk Vincent asked, "Hey dad, you know I've been thinking about the times when Cam and I were kids. Do you remember that bastard Jason Kebert?"

Peter just grunted in agreement. He also remembered at a very young age they called Carmella Marie, "Cam." It was easier for Vincent to say "Cam." He had a slight speech impediment and his lisp made some words difficult to form but "Cam" rolled off easily.

"Dad, do you happen to remember when that little prick Kebert called Cam a 'dago' and me a 'dumb guinea goomba?' I came into the house crying like hell and told you what he said. Cam didn't say anything. It was her way to just ignore any kind of malice or ignorance. After you saw me crying and I told you what happened, you didn't say anything. You went out and said something to Jason and you know, he never said another bad word to us again. What the hell did you say to him?"

Peter had just gotten out of Bureau training and they lived in Frederick, Maryland. Peter went out to the front porch and called the gangly twelve or thirteen year-old over to the porch. He asked, "You're Jason Kebert, huh?"

With a self assured and smug demeanor, the kid nodded.

"You live up the street in the white house with the red door and black shutters, eh," Peter asked.

"Yeah! So what?"

Peter continued,

"Well, I just wanted to know, because if you bother either of my kids again, I'm going to your house knock on the door until your father comes out and, when he does, I will knock him on his ass. When he gets up I might do it again then I'll tell him I did it because of what you did or said." Putting his hand on the young man's shoulder and looking him squarely in the eyes he continued,

"You have two choices; you can behave like a decent guy and let these kids alone or you can harass them again and get your father knocked on his ass. I think he might be upset with you for that. What do you think? What's it gonna be, Jason?"

The young man's eyes opened in shock. He didn't say a word, backed up slowly and then ran down the street as fast as he could. Peter called after him, "Jason, if you want, you can tell your dad we just had this conversation and he can come over now and pay me a visit."

John Kebert never visited and whether Jason told him of their conversation Peter never knew.

Vincent laughed and asked, "Christ Dad, what would you have done if Jason hadn't changed? Would you really have punched his dad in the mouth? I don't remember his father, what....I mean, shit, suppose he was some big guy who...?"

Peter laughed along with Vinnie and replied, "Fuck no, the guy was some little shit who worked in the Congressional Budget Office, and to answer to your question, I was ready, regardless of his size to knock Jason's old man on his ass. I figured anybody who'd raised a little bastard like that needed some punishment!"

Both of them were hysterical with laughter when suddenly Peter recalled the sobering sadness of his daughter's life, "Unfortunately, I couldn't be with Cam all the time. That's the greatest regret of my life—some of the stuff that wonderful kid endured and how totally powerless I was in the face of it."

There was silence for a minute, "You know Dad, Cam told me being different was a strange experience. On some levels because she didn't meet society's norms, she was ignored and felt obscure. Despite all that emotion and sorrow, she felt privileged for the person she had become. She liked who she was internally and felt good…confident about herself and her intelligence… and her soul.

Peter knew Vincent believed what he was saying, but Peter also knew his son was trying to prop his spirits. Peter was compelled to change the subject or risk descending into a black abyss of depression. He asked his son about his plans for the future.

Vincent replied, "Everything's working out as planned… I'm dating a great girl who's going to be a doctor."

"Vin this phone call is costing you a fortune. I'm going to send some money to help you out a little bit. We need to get together soon. By the way, say hello to your mom for me. Tell her I think about her often."

"No problem, will do, dad, I love you."

"I love you very much son. Take care."

CHAPTER FORTY-FIVE

Washington D.C., December, 1962

When Peter got back to his office, there was a teletype on his desk. It was from Bob Shannon in Miami. The message was brief,

Pete, call me.

Peter met Shannon a few years earlier when Shannon visited headquarters. Shannon graduated from Florida State University with a degree in accounting. He, like Peter, was a veteran of the war and also got his college degree as a non-traditional student. He was in the first wave in the invasion of Iwo Jima and was one of only eight-hundred first wave survivors. He developed a hatred for the smell of sulfur because the soil of Iwo was laced with the mineral and as a result, he would only use a Zippo lighter.

Peter was happy to hear Shannon's gruff voice respond, "I got your request and I gotta tell you there are Capos down here upset with the Kennedy's. Apparently, the Mafia had some serious cash in the casinos in Havana. Of course, when Castro came into power, he threw everybody out including the mob. The Trafficantes took a big hit and lost four casinos in and around Havana. They had some assurances from somebody somewhere how the Administration would take an aggressive approach in deposing our friend Castro. The Bay of Pigs signaled how weak our resolve was. Now, get this Pete, I am told someone from the C.I.A. contacted the Mafia to enlist its help in assassinating Castro! Can you believe that one?!!"

Peter said nothing for a few seconds and then, "I can believe the C.I.A. would get involved with something like that, sure. Christ, after Khrushev tried to put I.C.B.M.s in Cuba and then had to yank them out, there is no way we were going to invade Cuba, no way."

Shannon agreed and said, "The Family is angry and revenge is a powerful motive. Whacking the President, from a practical standpoint, would get Bobby off their backs. What else is there, right? ... practicality and revenge in one fell swoop."

Peter asked, "You don't have any ideas about where they might do it or who the hit men would be?"

Shannon, after a second, replied, "Sorry, I got nothin' about that. Pete, you are gonna need an informant. The stakes will be high, so you better have some big reward for someone to rat on these guys. If anyone catches wind of the rat, he's as good as in the cemetery. You know that, don't you?"

Peter thanked Shannon for his help. It was March of 1963, four months since his visit to Chicago, and he knew nothing more. He thought to contact someone at Secret Service in D.C. and see if they had identified any crazies who threatened the life of the president. There was always some nut threatening the life of the president. The Mafia could easily find three or four loonies to make an effective assassination team. The key was to get fruit cakes with the skills to pull the trigger. It would be great if the guys got killed during the act because that would silence them and no one would connect them to the mob since they were documented nuts. *Possible, oh yeah, real possible, but where are they going to find these nuts and how can I find them after they do? Where would you find someone who is crazy enough, smart enough, and skilled enough to kill the President of the United States? I'll call the Secret Service tomorrow and see what it has.*

CHAPTER FORTY-SIX

Mer d'Iglise, March, 1945

Peter couldn't get Kathryn out of his mind. When he was at Mer d'Iglise he was consumed by her presence. He remembered the walk from the Chateau to the village. He was floating. His heart was beating, he swore, out of rhythm and was pounding in his throat. He made the left turn at the intersection of the village, walked to the next block and finally arrived at Kathryn's house. He walked up the three steps to the stoop and tapped on the door three times.

She opened the door. He was breathless from excitement, the short jaunt, and her appearance. She had on a dark blue dress with a white top and a lace fringe. The top exposed her shoulder and came to a "v" at her cleavage. Her skin looked golden as though she was perfectly tanned. She smiled, asked him in, and he instantly smelled the meal she prepared. She led him into the dining room with the table set for two. The place settings were in china and what he assumed was crystal glassware.

"Would you like something to drink, maybe a glass of wine?" she asked.

He nodded.

"What would you like…white, red?" She asked again.

Finally, he found his voice, "I don't know much about wine. My father used to get a red wine. I'm sure you would think it was garbage. You know a lot more about what a good wine is than I do, so maybe you could get me something you think is ok."

She smiled again and looked directly at him and said, "I will be glad to do that but I am certainly no wine expert. I do know what I like."

She poured a little in the glass and offered it to him. He was uncertain what to do and she motioned for him to sniff it and take a sip.

He complied and she asked, "What do you think? Do you like it?"

Actually, Peter found it bitter but was not going to admit that and said, "Oh, it is very good. Yes, I like it. Can I have a bit more?"

She laughed out loud and said, "Of course, you can have a full glass. Did you think that was all you were getting tonight?"

Peter smiled and took another sip of the wine. She motioned for him to sit at one of the settings on a square table that would seat four. They sat next to each other around one of the corners. In the middle of the table was a vase with wild flowers. She had prepared a dish with fish and herbs. He could look at her for hours and be totally oblivious to everything else around him. She made small talk about the weather and what they were eating and he smiled, agreed, and offered inane conversation about the village's houses and the Chateau's architecture. The wine was going down much easier and he started to get giddy. When she served dessert, some crepe, Peter almost laughed out loud at his tipsy internal musing of the dessert called *craps*. He didn't share his word play with Kathryn for fear she think him some kind idiot.

Peter helped her clean up the table and bring the dishes to the sink. She was rinsing off the dishes with her back to him when Peter put his hands on either shoulder and turned her around to face him. He brought his face within a few inches of her and took her face in both his hands and kissed her. She eagerly returned the kiss and both embraced the other, as their lips parted. *This is wonderful. I'm kissing a goddess, and she is returning my kisses. I can't believe it.* His hands moved down her back and rested on her ass. Suddenly he stopped. He saw Millie and felt a strange mixture of guilt and lust.

"My God, Kathryn, I am so sorry. It must be the wine... it's been forever since I've had anything to drink...I guess it just got the best of me. I'm...I'm sorry."

She didn't say a word but simply took his left hand and led him toward the stairway. He stopped. Visions of Millie flashed through his mind again and the words, "I can't, I can't.....it's really not right," were barely spoken.

He weakly held up his left hand and his wedding band as though Kathryn had not seen it before that moment and said stupidly, "I'm...I'm...I'm married."

She was amused by his protestations and held up her left hand showing her wedding rings as well, and whispered, "I am too, Cherie... Moliere said, 'it is no sin to sin in secret, it is public scandal that gives offence'.... Come upstairs."

Peter didn't know who Moliere was but the argument had merit. Pulling on his hand, Kathryn noticed he was hardly resisting. Millie's face kept flashing through Peter's mind, but Peter was unable to stop himself.

She led him next to the bed and lowered the white blouse off her shoulders and down over her lacey bra. His heart was going to pound itself out of his chest as she unclasped her bra and exposed the most beautiful breasts Peter had ever seen. Thoughts of Millie faded rapidly and were replaced by thoughts of Mae. Peter was now very willing to commit adultery.

CHAPTER FORTY-SEVEN

Thoughts of Kathryn danced through his mind and Peter knew if he was to get any sleep he would have to expend some of the sexual energy these thoughts stirred. *Oh Christ, here I am, fifty-six years old and jerkin off like a teenager. Oh well, it beats tossin and turnin the whole night thinkin of some long lost lover,* and he immediately smiled at his choice of words.

The levity nearly got him out of the mood but he still felt the need to satisfy himself and completed it after some effort. He fell asleep and awoke refreshed. *Not so bad, maybe I should try that every night since I don't exactly have women lined up to get into my bed.*

Morgan was already at his desk when Peter got to the office. After he told Morgan he was going to call his friend at the Secret Service, Morgan laughed and said, "You mean the guy who said the President is always getting some strange tail? His name is Anderson Wellington, here's his number. Tell him I told you to call and that he should help you as much as he can. He owes me a few favors. Remind him of that!"

When Wellington answered, Peter identified himself and repeated Morgan's instructions. Wellington faked surprise and anger and replied, "Is he still working at the Bureau? I would have thought his inadequacies would have surfaced by now. Ok, I do owe him a favor, what do you need....what was your name again?"

Peter smiled and repeated, "Rinella....Peter Rinella. Do you have a list of anyone who might be considered a crackpot and has threatened the president? I know you have investigated all of them but I just want to revisit that list and see if something emerges."

Wellington took a moment and then replied, "I don't have that list at my finger tips, but I can get one, if it exists. You really are going to go over ground that has been covered many times. You have to realize if my boss finds out that I gave our information to the F.B.I. it will surely be my ass. You understand that, right?"

His statement was a plea couched in a question. "Of course, no one will know anything about what you give me. I have already forgotten this conversation," Peter assured him.

"Ok, give me a week or so to dig up what we have and call me back then, and tell Morgan 'thanks a lot.'"

When he got the list from the Secret Service and maybe some file information, he would be able to cross-reference the whereabouts of the "nut cases" with the travel plans of the president. As further refinement, he would assess skills of the possible candidates as well as any history of violence. The Bureau Field Offices could assist him in filling in any missing information and, if the list of potentials was too large, he might get the locals to help follow up on any leads. *I might also be able to run photos of any suspects past the guys at the Organized Crime Desk. If one of the nuts was seen visiting a Capo or a known Mafia member or at one of the "Social Clubs," that would really tie things up.*

Peter knew the Secret Service had access to a lot more information regarding the president and his security problems, but the Bureau had a better understanding of organized crime. Besides the Bureau's Field Offices were better than the Secret Service's. He needed to get the president's itinerary for the next six to eight months. He had no idea how much in advance those plans were made. *The Secret Service knows where he is going to be. I don't know anyone in the Bureau who would know that. I'm probably going to have to get some more help from Wellington. He's gonna love that!*

Suddenly, out of nowhere, the image of Kathryn and their first night popped into Peter's brain. *She was beautiful. What a magnificent body....Perfect tits, wonderful ass, everything was wonderful. No wonder I can't forget her.*

CHAPTER FORTY-EIGHT

Mer d'Iglise, March, 1945

He covered her with kisses. When he pleased her she whispered a barely audible "umm." When he really pleased her, the hum became a bit louder and extended to "ummmmm." She returned his kisses and embraces but let him take control of the lovemaking. As his kisses and attention became more intense, she seemed to be more excited, but not more animated. She might have climaxed once or twice, but he wasn't sure. He kept his boxer shorts on for most of the session. Finally, he ripped his shorts off and tried to penetrate her. He needed some help in performing the task. She willingly assisted, but soon after he penetrated her, he reached his orgasm.

"Oh shit, I'm sorry," he apologized. He didn't feel too badly because his foreplay was sufficiently skilled to make up for his poor coital performance, or so he hoped. She smiled, and, without saying a word, hugged him and got off the bed and started to dress.

"Nothing is worse than apologizing after sex," she offered. "I really enjoyed being with you," she added.

Peter, lying on his side, looked at her getting dressed and appreciated her wonderful thighs and tight smooth ass. He reached over, caressed them, and ran his hand up to her pubic area. She smiled again but continued dressing. After she was dressed, she said, "You really must be going. You have to get back and morning comes very quickly and Natalie will be by to meet me for our classes."

Peter asked quickly, "Can I see you tomorrow? I'd really like to do this again. I promise, I won't be such a disappointment."

She looked at him and took his face between her hands and said, "Yes, we can get together tomorrow about six thirty? And you were not a disappointment. Come on with you."

The next day when he saw Kathryn in the class, she acted as though nothing had happened the night before. That bothered him though he didn't know what to expect. *You need to start acting like a grown man not some love starved kid, what the hell do you expect her to do....smother you with kisses... you dumb ass!*

He tried to act just as disinterested, but inside he was on fire for her.

CHAPTER FORTY-NINE

Washington D.C., March 1963

The next day, when Peter got into the office, Morgan was there, phone cradled to his ear. He hung up the phone and asked, "Did you get a hold of Wellington?"

Peter replied in the affirmative and added, almost gleefully, "He said to tell you that you were a queer but he will do the best he can for me."

Morgan smiled, "You suck one dick and you're a cock sucker for the rest of your life, but do a great job on some ultra sensitive espionage deal and nobody calls you a great agent!"

Peter laughed out loud and asked, "When do you think Wellington will get back to me? "

Morgan replied, "Wellington is good about keeping his word. It'll be quick."

After a moment, Morgan asked, "Pete, as long as we've worked together, I never knew how you got into the Bureau and how you ended up in this Presidential Security stuff. How'd all that happen?"

Peter thought for a second and replied, "You got time? I'll give you the abridged version. After the war, I got my degree in political science at a small liberal arts school on the G.I. Bill. I graduated, had a wife and two kids and had to get a job. My cousin, Peter Rubino, was on the House Judicial Committee."

Peter smiled as he continued, "In my family, you have to be named Peter to be considered legitimate. Anyway, I asked my cousin for some help getting a government job. Since he was a member of the Judicial Committee, he had some gas in the Justice Department and got me a chance to apply to the F.B.I... I tested ok, got bonus points for being a vet, and got a job with the Bureau. I was assigned to D.C. on one of the General Desks assisting field agents with anything they needed."

Morgan nodded and asked, "So you didn't do presidential security from the start?"

"Hell, no, like most new agents, I did routine busy stuff. I expedited finger print I.D.s and shit like that. A little later I was assigned to security for Los Alamos and helped screen job applicants. I was back at Headquarters one day looking over job applications for Alamogordo when H.Z ran by and hollered 'anyone with a Bureau I.D. follow me.' There were only two of us there, Joe Peterson and me. H.Z. told us some Puerto Rican Independence sympathizers tried to kill Truman on his daily walk. He also told us Hoover wanted us at the scene of the attempted assassination, and to show our I.D.'s, pretending we were on the case from the start. The Bureau would get some good P.R. and maybe look like we had the whole thing figured out before the Secret Service did. The Secret Service and the Bureau had no idea there was a plot to kill Truman and both of us had shit on our faces. What mattered most was how the public and the president perceived the Bureau."

"You're kidding; he was worried about P.R.?"

"Oh hell yeah, we circulated through the crowd, flashed I.D.'s and made sure we 'accidentally' asked questions to reporters. At least we showed investigative presence and Hoover was satisfied. Hoover told H.Z. he never wanted the Bureau to be in such a bad way again and insisted we start actively providing presidential security to 'back up' the Secret Service. He knew the Bureau was on thin ice with another agency's mandate, and he emphasized all our activities be very 'low key and discreet.' H.Z. came over to our desks, Peterson was out of the office, and I got the assignment. I know as sure as hell, if Peterson was in he would have gotten the job—not me. When did a dago get a peach of an assignment? I finished Truman's term and both of Ike's. Here I am."

Peter finished his presentation with a smile and a wink and pushed Morgan's feet off the desk and commented, "You got the whole story. It's not exactly a case of great talent being rewarded. Is it?"

Any public discovery of the F.B.I.'s incompetence was not to be permitted. Advancement in the Bureau had more to do with not embarrassing it and being in the right place at the right time. Peter spent a few hours helping Morgan with some cross checking of I.D.s for one of his bank fraud investigations. It was trying, boring work and Peter was glad to be going home to a night of T.V. He flicked on the "Huntley-Brinkley Report" on channel three. Huntley kicked off the newscast with a segment on Berlin and the newly constructed wall separating east from west. Peter was getting tired of the nuclear brinkmanship and was convinced it would end in a nuclear holocaust. He let his mind wander to his time with Kathryn.

CHAPTER FIFTY

Mer d'Iglise, March, 1945

At six thirty, he went through the unlocked back door, but unlike the night before, there was no dinner on the table. He didn't care. He was only interested in making love to Kathryn. He climbed the stairs to her bedroom and looked around the partially closed door and saw her beckon for him to enter. He nearly ran in with excitement. When he got next to the bed, she flung the sheets aside and he saw her naked body. He tasted every inch of her. She seemed to climax with his fingers and lips but it was nothing like Millie.

He inserted himself and he thought he heard her say, "That feels good," though he wasn't sure.

He was able to extend his effort for at least three or four minutes, and when it appeared she wasn't getting more excited, he fell into an orgasm. He enjoyed the whole erotic situation, but on a strange level, it was unsatisfying.

He wasn't sure why. Kathryn seemed to enjoy their sessions but was oddly pedestrian. Millie was far more energetic and passionate. Millie loved making love to Peter while Kathryn enjoyed being made love to, but didn't reciprocate. Millie savored him without hesitation; Kathryn had to be directed to touch him and never made an attempt to orally please him.

Those thoughts washed over him in the aftermath of the episode, and Peter felt incredible guilt, sadness, and dissatisfaction all at the same time. None of that mattered though, because he was obsessed by Kathryn. Even before he was finished, he hoped for another time to be with her. He couldn't wait to ask if he might visit her the next night, yet was embarrassed to ask for another meeting. He tried to make small talk and told her how well he was doing with the art lessons—not true—and how much dexterity and hand skills he had recovered.

She laughed a hearty laugh and said, "Oh, you certainly have regained your hand skills but I didn't know art improved oral skills too."

He was pleased by the compliment, and it gave him the courage to ask if he could come by the next evening.

She thought for a moment and said, "Oh that would be wonderful, unfortunately I am going to visit some friends tomorrow evening and I won't be home until who knows when…no, not tomorrow night, maybe another."

She seemed really disappointed and Peter took no offence at the rejection and accepted it at face value.

"Ok," he responded, "We can get together some other night."

He walked slowly back to the chateau. He was bothered by her disinterest in both his body and his past. She never asked anything about how he was injured or what he did before the war… nothing.

He decided that the next night, he would go through the unlocked back door and be waiting in bed for her the way she had waited for him. Maybe, she might get over her shyness and become the lover to which he had been accustomed. He could hardly sleep thinking of what he was going to do to and with Kathryn. Those thoughts, and his guilt for what he was doing behind Millie's back, roiled his insides.

CHAPTER FIFTY-ONE

Washington D.C., March 1963

Peter's thoughts of Kathryn were interrupted by the ringing of the telephone. It must have been the fourth ring when he became conscious of the noise. On the other end of the line he recognized Morgan's voice.

"Hey Pete, just got off the phone with Wellington and he has some of the stuff you asked for. He wouldn't tell me anything because he is afraid someone in the Service or Treasury will find out he is sharing secrets with you. He said, 'the less people who know the better!' I don't know what he is telling you but I know it's something and that alone will get him fired from the Service. Anyway, he wants you to call him and set up a meeting. Oh, by the way, tell him I'm giving Doug Dillon a call to squeal." Peter smiled at the reference to the Treasury Secretary.

After the phone conversation had ended he turned his attention back to the T.V. and noticed that the Huntley-Brinkley report was finished and the series *Man from Uncle* was running.

It's strange how most people perceive spies and counter-espionage. Most of the time, it was mind dulling work with little or no excitement. Morgan had to hole up in a closet for almost two months to catch a Nazi spy in the act. The agents who worked on the Rosenberg's spent two years to tie up all the loose ends and even then missed Klaus Fuchs. Fuchs gave all the atom bomb plans to the Russians long before the English got him.

Despite his *inside* knowledge, Peter loved Robert Vaughn and David McCallum and quickly suspended reality when he watched the show.

He nodded off to sleep and awoke just as the show was ending. He pulled himself up, trudged off to bed, and tried to think positive thoughts. *Wellington will have a ton of names and schedules for me to work with and that will give me some direction. Yep, he is going to have some stuff that might get me on the road.*

His thoughts again turned to Kathryn. After nearly seventeen years, he remembered the night he was going to surprise her in flawless detail.

CHAPTER FIFTY-TWO

Mer d'Iglise, March, 1945

He entered her house off the alley at the back door, as usual. He noticed two dishes with bits of food on them and two glasses with a few drops of wine in them as well. *That's strange; I thought she was eating dinner at a friend's house. Maybe she had a change in plans and just went to visit and had dinner here.*

He walked through the dining room and started up the stairs when he heard some muffled sounds coming from upstairs. He climbed the stairs and heard what he thought was Kathryn. It was Kathryn, but she was never quite so loud or animated. It was more like a deep panting grunt. He knew instantly what was happening.

He crept up the stairs not wanting to interrupt Kathryn and the guy she was with to verify what was obvious. He made his way down the hall and saw a beam of light coming from Kathryn's bedroom. Quietly, he looked around the open door and peered around and saw two figures in the bed.

They were intertwined and writhing with passion exchanging feverous kisses. Kathryn was on top, but he couldn't make out the figure on the bottom. Slowly, Kathryn moved down the person and kissed their body. His angle wasn't good. Kathryn's damp body obscured the other lover. Finally, her head moved down and the other lover's legs started to part and Peter realized Kathryn was making passionate love to…Natalie.

His mind reeled. On the one hand, he was upset that his lover was cheating on him, with a woman no less, and on the other, he was strangely excited by the sight of these women making energetic love to each other. He knew he had to leave or be discovered. He slowly descended the steps as quietly as possible and when he got outside, he ran as fast as he could back to the Chateau.

CHAPTER FIFTY-THREE

Washington, D.C. March 1963

Anderson Wellington asked Peter to meet him at a bar two blocks away from the Bureau Headquarters. Peter arrived early and had a scotch and water, and as he sipped it, he was reminded how hard he had to work to acquire the taste for scotch. After a few more minutes, Wellington walked in and looked around the bar as though he was passing state secrets. Peter was amused by Wellington's furtive behavior, but wasn't foolish enough to say anything because he was the beneficiary of the younger man's efforts.

Wellington ordered a bottle of Budweiser. Peter was surprised. He was sure he would drink something more exotic. He was even more surprised when the young agent refused a glass and drank straight from the bottle.

"Rinella, I have a list of guys who have threatened the president. Some we think are Communist sympathizers. Others are right wing neo-Nazis, Ku Klux Klansmen, and nut case state's rightists. I did the best I could about getting their last known addresses but some of them disappeared. I don't know what happened to them. You asked for the president's itinerary, but we can't predict every one of his movements. Believe it or not, some of his travel is done at the spur of the moment. Meetings with heads of state are arranged months in advance but his trips within the U.S. are on a whim sometimes. Those kinds of trips put us in a very bad way. You should contact somebody on the White House staff who will alert you a few weeks before the president's going somewhere. We know, of course, but in these cases I'm busting my hump trying to do my job without worrying about yours."

He looked down at the folder he handed over to Peter and said, "Oh, for some of these guys, you will have to add the personal information about their history, we just don't have it and they haven't been assigned a 'high risk' threat. I don't have a clue about what constitutes a 'high risk' and what doesn't."

Peter looked from the folder to Wellington's eyes and didn't say a word. He had hoped for more information, but was satisfied with what he had been given.

After a sip of his drink Peter offered quietly, "Well, thanks for your work. I know it wasn't easy and I appreciate it. I promise if I find anything that represents an imminent danger to the President, I'll give it to you guys. If I can do something for you, let me know."

The young man nodded with mild pleasure. Peter knew if he uncovered any plot from any source, he wouldn't share it with Wellington or anybody at Secret Service. To stop an attempt to assassinate John F. Kennedy would be a coup for the Bureau and gain Peter the eternal gratitude of J. Edgar Hoover and a very easy road to retirement.

Peter walked slowly back to the Bureau, clutching the file folder as though it was solid gold. He had a feeling his future was somewhere inside that folder and somewhere among those names. He couldn't wait to get back to his office and start poring over the names and backgrounds. Kathryn's faced popped up out of nowhere. He couldn't figure out why, but often she intruded into his consciousness at the worst times.

He fought off the urge to think about Kathryn and Mer d'Iglise and forced himself to look at the material Wellington had given him. He looked at the thirty or thirty five names. Next to each name was *A Last Known Address* or the appellation *Not Available*. Only a few of the names had all the columns filled and more than half had only *A Last Known Address* and nothing else. Peter knew it was going to be a lot of work going through each name and filling in the blank columns with information. An address coinciding with a presidential visit flagged an opportunity to act. The *History* column was important because it showed motive and potential for violence. He was going to have to tap into the Bureau's location skills for the suspects if no address was listed and to verify current locations. He would also need assistance from Bureau for any record or history information. *The whole process is going to be a bitch and a lot of work, no matter how you slice it.* The president's itinerary was missing from the information Wellington gave him. Peter knew getting that would be difficult at best. Faced with the enormity of his newly found information, Peter's mind yanked him back to Kathryn.

CHAPTER FIFTY-FOUR

Mer d'Iglise, March, 1945

Peter avoided the art class. Instead, he waited for the class to end and all the G.I.s to exit before he entered the classroom. Kathryn was there and Natalie was picking up the supplies and returning them to a closet in the corner of the room.

Peter approached Kathryn and asked softly, "Do you have some time to talk? I need to talk to you for a few minutes….alone."

Kathryn looked directly into his eyes, said nothing for a few seconds and then, "Natalie, please go over to the supply room and see if there are any new sketch pads and charcoal."

Kathryn waited for Natalie to leave and then asked, "Why weren't you in class today?"

Peter was caught off guard and simply ignored the question and began,"I came to your house last night and found you and Natalie…. in bed together….. I was….shocked."

Kathryn said nothing but continued to look him directly while he continued, "I….I don't understand how you can make love to me one night and the next with her. I…..I mean, what the fuck is going on with you? I know some women prefer the company of other women….that doesn't seem to be you…..and…it's none of my business but what about your husband? How do I fit in this picture?"

His voice quaked with emotion and he couldn't get the words out of his mouth. Kathryn was quiet for a minute and finally responded, quietly, controlled, "Oh. I see. It was ok for me to cheat on my husband with you but not ok to cheat on both of you with Natalie? Didn't I cheat on Natalie with you?"

Peter's mouth was open and he was unable to respond. He felt his chest and throat start to tighten with sorrow and disappointment as Kathryn continued, "Women's bodies are more beautiful and interesting. They excite and intrigue me. I like men but find them less aesthetically pleasing. As for my husband, I love him with my heart and soul, but I crave Natalie. We have been lovers before and during my marriage. And you are right; it's none of your business."

Peter's voice grew louder, "Great, great, but where do I stand.... in this wonderful little play?!"

"You are where you were when we met. What, you were going to leave your wife for me? I can't give up my husband and Natalie for you; Peter, I never was going to; you knew that, didn't you?"

She was right, but he felt hurt and betrayed. He was rejected for two people with whom he couldn't compete, and that was galling, frustrating, and painful. Peter had nothing left to say and neither did Kathryn.

Peter offered a weak smile and said, "Have a nice life. I hope everything works out for you."

He realized Kathryn said nothing because she didn't care enough. He also realized, finally, that she appeared disinterested during their love making because she was not attracted to his body, or more importantly, to him as a person. That hurt more than anything that had transpired. He made his way to the administration office knowing what was left for him to do. He stood next to the secretary's desk and said, "I'd like to be reattached to my unit. I'm ready to go back."

She pulled out his file and said, "Are you nuts Corporal? You can have another two or three weeks here. Patton is well into Germany and who knows, maybe it'll be over in two or three weeks and you could still be here."

Peter nodded and said, "Please take care of the paperwork."

CHAPTER FIFTY-FIVE

Washington, D.C., March 1963

As Peter looked at the list of names, he decided to start with the ones that had *Address* and "History" information. He needed to verify the information and see any correlation with a Presidential visit. To do the matching, he had to get Kennedy's itinerary. On an attached page, the *Record and History* section, he began reading,

> **Atwell, Donald**; *born 1924, Macon Ga.*
>
> *Graduated Macon School System.*
>
> *Drafted United States Army 1942. Honorably Discharged 1946.*
>
> *Member Southern Order of the Ku Klux Klan Circa 1948.*
>
> *Picketed White House five times with placards and sent racist and violent letters to Pres. Truman on passage of Civil Rights Legislation.*
>
> *Demonstrated against Kennedy campaign and made threats to then Kennedy candidate.*
>
> *Sent letters to President 'hoping his death' was imminent.*
>
> *Potential for Violence: Moderate.*
>
> *Last Update: 1/30/61*

Peter decided to call the field office in Atlanta. He asked Agent in Charge, John Harrison, to follow up on Atwell and try to find his current whereabouts. Harrison was not pleased but agreed when Peter explained why the investigation was necessary. He told Harrison, because of his Southern location and the number of KKK nut cases, he would be getting more names to look up.

"Sorry, John, but I promise not to hit you with too many, just a few at a time. I know I could really consume your office with this stuff. "

Peter scanned the list and noticed almost all of the names with complete information came from areas covered by Harrison's field office.

He supposed an informant had been planted in the KKK and some of the other radical organizations down there. With constant monitoring, those suspects could be controlled. Going down to the next name on the list, he read.

Barger, Jerome C. *age 45, Minneapolis Minn. Attached: Barger, Jerome Charles, nee Duluth 1917.*

Employed as machinist in Minnesota Tooling Corp. Doing War supply and munitions products. Joined Communist Party of Minnesota 1937.

Maintained Membership until 1948.

Potential for Violence: Low

Last Updated, 6/60.

Peter had no idea why his name appeared on the list. Perhaps, his membership in the Communist Party set off a flag. He was not a violent person, and had made no menacing or violent threats. He called the Minnesota office and asked them to update his whereabouts and if anything had changed to indicate he was a threat to the president. The Agent in Charge, Peter Nielson, like Harrison, was unhappy, but knew it was pointless and career ending to refuse a request from a D.C. special agent and quietly agreed to Peter's request. Peter went down the list and culled out the *Completes*. In all, the Atlanta Office had six and all others totaled five. Three of the names would be referred to the New York field agents and one would be given to New Orleans. New Orleans triggered remembrances of Capt. LeLuc, the Cajun, who Peter met shortly after he left Mer d' Iglise.

CHAPTER FIFTY-SIX

Germany, March 1945

He jumped off the back of the troop carrier with his new duffle bag slung over his right shoulder. He lost all of his equipment after his injury and had to be given everything from scratch. He looked like a new recruit in a pristine uniform, helmet, and boots. The dog faces in the platoon, by comparison, looked dirty and well worn. Walking toward the group, he saw the deeply scarred face of Despuerto.

"Amigo," Peter screamed, "como esta?" The only Spanish he knew. "What the fuck are you doin here?! I thought they were sendin' you home?"

"I thought I was too, goddamn it! Patton won't let anybody go home. Why're you here? I heard you got your brains scrambled, yeah?"

Peter was so happy to see Despuerto he almost didn't answer the question, "Yeah, I got a concussion and some brain injury, but I didn't have much to get hurt so my recovery was fast. Patton apparently wanted me back too, so I'm here with you till the bitter end."

They laughed and Despuerto introduced Peter to his fellow platoon members and Captain de Luc. Despuerto and Peter shared stories about Perkins and Forrester and the terrible day in Belgium. Peter sat silently as he thought about the Chateau and Kathryn. He wondered if he would ever be able to forget her and how his relationship with Millie would be affected. The more he thought about the difference between them, the more he remembered Millie's lovemaking. Some of his sorrow over Kathryn began to fade but was replaced by an aching guilt. He would never mention what happened between him and Kathryn. He would file it away and visit it whenever he wanted. Sometimes those thoughts aroused him, other times they saddened him, and as time progressed, they became easier to manage.

CHAPTER FIFTY-SEVEN

Washington, D.C., March 1963

As he looked over the list Wellington gave him, no one jumped out as someone who had the extreme motivation or ability to carry out an assassination attempt. If the Mafia was looking for a non-conventional hit man, he would have to have the motivation and basic skills. The mob would provide the necessary organization and material support for a hit. *Whoever they get, he will be someone who has no ties to them. Hell, he really should be some goof with a crazy political philosophy or nutty cause. Then he would be the perfect patsy.*

All the guys on the list were crazies, Peter knew he had to find the craziest. Thinking more, *the assassination of the President of the United States is a gigantic, statement. How nuts would you have to be to think you could pull it off?* Without complete histories on the whole list, he was only looking at part of the picture. He decided to send those names over to Maggie Johanson and ask her to provide as much information as possible.

"You know, agent Rinella, this is a lotta work not to mention all the requests to the Field Offices you made are comin' here too. You have to realize that you aren't the only agent in the Bureau!"

Peter replied meekly and pleadingly, "Mag, take your time. I know you guys are worked to death. It's just that you are the only ones who can get it done."

She calmed down, "Ok, ok, we'll do our best but please be patient."

Before she could hang up, Peter asked again with deference, "Mag, who could I talk to about the president's itinerary for, say, the next year? Do you have any idea?"

Maggie got upset again and spat out, "Not me. I have no idea what his schedule is!"

Peter knew he couldn't piss her off and promptly added, "No, of course, I didn't mean that you would have his schedule, but do you know anybody in the White House who might, or know anybody who knows somebody who could help me?"

Maggie thought for a minute, "I have a friend who works in the White House. She might be able to give me a name for you. I'll call you back with any info. Remember, give me time!"

Peter was genuinely grateful, "Mag, thank you so much, hey, by the way, are you married?"

She quickly responded with a chuckle, "Forget it agent Rinella, you're not my type."

Peter smiled and bid good bye, "I love you too, Maggie."

Peter knew that most people avoid work. Maggie was no different. *It was like being in the army, whatever it took to coast through without breaking a sweat.*

After he was re-attached to his unit, he was especially aware of *do as little as possible and volunteer for nothing.*

CHAPTER FIFTY-EIGHT

Germany, March, 1945

The Germans knew everything around them was crumbling. They were encircled by the Americans and British on the western side and the Russians on the eastern side. Defeat was inevitable and the Germans realized it was far better to be a prisoner of the Americans and British rather than the Russians. Germany was responsible for the death of twenty million Russians and would be the object of terrible revenge. The Russians were facing stiffer resistance than the Americans and British, who were having an easier time advancing on Berlin.

Sitting on the back of a Sherman tank, Peter, Despuerto, and four other G.I.s were astounded by the total destruction of the villages. Buildings were completely flattened, or in some cases, a wall jutted up from a foundation. Millions of pounds of rubble lay everywhere they looked. People with carts and huge bags made of sheets or blankets were walking in the opposite direction of the Americans.

Despuerto asked, "Where are they goin? Shit, there ain't nothing where we just came from. It looks like they got their whole lives on their backs."

The further East they advanced, the larger the number of refugees.

"I'll bet they're tryin' to get away from the Ruskies. I know I'd be afraid of those cocksuckers and be gettin' out of town, too," Peter said.

About 90 miles west of Berlin, Patton stopped his advance. They set up more permanent camps and supplies and support material began to arrive. Meals were hot, showers were set up and the G.I.s tended to shaving and bathing. Jonathan Lewis, a slight Jewish kid from Albany entered a tent where Despuerto and Peter were laying on cots and said, "I don't want to be the last guy killed in the goddamn war."

Despuerto laughed a hearty laugh and said, "You aint gonna be, I guarantee it. It'll be me or Rinella. We got the worst luck of anybody in the world. Look how messed up we got. Anyone else goes home and sleeps with mama. Not us, we're here with you assholes. If anybody gets it in the ass, it'll be us, the last casualties of the war."

Everyone laughed but Peter because he believed Despuerto.

CHAPTER FIFTY-NINE

Washington, D.C. March, 1963

The phone rang and he instantly recognized the gravelly voice of Maggie Johanson, "Rinella, you have to appreciate my concern for you," He could hear her take a drag on her cigarette, "I mean only a day after you asked, I got a name for you in the White House."

Peter was surprised and pleased, "Mag, nothing you do surprises me. I don't know anyone who is as dedicated and efficient as you."

Peter knew she was flattered by his honest compliment as she continued, "Yeah, yeah, I'm sure. Anyway, there is a kid who works in the White House for Schlesinger. His name is Mahmoud El-Youssef."

Peter started to laugh out loud. "Come on Mag, you gotta be kiddin' me? What's an Arab kid doin' workin' in the White House?"

Maggie enjoyed Peter's incredulity, and with an audible laugh, continued, "No, no that's his name, no kidding. He's second generation born and raised in Dearborn, Michigan. Dearborn has a huge Arab population and this kid, who graduated from Harvard, registered nearly all of 'em Democrat and then delivered a huge turn-out for our beloved Irish-American President. And, if that ain't enough, his old man is a doctor who treated Joe Kennedy for some stomach problem. Anyway, the young man got a job with the transition team and then a job in the White House."

Peter smiled and said, "God Bless America. All you have to do is get a degree from Harvard, help elect an Irishman, and have your old man help his old man and boom you're in the White House. You gotta love this county."

Peter heard Maggie take another hit on her cigarette as she gave him the direct number for the young man and added, "Rinella, his non-Arab friends I'm told, call him Mimo."

"Well if he can give me the information I need to put this stuff together, I'll call him Jesus, if that's what he wants. Get it Mag, an Arab, Jesus?"

"I get it agent Rinella. Just call the guy and do what you gotta do."

Peter asked before they hung up, "I know it's soon, but you don't have anything on the list I gave you?"

Maggie grew agitated, "I told you, it's going to take some time. I'll get back to you when I have something. I'm doing the best I can with our limited resources."

"Ok, ok, I gotcha. I'll wait."

Maggie felt guilty about her stern reaction, "Tell you what I'll do. I'll send over five or ten names at a time as soon I get em done. Ok?"

Peter was very pleased.

CHAPTER SIXTY

Germany, March, 1945

Peter would call Despuerto, *Pancho*. Peter couldn't remember Despuerto's given name and "Pancho" seemed like a good name for him anyway. Despuerto didn't take grave offence at the misnaming but lectured Peter on Hispanic name derivation.

"Goomba, 'Pancho' is a Mexican name and I'm Puerto Rican. If you are going to fuck around, at least call me Puerto Rican name, like... Roberto."

Peter laughed, ignored Despuerto's lesson, and immediately referred to him as Pancho. After a lazy day sitting around and doing nothing, both considered their good fortune.

Peter laid on his cot and mused, "Pancho, DeLuc told a few guys that he heard at a staff meeting Patton was fuming about having to pull up here instead of driving right through to Berlin. DeLuc heard Ike tell Patton that the Ruskies are supposed to get there first and we and the English are to come in later like two teenagers at a gang bang."

Despuerto smoked a Camel, sipped coffee, and nodded. He rubbed the right side of his face where a scar ran. After silence of a few minutes, he asked, "Rinella, can you make out the scar on my face?"

The scar was prominent, but more noticeable was the way Despuerto's face had been affected by the scar. His right side seemed frozen and didn't move with the other side. The lips on the right side were slightly paralyzed as well, like someone who had a hair lip repaired.

Peter replied, "Fuck no, Pancho, I can't see hardly a thing. I mean you are just as ugly as before, no doubt of that, but I don't notice the scar."

Seemingly satisfied with Peter's lie, Despuerto settled back on his cot, closed his eyes, and rubbed his scarred face.

Peter thought out loud, "This thing is coming to an end, you know. When the Russians get to Berlin, it's all over but the signing and we can go back home. I can't wait!"

Despuerto was dozing. Lewis, who had just entered the tent and had heard what Peter said, replied loudly, "You're goddamn right this deal is coming to an end but you are forgetting about the Japs. That shit is still goin' on and it looks like our asses might be over there for an invasion of Japan."

Peter exhaled his Pall Mall, "Do you know how many goddamn guys are gonna get killed by those fanatics! It' gonna be a goddamn meat grinder before this thing ends!!!"

Lewis nodded in agreement. Peter's temporary elation was quickly tempered by the realization of dying in Japan. He was sickened by the thought of never seeing his family again. He prayed, *please God, let this thing last another month or two and then another four or five months or a year even to get us over there. Shit, a lot of stuff can happen in a year and maybe it'll be over by then.*

The Japanese would fight to the death and could easily last another five years if they had to protect their homeland.

Out loud in Lewis' direction, "Jesus Christ, I sure hope something happens to get all of us home."

Despuerto started to snore and Lewis nodded again, and said, "It'll take a goddamn miracle for that to happen, a goddamn miracle."

CHAPTER SIXTY-ONE

Washington, D.C. March 1963

Peter dialed the number Maggie had given him and when he heard
Mahmoud, Peter was surprised at how young he sounded. He introduced
himself and explained he had gotten the number from a friend of
Maggie's and exchanged pleasantries.

"Maggie said you're from Michigan and a Harvard graduate?"

The young man answered in the affirmative and quickly asked
Peter the nature of his call. Peter ignored his question,"She said I can call
you Mimo—is that ok? I mean, she told me that's what your friends call
you. Not that we're friends or anything, but it's a little easier."

Mimo, distracted by other matters, "Yes, that's fine, but what did
you say I can do for you agent......Riffulla?"

Peter smiled to himself, "It's Rinella and I'm wondering if you
can give me the president's schedule for the next eight to twelve
months?"

Mimo remained silent for a few seconds, "Well normally that sort
of thing goes to the Secret Service...Don't they share that with the
F.B.I.?"

Not knowing how to respond, "Er.....sometimes they do, yes,
but not always. I need the president's schedule in connection with other
matters we are investigating and their relationship with the president's
safety. Of course, the Secret Service has the lead in the president's
security, but the Bureau often times helps out as well."

Peter knew this was true but neither agency would care to admit
it. Mimo thought a minute or two, "I'll get you his planned schedule but
we are going to have to meet in person so I can see if you are who you say
you are."

Peter was surprised by the younger man's caution but understood
it, "Sure... sure that's no problem. Oh is there a way you can notify us...
me if anything pops up and the president has a spur of the moment trip?"

Mimo dropped his composed and assured manner, "Geez, I don't
know about that. I mean... sometimes it just happens and we barely have
time to let the Secret Service know."

Peter pressed, "I know, I know, but it would be helpful if you could include us...er, me, in on that kind of information."

Mimo was convinced and reverted to his cool demeanor, "Yes, I guess I can after I'm sure you're an F.B.I. agent. We can meet at the White House in a few days...I'll make arrangements to have the president's tentative trip schedule and you have your I.D. and...while I'm thinking about it, an authorization from your immediate supervisor."

Peter laughed, "Man, you don't fool around do you?"

Coolly, Mimo responded, "Based on what you want to know, you're lucky I don't need a letter from Director Hoover."

Not wanting to sound ungrateful, but also assertive, Peter replied, "I can guarantee you this, Mimo, if needed, I'm sure Director Hoover would comply with your request."

"That won't be necessary, can I have a number to reach you, agent Rinella?"

CHAPTER SIXTY-TWO

Germany, April-August, 1945

Patton's army was on the move again and faced no resistance as it drove toward Berlin. The Russians were close to overrunning Berlin and the massive artillery and rocket attack on the German Home Guard was audible even to the Americans twenty miles away. The devastation was complete and terrible. Not one building was intact and the flow of refugees was unending. After a few days, the American advance came to another halt. Rumor had it a symbolic meeting between East and West was going to occur near the center of the city. In the late afternoon, the Americans saw the approach of Slavic, and, curiously, some Asian faces. Their noses and cheekbones were broad with correspondingly thick lips. Cameramen and film photographers were stationed around the event to catch it for the home front. Interpreters were positioned around the milling soldiers and tried to help in communication, but everyone spoke at the same time and the interpreters were useless. Rather than speak, some soldiers removed their helmets and hats and exchanged them and posed for pictures. The Americans offered the Russians cigarettes and the Russians brought out bottles of vodka. Peter asked why some of the Russians looked Asian and he was told that over fifty per cent of the first wave of invaders was Mongolian. Soldiers were drinking directly out of the vodka bottles and shared long swigs. The vodka burned Peter's throat as it went down and he felt the instantaneous warmth spread through his stomach and entire body. After a few more hugs and pats on the back, the allies waved to each other and retreated back to their home camps.

On April 15, the Germans surrendered officially. Germany had been vanquished and only the Japanese were left. Peter knew the War in the Pacific was waiting. At the Potsdam Conference, Roosevelt, Churchill and Stalin, insisted on the *unconditional surrender* of Japan.

Peter sat on his cot when he heard Lewis ask anyone who would listen, "Did you see what happened on Okinawa? The Japs and civilians dove off the cliffs rather than surrender. Shit, marines cooked them with flame throwers and they came out on fire shooting their goddamn guns."

Fortunately, the occupation of Germany took some time and *repatriation* even longer. The allies had to sift through the former combatants and filter out any potential war criminals. Al Allegretti, a kid from somewhere in Pennsylvania too, told Peter he was going to work the War Crimes Trials. He was an M.P. and was going to guard the German captives, probably in Nuremberg.

Nuremberg sounded a lot better than Japan and Peter wished he was offered that duty. Instead, he and the other dog faces were awaiting their transfer for the Japanese invasion.

The evening of August 7th was muggy and the humidity was oppressive. While on the way to the latrine, Peter passed Capt. DeLuc who excitedly told him, "We dropped one mystery bomb yesterday on the Jap city, Hiroshima and the goddamn thing flattened the whole city. Christ, they say 75,000 people were killed by one bomb. Can you believe that, Rinella!? Truman called it an atomic bomb."

Peter didn't believe one bomb could destroy an entire city and didn't much care as long as it would bring the war to a merciful end. On Armed Services Radio, on August 9th, they heard Edward R. Murrow announce,

"The B-29 bomber *Bock's Car* dropped another atomic bomb on the Japanese city of Nagasaki. Although the bomb was slightly off target, most of the city was destroyed and 55,000 Japanese perished in the explosion and subsequent events. President Truman has issued another statement to the Emperor, 'for the unconditional surrender of the Imperial Government of Japan.'"

Three days later, the Japanese surrendered and every G.I. breathed a collective sigh of relief.

CHAPTER SIXTY-THREE

Washington D.C., March 1963

The cab pulled up to the service entrance of the White House. Inside the entrance, he identified himself and told the officer at the desk he was there to see, "Mahmoo.....er...Mimo."

The guard smiled and phoned for Mimo who promptly arrived to greet him. Peter immediately offered his F.B.I. badge and I.D. as well as a letter from H.Z. asking for his cooperation in Peter's request. Scanning the documents for a minute, Mimo looked directly at Peter and pointed to an elevator. Standing in the elevator, Peter noticed how slight the young man was. His brown hair and coal black eyes were deeply set in a very dark face. His lips were full and his nose was thin, straight, and fairly long with a little hook in the bridge. Peter was surprised that Mimo's formal attitude had been supplanted by a more casual and pleasant one. He had an easy smile as they made small talk on the way to the basement cubicle, the young man called his office. Mimo handed Peter a file folder with thirty or forty entries indicating "scheduled visits" the president would be making in the next eight months.

"You know, these are just tentative and some may be added or deleted, depending upon the president."

Peter's head was spinning, "Holy shit, Mimo, this is far more travelling than I expected. I really don't know how I'll handle all these."

Mimo shrugged, "Well, that's what the Secret Service is for, right? I would think between the two of you this should be pretty easy. Oh, by the way, I'll try let you know if any special travel plans crop up."

Mimo looked down at his watch and Peter knew it was time to leave. He had to get the list back to his office and start the arduous task of matching suspects with cities. *Shit, he thought, this is a helluva lot of work.*

CHAPTER SIXTY-FOUR

Meadville, November, 1945

It was a Sunday afternoon, the wind was blowing from the North, and for November, it seemed especially cold. He walked up his front steps, his olive green duffle bag slung over his shoulder. His bus got in earlier than he anticipated, so he took a cab home.

He knocked on the door. Hearing his kids on the other side and Millie call out, "Wait a minute, please. Cam, Vin quit making a mess damn it, your dad is going to be home soon! I'll be right there," he knocked again.

Her voice sounded wonderful, something he had yearned to hear for nearly three years. Milly saw him through the door and screamed with excitement, "Peter, Peter, Daddy's home. Peter, Peter, Oh my God."

She threw open the door and hugged him around his neck and kissed him on the lips, neck, head, anywhere her mouth could reach. He returned her kisses and squeezed her waist so hard he pushed the air out of her lungs.

He panted between kisses, "Oh Mil, I missed you….and the kids so much I….thought I was gonna die from missing you!"

The children came running up to him and he left Millie's embrace to wrap his arms around the pudgy Cam and the reedy Vincent. They screamed with joy for the man they had seen only in pictures. He squeezed all three of them into his chest. In those moments, he experienced a complete and enveloping euphoria. They quickly gathered the kids and went down to visit his father and the whole scene was replicated.

"Oh, Papa," Peter murmured, "It's wonderful to see your face."

Tears streamed down his father's worn face. Tears started to well up in Peter's eyes and he started to laugh hysterically.

The entire Prutto family arrived to welcome Peter. Mrs. Prutto came armed with a huge bowl of pasta and Giacomo fetched a bottle of Mr. Bergamasco's wine. Dishes were heaped with pasta, glasses filled with dark red wine and Peter kissed everybody, including his father-in-law. Amazingly, the old man offered no resistance. Peter looked at

Millie, with her wonderful lips curled in a delicious smile. He saw her staring back at him and felt his love returned.

He hollered to her above the din, "Hey Mill, this is heaven isn't it?"

She nodded in agreement and shouted back, "It's real close!"

CHAPTER SIXTY-FIVE

Washington D.C., March, 1963

Peter rushed back to his office and realized that the schedule Mimo had given him included a few visits out of the country and they would not be his concern. The president would be visiting Germany on June 26 and June 27 and then his ancestral home land in Ireland June 27 through June 29. The Secret Service and the C.I.A. would have those sites covered. Other *safe* visits were the president's trips to Hyannis Port in August and West Palm Beach in mid-November. Those locales were locked up tightly by the Secret Service since Kennedy spent a good deal of time at both and were nearly impenetrable. Kennedy's visits to the Air Force Academy on June 10 and the Naval Academy on August 1 were safe because the crowds were hardly *public* and as safe as any U.S. military base. For the same reason, his visit to MacDill Air Force Base in Tampa was another *safe* visit. Of course, any visits within the D.C. area were secure because the Secret Service worked all of D.C. on a daily basis. That meant he could eliminate the speeches at the World Food Congress on June 4 and American University on June 10. The President was scheduled to make a speech in Newport Rhode Island on September 15th and Amherst College in Amherst Massachusetts on October 26th, and the Hyannis safety net would be cast over those events. *Where would be the best place to whack the President of the United States?*

He listed them on a pad:

May 18, Speech at Vanderbilt, Nashville, Tennessee

June 6, Meeting with Vice President Johnson and Gov. John Connelly, El Paso, Texas

September 20, Speech at the UN, New York

September 26, Speech at the Mormon Tabernacle, Salt Lake City, Utah

September 28, Speech Las Vegas, Nevada

November 8 Speech at Protestant Council, New York

November 21 and 22 San Antonio, Houston, Fort Worth, Dallas, and Austin Texas.

Peter mused to himself. *Where would I get Kennedy? Not in a city where the organization has a high profile. That eliminates New York and Las Vegas. What's left, Nashville, Salt Lake City and the Texas cities?*

He had managed the list to a workable one and knew he could concentrate on the *target* visits by contacting all the field offices and forwarding to them a list of "suspects." *Rinella, you aren't the dumb-ass everyone makes you out to be. Actually, you're a pretty smart guy.*

CHAPTER SIXTY-SIX

Meadville, November-February 1945-46

The first few months at home were like a second, third, fourth and fifth honeymoon. Peter and Millie made love like teenagers in every possible place. Millie seemed far more responsive to him than before he left. Thoughts of Kathryn intruded on his consciousness at the most inopportune times, but her passive performance and Millie's incredible passion made repressing those thoughts easy.

It was the best of all worlds. When he wasn't having incredible sex with his wife, he was surrounded by his adoring kids and eating the most wonderful meals Millie had ever cooked. After a few months, though, Peter grew restless.

He felt lousy as Millie went to work every day and he stayed home with the kids. He felt even worse when he dropped the children off at the Prutto's. Millie's parents didn't say anything, but he knew they thought he was a jerk to let his wife work while he sat at home. Millie had gone back to night school and sharpened her typing and learned short hand. She was able to get a clerical job at the factory, and mercifully got out of the core room. She advanced from a simple clerk to the secretary of the plant manager. She made more money in the office than in the plant and her hands were far softer now than when he left. Peter also noticed how more refined Millie had become. Working in the office gave her an appreciation and introduction to other ways of expression and attitude.

Millie wasn't smoking as much and had begun to smoke filter cigarettes because she said, "I don't want to get tobacco on my lips. Those tobacco bits look really ugly."

She dressed in a skirt, blouse and stockings. She got up an hour earlier to put on her make-up and lipstick and fix her hair. When she worked in the factory, she never spoke of her job and fellow workers. Now, that was all she talked about—her job and the people she worked with, both men and women.

The constant discussion of her work irritated Peter who felt hopeless at home. He could draw twenty dollars a week for fifty-two weeks as a *Separation Allotment*, but decided to waive that and get a factory job and use the newly announced G.I. Bill to pay for his tuition and living expenses in college. Even though he worked, the G.I. Bill paid him seventy-five dollars a month which also helped with expenses.

He proposed this to Millie and she gushed, "Oh, Peter, that is fantastic, absolutely great. We'll be able to stay ahead of our bills and after you graduate, you can get a decent job. Who knows what sort of management job you can get? Then, we'll be able to move out of this apartment and buy a house of our own with a nice big yard and garage for our car."

Peter smiled at Millie's reaction because she wanted her husband in a *respectable* job, adding, no doubt, to her social standing at the office.

He asked, "If I can get a good paying job, what do you think about quitting and staying home with the kids and taking care of the house?"

Immediately, she replied, "No Peter. I love my job and don't want to leave it. I don't care how much money you make. The kids are doing fine with mom. You don't look like your losing any weight so I must be able to keep up with the meals…..and we can use the spare money from my job."

He realized how things had changed in his absence, some for the good and some for the bad. In either case, it had become a very different time.

CHAPTER SIXTY-SEVEN

Washington, D.C., April, 1963

Peter was sitting at his desk, two days after he vetted the list of presidential trips and got a call from Maggie.

"Rinella, come upstairs and get some of the info you asked for. I wasn't able to complete all the whereabouts and personal histories of every name you gave me. Four or five of them are in jail and another three, I think, went and died on us. Those seven or eight were the easy ones."

She laughed at her own joke and Peter laughed along with her, not because it was funny, but because he was trying to humor her. She continued, "Ok, not much time to talk, come on up in say, a half-hour, and I'll give you the list. Please, don't ask a lot of questions because I listed everything I could. I didn't keep anything back."

Peter, replied, in the affirmative and could hardly wait the thirty minutes to get up to her office and got there five minutes early.

"Well, here's your list," Maggie announced proudly, "I've forwarded the information on last known residences to the correct *Office of Origin.*"

Maggie was referring to the Bureau policy of giving primary jurisdiction to the Field Office where the subject lived. If the person moved to another city, that Field Office was called an *Auxiliary Office* and had to request, in writing, to have the suspect's file moved to them and that office would become the *Office of Origin.*

Peter appreciated her efforts. While she was explaining how much work he had caused her, he looked at her with discretely. She was nearly six feet tall. Her hair was light brown with streaks of a faint blond here and there. She had large breasts, and in her youth, she must have been athletic. Peter looked down to see if she had a wedding ring on and noticed she didn't. He had heard rumors that Maggie was involved with another woman, and like most men, assumed that was so because she hadn't found the right guy yet. He was certain if she was with a woman, he'd be able to convert her. The irony and folly of this thought came crushing down around him as he had a flashback of Kathryn and Natalie. He almost busted out laughing at himself for the over-estimation of his skills. Given the conservative nature of the Bureau, he couldn't believe Maggie would be living such a divergent life-style and still be employed by the F.B.I.

He was brought back to their meeting by Maggie saying, "Rinella, all you will have to do is to call the *Office of Origin* if anybody stands out to you. I supplied the number of the office for you, as well. You know, I am way too good to you."

Peter looked into her blue eyes, "You are. Maybe, for all your hard work and help, I could take you to dinner? I promise nothing serious, no strings attached or anything."

Maggie's face softened and she brushed her hair back with her right hand and Peter knew she was pleased by the invitation but she replied in the negative.

"Well uh, thanks Peter. I really appreciate the invite, but I'm 'involved' with someone and it really....I really can't," her voice trailed off as she let the rejection simply fade out into nothingness.

Peter smiled back, embarrassed by the turn down, "Oh, sorry, I didn't know. If anything ever changes or if you change your mind, let me know. I really appreciate all your help with this stuff."

When he got back to his office, he immediately called the Nashville Field Office with the number Maggie supplied. The Field Office was managed by Paul Johnson and Peter reminded him of the list Maggie mailed to him and to have some of his field agents interview the subjects as quickly as possible. He also told Johnson to feel free to watch any other 'possibles' and maintain physical contact with all of the suspects. He reminded Johnson of the president's arrival for his speech at Vanderbilt and asked him to have the motorcade route from airport to the University clearly secure.

Johnson asked, "Great, what is the Secret Service gonna do if I do all their work?!"

Peter agreed and told him to contact them and get the all the details they would share. He told Johnson he would be arriving in Nashville two days prior to the president and asked to be picked up at the airport by an available field agent. Johnson agreed to all Peter asked.

"I can't wait for the president's visit to be over and done with, goddamn it." he said tiredly.

Peter knew exactly how he felt.

CHAPTER SIXTY-EIGHT

Meadville, September 1947-October 1949

Peter was accepted at Allegheny College and got a job in the second shift at Viscose Fiber Company. He knew he was accepted not because he had distinguished himself as a high school student, because he hadn't, but because Allegheny gave preference in admission to Meadville residents. He took classes during the morning and early afternoon and got to work by four o'clock when his shift began. He worked until twelve and studied for a few hours before getting some sleep. Throughout his college career, he was aware of his school and home personalities. He knew in school he responded in a modulated mid- western American way. At home, he could adopt the gruff, Italian-American vernacular. When he went out in the neighborhood, he drifted into the profane, neighborhood slang.

He and a dozen or so other G.I. Bill students were different than the traditional students. All of them were married and not in the hunt for the female students. Fundamentally, they were also different at their core than the young men just out of high school. Most of them had witnessed the barbarity of war at the expense of their personal lives and social issues--fraternities, football games, and class offices--were irrelevant to their experience. They lived off campus and, in addition to looking older, were physically separated from the other students. The basic differences, though not expressed, were felt by both groups. The professors accepted the older students without reservation. Some of them were returning veterans, as well, and sympathized with the "new" students and the difficulties of combining work, family, and education.

Peter knew he wanted to major in Political Science because he felt unable to do the physical sciences. He wanted to be a lawyer and a Poli-Sci degree was as good as any to get into law school.

He had to balance the artificial environment of Allegheny and the ugly real-life world of the Viscose. The first day he started at the Viscose he was overwhelmed by the pervasive odor of rotten eggs. He was assigned to the Spinning Department where the rayon fluid was turned into yarn and had to be joined strand by strand to make a larger more manageable string. The smell of eggs came from the use of sulfuric acid which was used in converting cellulose into rayon. Peter worked next to Andy Kozloski, another newly returned veteran.

"Hey, Andy," he hollered over the factory noise, "how the hell do you get the smell of this goddamn place out of you!?"

Peter leaned closer to Kozloski to hear his answer, "Try taking a shower before you go home and bring a change of clothes."

Peter laughed out loud and replied, "No shit, I mean besides that. I still smell like the sewage plant after I leave here and the clothes in my locker clean or not, pick up the smell of the place for Christ's sake."

During the weekend and away from work, the smell dissipated. The grind of work and school was clearly having an effect on his family life. He was nearly as absent as when he was in Europe. He never saw his family awake and when they were awake; he was studying, reading, or writing something for school. He caught glimpses of his marriage change with his absence.

It wasn't as though his relationship with Millie was strained, but it was less intimate. Slowly their relationship became quieter. His attention to Millie was saved for Saturday and Sunday and then they visited family or the kids were awake and screaming for attention. Physical intimacy between them became rare, and strangely, because of their busy lives, neither seemed to care. Peter and Millie got used to his absence and neither complained about it.

He maintained a low "B" average and considering his situation with work and family was pleased with his performance. The next three years grew easier. He learned how to evaluate what professors were looking for and how to study and write efficiently. As he got deeper into the Poli-Sci major, he made the friendships with all the Department's instructors.

CHAPTER SIXTY-NINE

Nashville, May 16-18, 1963

The flight to Nashville was nearly empty and Peter was seated by himself. He was able to mull over his thoughts without any intrusion. Out of nowhere, Peter was struck by the way his life had flown by, and more depressingly, how little time he might have left. *Jesus Christ, I'm nearly sixty years old. How much more goddamn time to I have? What, another ten or fifteen years if I'm lucky?*

He was met at the gate by a young agent whose drawl was as thick as syrup.

"Welcome down here, my name's Albert Gruzzard. I got out of the training school about three weeks ago. I'll get you to the office and take you wherever you got to go."

The agent looked like he was fifteen years old and Peter nearly asked to see his driver's license. When they got to the office and exchanged pleasantries, Office Director Johnson reported to Peter the status of their inquiries,

"Atwell, the name you gave Atlanta, has been located and we have asked them to maintain a visual surveillance of him. Miss Johanson didn't have any names in our Office of Origination but some in four others. We have contacted Wheeling, Jacksonville, Birmingham, and Biloxi and reminded them of Washington's directives and asked them to verify location and maintain visuals on all the suspects. That takes care of all the potentials in the South East region, at least any which have a threat for violence."

Peter looked beyond Johnson, and thinking out loud, "Of course, who's to stop some goof from hopping on a plane to pop the president?"

After a minute, "Rinella, who in North Dakota knows Kennedy is going to make a speech at Vandy? No, it would take some big conspiratorial group to arrange that kind of mission. Anyway, you notice most of these guys are loners or losers who have some right wing or KKK connection. You don't have those guys in North Dakota do you?"

"No, the KKK guys aren't in North Dakota but the John Birchers are there and who knows? Speaking of right wing, do you guys have any leads on who tried to plug Edwin Walker? Jesus Christ, Walker was the guy who tried to stop the integration of the University of Georgia, wasn't he?"

Johnson laughed out loud, "Rinella, that happened at his house in Texas, and you know we aren't the Office of Origination for that area. And, if I might add, it'd be a local police matter."

"Johnson, what's the weather supposed to be like in two days when the President arrives to your beautiful city?"

"Why....what difference does the weather make?"

"If it's raining, the president will have the glass bubble on the Lincoln. If it's not, he'll have it off and be an easy target."

"Gotcha. We'll check and hopefully it will be raining like a mother and all of us can rest a little easier. Is that bubble bullet-proof?"

"No, not really, but getting an accurate shot through it is a little harder and shooting through a rain storm is a helluva lot harder. Can your agent take me over the motorcade route? Maybe we can see if anything sticks out that the Secret Service may have missed?"

May 18th came with heavy rain storm; Kennedy got to Vanderbilt, and made an inspiring speech to the graduating seniors. More importantly, he got back to D.C. in one piece. Peter thought *one trip down, a few more to go and 1963 will be history.*

CHAPTER SEVENTY

Frederick, Md., 1950-1954

After four of the longest years of his life, Peter graduated with a B.A. in Political Science. The four years had taken a toll on his marriage. Millie grew more remote and bothered by any attempt at intimacy. He was seldom home and she treated him as though he was a stranger in their house. Now that he had graduated, he was sure all would be different. He needed to find a job that would make her proud to be his wife.

True to his word, Peter Rubino got him into the F.B.I. and Rinella went to the Bureau's Training School in Quantico, Virginia. He was gone six weeks for training, not good for their marriage, but when he returned he had an assignment. During the intensive six weeks, the candidates learned some law enforcement principles, Bureau policies and standards, self-defense, investigative procedures, arms training and, most importantly, Bureau forms and their completion protocols. Prospective agents were also required to maintain physical fitness standards and complete a test that combined fitness, cognitive and shooting skills. The program got him back in shape quickly.

Two days before the official completion ceremony, he was assigned to the D.C. headquarters and the Rinella family had to move from Meadville. Peter excitedly told Millie, who didn't say much and just nodded in agreement. Her attitude was compliant but not enthusiastic. She hated to leave her family and job, which she constantly told him she loved and would miss. They found a house in Frederick Maryland and moved completely about a week before Peter started his job in D.C.

As a new agent, he worked a desk to assist Primary and Field Agents with their investigations. He rode along with them on interrogations and assisted on occasional arrests. He worked with the Santa Fe Office in the security clearances for the Nuclear Bomb facility at Alamogordo. Ten to fifteen days a month, he had to make a trip to New Mexico. He was responsible for checking references and backgrounds for every newly hired employee to make sure all of them were trustworthy Americans. The Russians detonated their first Atomic Bomb and it became apparent how much of their bomb's development was assisted by spies planted in the Alamogordo facility during the war years.

The nuclear physicist, Klaus Fuchs, gave the Russians the entire design of the "Bomb" and incredibly got through three security checks. The Bureau was responsible for security, and to Hoover's dismay, took the blame for all the espionage leaks. The director was hysterical with anger and punished all the agents responsible. Into that paranoid atmosphere agent Rinella began his career. While America was developing the Hydrogen Bomb, pressure was especially intense to preserve the security of that project. Even when he wasn't in New Mexico, Peter worked ten hours a day poring through employment records and personnel data. After he was finally able to pull himself from the thousands of documents, he had to drive an additional two hours back and forth from Frederick. His visits to Alamogordo actually took less out of him than his work at F.B.I. headquarters. Again, he was seldom home and Millie began to complain. She told him, when they did speak, how she felt suffocated in a house she hated, away from her family, friends, and her beloved job. Peter hardly listened and if he did hear her, he couldn't answer her despair.

He answered her complaints with, "I'm making a career for you and the kids. This is the price we gotta pay to get our lives moving in the right direction."

One evening completely without warning, Millie quietly announced, "I'm taking the kids and we're going back home. I can't stand it here any longer and, to be honest Peter, I don't even know who you are anymore. Why should I stay here with a total stranger?"

The thought of his wife and kids leaving him literally took his breath away. He felt like he had just gotten punched in the stomach and the fist was still there.

"Fuck it, Mil, I'll quit my job and we can move back home if that is what you want. I know it's tough on you here. I'll take care of that."

He hoped the offer alone would pacify her and she would relent and stay with him in Frederick. He might be able to juggle his work schedule to mollify her crazy demands. Instead, Millie just shook her head no and whispered,

"No. Peter, that's not what I want. It's too late for that. I want to go back without you. I don't feel the same about you or us anymore. I want to try it with the kids....alone....alone"

"Why, Millie? What's going on; I mean what did I do or not do to......make you want to leave me like this?"

Millie murmured as though Peter might be less hurt by the bad news if she quietly spoke, "Peter, there is and has been somebody else.

Before we left Meadville, I met somebody....and I think we love each other. I want to go home to see if we have a future."

She looked down, ashamed of the confession and was forced to hear Peter scream, "You've gotta be kiddin me. Who's the guy who'd go with a married woman with two kids? How could you do this to me and our kids? Tell me who the guy is; I want, I need to know, goddamn it!"

Millie never raised her eyes and whispered, "Ray Ward."

Peter's face was flushed with anger and he screamed again, "Ray Ward, the little American guy who manages the plant? The guy was a *Four F* and sat his ass back home while everyone else was getting their asses blown up. Tell me you're kiddin me, for Christ's sake! What kinda man can he be?"

Not knowing how to respond, Millie simply said, "I am going back home as soon as possible."

Peter was beside himself with rage, frustration, and shame and spit out, "Your old man was right Millie, you're a whore and I hope you get paid back in spades some day. "

Peter knew in his heart that this was a payback for his time with Kathryn, and, in some strange way, that he had brought it upon himself with his act of adultery.

Two days later, Peter watched out the living room window as Millie, Cam and Vinnie got into a yellow cab with all their baggage. The children kept looking back and waved to him. He waved back, tears streaming down his face. Millie looked forward and never turned around. The cab pulled off and Peter discovered just how cruel a woman could be, and later discovered how lonely it was without her.

CHAPTER SEVENTY-ONE

Washington, D.C. May 1963

Peter knew he had time to consider the president's visit to Salt Lake City. It was nearly four months away, and depending upon what was planned in Utah, he might even get ready for that trip as well as the November visits in Texas. The CIA and Secret Service were ultimately responsible for the European visits and he could concentrate on the high exposure American visits left in 1963. He phoned the Salt Lake City Field Office and immediately made an enemy.

He asked Office Director William Rounds, "Are you aware the president will be arriving in Salt Lake City on September 26th, Bill?"

"It's William, agent Rinella, and yes, of course, I am aware of his visit. We have received two or three names of possible troublemakers."

Peter was taken aback by Rounds' corrections, "Do you have anyone else who might be considered a threat or maybe some crazy Mormon or Polygamist who might want to snuff the president?"

There was a long silence until Rounds replied, "Agent, I am a Mormon and I can assure you Mormons are not interested in 'snuffing' the president. I can also assure you that if we have any suspicion of any threat to the president we will follow up on it prior to his arrival."

Peter was nearly at a loss for words but was finally able to get out, "Oh, just kidding, no offense meant, just trying to lighten the air, so to speak. I'm sure you're being proactive with the president's visit it's just I'm trying to follow Director Hoover's instructions as to the protection detail of the president."

Peter was blowing smoke because he knew very well that Hoover had not given any specific instructions in the protection of the president other than he was to be kept safe. By dropping Hoover's name, he was hoping to impress the Mormon and change the dynamic in this otherwise bleak conversation. It worked a little because Rounds seemed a bit more helpful.

"Everything in the Tabernacle itself will be manageable and security will be easy. Any trouble, if there is any; will come from the trip to the Tabernacle or the trip back to the airport. We'll secure the motorcade route; there should be no problem whatsoever. Of course, the Salt Lake City Police and the Secret Service will take care of most of that."

Peter was pleased with Rounds' assessment, "What we've done in the other locations, and are asking of you, is to maintain visual surveillance of anyone on the list and of course anyone else you think is a threat. If you have to throw them in custody for spitting on the sidewalk do it, but don't lose them until the President is gone."

"Agent Rinella, you're assuming we have every possible assassin on our list in Salt Lake City and are able to locate them. You how some people are constantly on the move from one city to another and our system of office responsibility can let one of these bad people fall through the cracks."

Peter agreed and was constantly frustrated himself by the Bureau's mail system. The mail was always days behind an event.

"Yea, yea, I know, but we have to deal with it the best we can, so keep an eye on all of them, and hopefully, no one has 'fallen through the cracks.' Oh by the way, I'll be coming to Salt Lake City on September 24th. If you can have someone meet me at the airport and maybe get me around during my stay, I'd be most appreciative."

Peter sensed Rounds was trying to get rid of him and ended the call. He decided to start working on the Texas visit which would encompass two solid days of presidential activity. The president would begin his trip on November, 21 with a visit to San Antonio then move on to Houston followed by Fort Worth, Dallas and finally, Austin. He had to contact all the offices in those cities and co-ordinate their activities to pull in all possible threats. The offices were part of the Dallas Division so many of the logistical issues could be solved at that level. He had six or seven months to get things going.

As an after thought, he planned to call the Field Office in Tampa to make arrangements for security for the McDill trip. It would be nice to get out of D.C. in November and in the Florida sun. Other things intruded into his mind and brought on sadness and anxiety. *My mind just can't stand prosperity.* This time his mind stirred up thoughts of his desolation after Millie's departure.

CHAPTER SEVENTY-TWO

Meadville, September, 1954

A month after Millie and the kids left, Peter made a trip back to Meadville to try to convince Millie to come back with him. He was willing to forget about Millie's indiscretion. After some conversation, Peter finally realized Millie was not coming back and that she intended to marry Ray Ward.

"Shit, I've been completely faithful to you. You can't say the same thing can you? You and that little fuck Ward were having a great old time at my expense, weren't you?"

Millie got angry, "We probably never should have gotten married. I expected more out of marriage. You could never be more than you were or become what I wanted."

"So that's why you started with your little American, huh, to get what you expected?"

Millie raised her voice, "He listens to me! Do you know how nice that is for a change…. to have someone care more about what you think and want instead of what they want?!"

Peter didn't have an idea what Millie was talking about. He couldn't think of a time when he was selfish or not sensitive to his family's needs.

Just as he was walking out the door, he spat at Millie, "It sounds to me like you're the selfish one. Take a look at your kids and see all the shit you started and what it's doing to them. Think about that when you get in bed with him and spread your legs… tell me then who is selfish!!!"

Peter had nowhere to go but his father's. He walked in and the old man was listening to the news on the radio. Giacomo's radio was up full blast. His face lit up when he saw Peter and didn't protest when Peter immediately turned the volume down.

"Pa you heard about me and Millie, huh?"

The old man said nothing and nodded.

Peter continued, "She's got a boyfriend, some guy she met when she was working at the plant. Of course, she says it's my fault because I didn't pay attention to her and wasn't what she wanted in a fuckin husband. Pa, I think she's losin her mind, but there's nothing I can do about it."

The old man said nothing for a while, "Pio, once a woman goes to bed with a new man, love for da olda one--it's a gone. No woman will have sex with a man when she still love another. So, I think she probably losta love with you before she take up with the Americana, but once she get in the bed with quista Americana, no way she gonna love you."

Peter whistled in agreement and cursed Millie and her lover under his breath. Moments later, he noticed his father staring strangely into space. His gray eyes were wide open but unfocused. Peter shook Giacomo to get his father's attention, but to no effect. He finally focused his eyes on Peter and tried to speak, but only unintelligible sounds came out. Giacomo slumped back into his chair and his right arm dangled over the side.

Peter called for an ambulance and they got the old man to Spencer Hospital. Doctor Mangione met Peter in the hallway,

"I'd say he's had a stroke. He has no reflexes on the right side and like most stroke victims he is aphasic, can't form words even though he still seems to have cognitive ability. It really doesn't look good, but if he survives the next twenty-four hours, he may get through it. I can't tell you that if he makes it he will have any use of his arm, leg, or for that matter, if he'll be able to speak."

Giacomo was in a room with an oxygen tent around him that looked like a transparent blanket, but he became agitated with it. A nurse removed it and placed tubes into his nostrils. Peter held his father's right hand in his two hands. The old man's hand was rougher than the leather he worked. His fingers were huge compared to Peter's. Peter brought his father's hand to his cheek and cradled it between his face and his hands. Tears started to stream down his face and onto his father's hand.

He whispered, "Pa….I love you. I love you."

Giacomo raised his torso and saw Peter, looking right through him, then quickly slumped back onto his pillow. He gasped twice and stopped breathing. Peter rested his head on his father's hard chest and sobbed.

142

CHAPTER SEVENTY-THREE

Washington, D.C., 1963

Peter hated to admit it but Rounds had Salt Lake City well in hand. The trip to Texas was a lot more complicated because it involved at least four venues and the entire state of Texas. Fortunately, he had a lot of time to get things organized. He called the Dallas field office and spoke with John Fain. Fain was more co-operative than the Mormon, Rounds. He even offered to expedite the communications with the other offices, and told Peter of an additional name or two which should be added to the list of suspects. What was more helpful was the offer of the use of Jim Hosty, an experienced field agent.

"We hope you'll be able to come down sooner rather than later. I'm retiring in a couple of months, but I'll take it as a personal mark on my career if anything happens to Kennedy here. Hosty's a great agent but mighty busy. He's working about thirty or forty cases, but he'll put those on the back burner and he's smart enough to hook you up with locals, if you need it."

"John you got the names from headquarters, right?"

"Yep got em about a week ago, but really didn't see anybody who jumped out as a possible assassin. Of course, there are some guys, who given the right circumstances, could do the job. Those are those guys we have to watch. Anyway, Jim'll be able to help, and I gotta tell you, the Secret Service in Dallas isn't bad. We share information pretty well. There is a young Secret Service agent who manages the Dallas office. His name's Henry Biggs. He's from the area and seems to be pretty bright. I suggest you get a hold of Biggs. He'll fill in some blanks about the president's schedule. Every time I've had anything to do with the kid, it was ok."

Peter felt good about their conversation and decided then to take a week off and go back home, while the president was in Europe. Late June in Meadville was a beautiful time of the year. It was five or ten degrees cooler than D.C. and the air clearer. He was able to jump on the Pennsylvania Turnpike. President Eisenhower promised a complete national system to be completed by the end of the 1970's. The Pennsylvania Turnpike was the prototype for the new Interstate Highway system. The trip back home to Meadville was shortened by an hour using the Turnpike. The drive allowed his mind take him where ever it wanted to go. Sometimes it was pleasant, sometimes it wasn't. This trip in 1963 reminded him of his drive home in 1954.

CHAPTER SEVENTY-FOUR

Meadville, 1954

Peter had to sell the old house and most of the stuff inside it. He decided to take time off from work and tie up any loose ends of his father's estate and get some time to spend with his children. He phoned the Pruttos' to speak to Millie and arrange visiting times, but instead got Mrs. Prutto. She took pleasure in telling him that Millie and the kids had an apartment of their own. Peter phoned the number his ex-mother-in-law had given him and a voice pleasantly answered, "Hello, Ray speaking."

The voice pierced Peter's heart and stomach and he nearly hung up, but after a minute croaked, "This is Peter...is....Millie in?"

The voice answered as though nothing was out of the ordinary, "Sure, I'll get her."

Peter's head pounded with anger and sadness. When Millie came to the phone, he couldn't resist, "Jesus Christ, Millie, it didn't take you long to move the dog shit in with you to play house, did it?"

Millie ignored him, "What do you want? Why are you callin'?"

Peter wanted to continue the discussion of Ray Ward's presence but knew it was pointless, "I'm in town to clear up some of my father's affairs and wanted to know when I could spend some time with my kids? With work, it's hard to know when I'll be able to get back."

"That's ok, I guess," she replied, "I'll drop them off at your dad's or wherever you want....You don't have to come and get 'em."

Peter was amused by her comment, "What's the matter, afraid I'm going to pop your little friend? Don't worry Mil, your guy isn't worth the effort."

He and Millie arranged a drop off in the morning. Peter looked around the old house and saw his father everywhere and was overcome by sadness. The furniture and the old man's bed, Peter's room, the dinnerware, everything was frozen in time and it all outlived Giacomo. Peter sat down in the living room next to the radio. He picked up his father's pipe and touched the worn, whitened end of it. *How the hell did he do that, for Christ's sake, he didn't have a tooth in his head. He must have gummed it down or maybe it was the same pipe the old man had when he had teeth. Hmm, what a guy he was. Oh Christ, had he been born thirty years later and maybe gotten an education, I wonder what he'd have done.*

Peter felt a deep sadness selling all the things Giacomo knew, touched, and lived with, but knew if it wasn't sold, it would rot into nothingness. He went into his old room and lay on the bed he used until he left the house to get married and quickly fell asleep. He felt his father's presence. He awoke the next morning refreshed and hopeful.

CHAPTER SEVENTY-FIVE

Meadville, 1954

Millie dropped the kids off at the door and Peter saw she was alone. He also noticed she drove a black Ford Sedan.

"Whose car Mil?" he asked, "your friend's, huh?"

"The kids would like to go to the movies; if you could oblige, that'd be great. Ray has given Cam some driving lessons and she wants you to see how well she is doing, if you have time."

Peter noticed the sarcasm in her voice but, like her, chose to ignore it, "No problem, Mil, I'll do my best. Glad your friend is stepping right in to the fatherly chores. Yes sir, he's one upstanding guy."

Millie asked, "Will they be spending the night here or at home?"

Peter nodded, "It's up to them. We'll call and let you know what they decide."

Millie turned on her heels, said nothing and left the porch without a good bye. Cam was quiet and after her mother left, put her arm around his waist and asked, "How have you been daddy? I think about you every night."

Peter put his arm around her shoulder and brought her deep into his body and replied, "Don't worry about me, honey. What's more important, is how are you doing? How's school?"

"Fine, actually, it's great. I love to learn new things, dad. Learning is exciting. I have a couple of friends, it's nice. In the very back of my mind, though, is that you're not home. I hate that."

He looked at Vinnie who was the polar opposite of his sister. He was bone thin, constantly on the move, and as brash as Peter's uncle Guidano.

"Ok, Vin, settle down, and tell me what is going on with you since your mom and I have…a… separated."

Vinnie seemed hardly fazed by the change in his parent's marriage.

"Everything is going fine, dad. I'm playing on a Little League team and am the starting catcher. Dad, I might make the all-star team.

The problem is Jeff Roberts is a catcher, too. His dad made the majors and everyone thinks he is better because his dad was a pro. What a bunch of bull!!"

Peter laughed and said, "Tell 'em your dad is an F.B.I. agent and will arrest his father's sorry ass....oh, shit I didn't mean to swear...don't repeat that, Vin, ok."

"That's a great idea dad, go on and arrest old man Robert's 'sorry ass,' I won't say a word."

Stifling any sort of humor Peter lectured, "Don't swear, Vin, your mother will know it came from me."

Cam looked at Peter and hugged him again and said, "I really am glad you're home dad, gosh I miss you."

Peter squeezed her as hard as he could and simply said, "So am I honey. You guys'll never know how much I miss you."

CHAPTER SEVENTY-SIX

Meadville, March, 1957

He went back to Meadville three or four times a year. He was able to repress the unpleasant thoughts but sometimes he couldn't and the ugliest jumped out. The morning of March 19, 1957 was his blackest memory; one he was incapable of controlling. He was awakened by the phone and Vinnie's hysterical voice,

"Dad, Dad, Cam died last night. My God, Dad, Cam died last night. She went to bed and just never woke up. She's gone!"

Peter couldn't process the information. The words didn't make sense or he simply refused to accept their meaning. Finally, he heard a voice screaming with intensity and bitterness, "No! No! No! Noooooooo!!!" It was his.

He collapsed on his bed screaming agonized moans. *It's a nightmare.* He slapped his face to awaken himself, but realized *he was awake and was living the nightmare.* The horrible reality, that his child was dead, trickled into his being. Again and again, he screamed as loud as he could to vent his anguish and anger but nothing helped. He wanted desperately to get back to Meadville, see Cam and embrace Millie and Vinnie. He had to get home as soon as he could. The trip back took forever and anguish travelled with him and covered him like a pall. Every twenty or so miles, he thought of Cam and his heart would grow leaden with sorrow and regret and his reaction was an angry, uncontrollable sobbing.

He arrived at the Prutto's and found Millie, Vinnie, and Ward there with his ex- in-laws. All of them were in shock—the same look he recognized in soldiers who had felt and seen too much to comprehend.

He embraced Millie so tightly he cracked her back and he murmured in her ear, "I can't believe she is gone. Mil, please, please tell me this isn't happening I can't believe Cam is gone."

Millie was totally silent and collapsed in his arms. He didn't attempt to lay her down and he kept hugging her limp frame that now resembled a life sized doll. Vinnie and the Pruttos were crying, Mrs. Prutto rocked with grief. Ray Ward stood in the corner, his eyes red from sorrow, but not intruding on the horrible scene.

Strangely, Peter remembered the scene at his father's house after his return from Europe and if that day was heaven, this day was surely hell. Those days were filled with the darkest and deepest despair of his life. Sometimes, he would recall the whole terrible event and sometimes only snippets would emerge. It would take him hours, literally, to compartmentalize the terrible memories and rip himself from the unending and unrelenting sorrow.

The drive back to Meadville for his vacation brought back that ugly time again. Six years had passed since that terrible day and it seemed like yesterday. On this trip, he decided to stay at the David Mead Hotel in downtown Meadville and walk the town at his leisure and maybe erase the horrible thoughts or at least put them away for a while.

CHAPTER SEVENTY-SEVEN

Meadville, August, 1963

He walked to Miss Flossie's *house* on West Street and noticed how it now resembled the other houses around it. It no longer stood out as a beacon and was nearly as ratty as its neighbors. An attractive light skinned Negro woman was sweeping the porch and casually glanced over her shoulder at Peter as he approached.

"Excuse me," Peter ventured, "I don't suppose Miss Flossie is still around is she?"

Hardly looking up, "She's my grandma. Why is it you are looking for her?"

Peter smiled, "My name's Peter, Peter Rinella, and I knew your grandmother from when I was a kid. We were....friends, I think you could say. What's your name?"

She continued sweeping and didn't look at him. She was probably twenty-five and had to be six foot one or more and towered over him. She had long curly hair. She had high cheek bones, nice full lips, and a beautiful ass.

"Bridget Buchanon's my name and I've been living with my grandma for some time. If you are a friend from when she used to make a livin in this house you have come to the wrong place at the wrong time, got it!?"

Peter laughed out loud, "Oh, no, I'm not here for that. I just wanted to visit with your grandmother and pass some time. I can see things are different now, Bridget, a lot different."

Bridget looked up and down Peter and warily, "I'll go see if grandma has a minute to spend. Peter, what's your last name again?"

"Rinella, Peter Rinella, I was Giacomo's son and Guidano's nephew, she'll remember."

Muttering to herself as she went through the door, "Asked him his name and he gave me his fuckin' family tree. Goddamn white guys are full a shit."

Flossie emerged on the porch looking much thinner than he remembered. Her hair was stark white, but fashionably set. She still wore the dark red lipstick and rouge on her cheeks, but now they were creased by wrinkles. She moved slower and walked with a cane.

She focused her eyes on Peter and said, "My granddaughter says I should know ya from many years ago and I thinks I do. I remember yo father would come by occasionally but yo uncle, bullshiter that he was, would come by once, twice a week. All the girls tried ta avoid him because he always tried to get outta' payin'for anythin'. We had ta get paid upfront wit him an then git him wit one a the new ones. He was sumptin, sure was."

Peter nearly howled at the precise description of his uncle. He asked timidly, "Do you really remember me? I came here when I was a teenager and into my early twenties. I would spend all of my time with Mae."

The old lady thought about it and said, "Yea…..yea I do. You got yo first here wit her, right and you uncle paid fo it, right?"

Peter jumped in, "Right…right…you picked her for me because we were close in age and I didn't know my ass from a tin cup. And, she helped me, a wonderful selection, I gotta add Miss Flossie, she was amazing. What happened to her?"

Flossie thought a while, "She married to one of her clients…a nigger black as coal and 'bout fifteen years older 'n her. He beat the shit out that po girl. He was one crazy fuckin nigger, fo sure. One night whilst he was sleepin' she cut his fuckin' throat and killed his ugly black ass right then and there. A course she got rested and sent ta prison….still there as far as I know."

Peter was stunned by the ugly news. He had to sit down on the steps to absorb the shock. He tried to compose himself by making inane small talk, but realized it was pointless. He had to leave.

He hugged Flossie and said good bye to Bridget who was looking around the door and lamely said, "Thank you for everything Miss Flossie, I really appreciate all you did for me. Nice meeting you Bridget—your grandmother is quite a woman. Both of you have a nice day."

The news about Mae was eating at his stomach. He was in a daze when, a half a block away, he found himself at the old wooden Catholic Church that had marked much of his life.

St. Mary's was the church where all the Italians went. The Germans went to one parish, St. Agatha; the Irish to another, St. Brigid;

even in their Catholicism they discriminated against one another. The Irish and the Germans both hated the *guineas* or *dagos* on the other side of the tracks.

St. Mary's was founded by an Italian immigrant priest around the turn of the century and Peter was sure it was established to keep the Italians in their own community and neatly away from the other, lighter skinned, northern Europeans. The Italians, for their part, were happy with the arrangement and preferred their prayers with *their own kind*, in their own language. They liked always being assigned an Italian priest. Father Catalano, who married Peter and Millie and buried his father and Cam, had been at St. Mary's for years. While most priests only stayed for four or five years before being transferred to another parish, the Italian priests didn't have the same parish mobility and stayed longer in their ethnic enclaves. St. Mary's literally was on the *other* side of the tracks at the end of a narrow brick street. He forgot how close it was to Flossie's house and the neighborhood where all the *shines* had moved.

The Italians moved out and made their way slowly up-town, the Negroes moved in, but St. Mary's maintained its Italian core membership even though its parishioners had moved out of the neighborhood. The church was an old frame building with a matching wooden steeple and the prerequisite cross as the spire. The whole building was a dull gray and desperately needed a paint job. Peter walked into the church and it seemed smaller than he remembered, even though it was only a few years since he had last been in it. The church was dark except for a few blue glass intention candles and a ray of light streaming in through an old stain glass window. It was all bathed in a surreal blue cast. He sat in one of the narrow pews, five rows back from the communion rail. The smell of candle wax from the few intention candles enveloped him.

He was lost in thoughts about his father, daughter, where his life was and where it was going, when he heard a deep, scratchy voice, "How are you doin', just thinkin' or maybe prayin'?"

Peter looked up with a start and saw a man dressed in a black cassock buttoned completely from his neck to well below his knees. His large belly stretched the garment to its fullest and almost popped the black round pearl buttons trying to restrain it. His hair was thinning and combed over to one side hiding his obvious baldness. His skin was dark olive. He had a large bulbous nose and dark eyes sunken and framed with large bags under them.

Peter looked at him, "Just thinkin', I guess. I don't pray much anymore. Where's Father Catalano? Is he still the pastor here?"

The priest sat in the pew in front of Peter and rested his arm on the back of it and leaned toward him, "Father Catalano has been gone for awhile. I'm only here for a day or so. So what brings you here? What's your name?"

Peter felt comfortable with the stranger maybe because he looked a little like his father and, oddly had Cam's quiet, friendly personality… and he was not a little guy…Cam would have liked him.

Peter without thinking said, "My name's Peter Rinella. I have been coming to this church, on and off, my whole life. I was baptized, made my first communion, got married, baptized my kids, and buried my mother, my father and……my daughter here. Some of the happiest and saddest times of my life have been inside these walls; this is kind of my home, Father."

The priest just listened and looked Peter directly in the eyes. His coal black eyes were piercing but also comforting so Peter continued without filtering his most intimate thoughts.

"My life has been a disappointment, I guess. I have messed up a little and to be quite honest, Father, I don't know if I believe God even exists. What if after this sad life is done, there isn't anything after it? Not so much for me but the people I'd have given my soul for."

After a few moments of silence, the priest said, very quietly—just above a whisper, "Belief in God or the hereafter is a personal choice. There's no way, of course, to prove our choices right or wrong because no one can prove or disprove the existence of God or life after death."

There was a silence that lasted for minutes when the priest continued, "A wise woman once told me 'it takes as much faith and effort to disbelieve as it takes to believe' and it's just a matter of pure blind faith in either case. I choose to believe, Peter, because it makes my life more bearable and worthwhile. My belief in God gives me purpose and fills a void that disbelief not only leaves vacant but makes larger and uglier."

Peter couldn't take his eyes off the priest. Never in his life had he been so transfixed.

After what seemed minutes of silence again, "Peter, I feel a whole lot better believing the people I love the most are still alive in some form and not rotting away in an unconscious existence."

Peter couldn't argue with him because any counter argument had been pre-empted by *the no proof either way* premise, but also because what the priest said gave him some comfort. He and the priest stared ahead at the altar and the crucifix in the middle of it.

Eventually, the priest spoke, quietly again, "You know, if an atheist wanted to live a good and just life in this world, all he would have to do is follow Jesus' example. He wouldn't have to make any grand statements about his beliefs or lack of, but he would make a tremendous difference in this life, huh?"

Peter thought awhile, "Yea, I guess so, but for me Father, aside from all the philosophical stuff, there is a lot of comfort in the rituals we practice. You know, Father, even when I'm having trouble with what's going on in my head, believing in the existence of God and stuff. The rituals make me feel good, nuts huh?"

The priest laughed, "You won't get an argument out of me on that one. I made a living with those beautiful rituals."

Peter smiled in response and they both were quiet for a long time when Peter finally got the courage to whisper, " I had a very short affair when I was in the army and would still be having it this many years later, if that was possible. My ex-wife said I was only worried about myself. She might be right. I think somehow I got punished for my sins with the loss of my marriage and, especially the loss of my daughter. I'm in such pain, Father."

The priest pondered his response, "God doesn't punish or even have to punish us in this lifetime. We do a good job of punishing ourselves and seeing God's role in our agony. We're the instruments of our own punishment. Sometimes, Peter, the very things that break our hearts have the potential of saving our souls."

Again they both looked straight ahead and spoke nothing for minutes when Peter said, "Father, I'd like to go to confession. Maybe we could go into the confessional over there."

The priest turned slowly to him, "That's not necessary, Peter, you have already confessed. I've heard them, felt them."

Relieved, Peter pulled himself up with the pew in front of him and offered his hand to the priest who took it in both of his.

"It was a pleasure spending time with you, Father."

The priest gave him a gentle smile, "Peter, it was wonderful spending time with you too."

As he was walking down the aisle to leave the church he turned to the priest, "Father, you forgot to give me penance for my sins."

The priest responded, but Peter couldn't hear him and drew closer to ask him to repeat himself. In a very soft whisper, barely audible the second time, "Peter, you've already done your penance. You've done enough."

Peter didn't know what to say but "Thank you," and hurriedly left the church. He walked down the steps and it occurred to him that he forgot to ask the priest's name. He felt like a dumb ass for not asking, and ran back into the church. It was totally empty. His called out for the priest, but there was no response, only the blue candle lights and their pleasant aroma were there.

On his way back out, he saw Mrs. Diluvio, a longtime parishioner and he identified himself, "Mrs. Diluvio, I'm Peter Rinella, do you remember me? Giacomo, the shoemaker, was my father. Who's the heavy set priest who's here now?"

She looked at him as though he was nuts, hurried up the steps to the church and said, "We havea no priest since Catalano lefta."

He decided to walk back to the hotel and leave the next day for D.C. It was time to get back to reality and tell no one about his meeting with the priest.

CHAPTER SEVENTY-EIGHT

Salt Lake City, September 25, 1963

The flight to Salt Lake City was miserable. The packed airplane rocked and rolled like a roller coaster as it hit every bit of turbulence from D.C. to Utah. *Who the hell would think a flight from D.C. to Salt Lake City would be full. Is September 25th the day all Mormons on the East Coast have to make a pilgrimage to Salt Lake City? Oh, Christ, I bet ol Bill....er..William Rounds will be in fine humor after I get there. Who knows, maybe he'll have to miss a Mormon holy day.*

Peter laughed at his own religious intolerance. After six agonizing hours of lurching, the plane made its approach to Salt Lake City and Peter realized how easy security for the president would be. Salt Lake was in a huge basin and the route from the airport to the Mormon Tabernacle would be along a very flat and easy to secure wide open road. *William and the Secret Service will have no problem locking up this little ride. I think Rounds is right about the Tabernacle too. Security can be stationed at all entrances and everyone coming in can be searched and cleared.*

Peter saw an older man with a large placard in front of him with "Rinella" on it. Peter approached the graying, heavy set guy with his hand out and said, "I'm Special Agent Rinella, and you are Agent...?"

The man looked surprised, "I'm Jerry Riggs...I'm not an agent... I'm just a driver the F.B.I. Office sent over to pick you up."

Peter just whistled between his lips and thought, *sonofabitch didn't have the decency to send an agent to pick me up. He fucked me over for the Mormon comment.*

When he finally got to the field office, he purposely didn't exchange pleasantries with William Rounds.

"I'm Special Agent Rinella. I'm sure you have made all the necessary preparation for the president's visit?"

Rounds was forty-five or fifty and had deep red hair in a severe flat top. He must have been six foot one or two and looked very fit. He wore the required gray or dark suit and dark tie.

His attitude to Peter was equally strained and he responded tersely, "Everything's ready. I can tell you the two names we were given,

Wilson and Guerard are under surveillance. We contacted the Secret Service and they're well in control of the Tabernacle. Rinella, I think you wasted your time with the trip out here."

Peter agreed with Rounds, but wouldn't give him the satisfaction of that and said, "Director Hoover is very precise about what I have to do in taking care of the president's safety."

What a bunch of bullshit that is... I should've stayed in D.C. instead of putting up with the most miserable flight and the biggest horse's ass in the Bureau. He couldn't wait to get the president out of Utah so he could quickly get back to D.C. and plan the much harder trip to Texas. He was still uncertain if he should go to Tampa a week before the Texas trip.

CHAPTER SEVENTY-NINE

Washington, D.C. September 30, 1963

After he got back to D.C., Peter was sitting in his office across from Morgan, who had assumed his usual position of feet on the desk and phone next to his ear. Peter was glad the trip to Salt Lake City was over but really was wishing 1963 was over as well. He felt good that the Dallas field office was cooperative. He also felt encouraged that the Secret Service office in Dallas would be very helpful and planned on giving Henry Biggs a call.

"Pete, I wanted to ask why you didn't stay in Pennsylvania longer." Morgan asked idly.

"I did what I wanted to in a couple of days and felt stupid just staying in another hotel room. What a waste to spend another night doing nothing...with no one to see or hoping to see me. You know, maybe Millie and that little fuck Ward could have invited me to dinner?"

Peter laughed at the ridiculous possibility of a civil and enjoyable meal with the Wards. "I had to make a trip to Salt Lake City and wanted to get ready for that. Thank God that's over. What an asshole Rounds is."

Morgan smiled at Peter, "How 'bout you comin' over to my house for a cook-out tonight? Patty will be thrilled for me to grill and the girls will be glad to have such an interesting guest for dinner. We just got a new swimming pool. It's heated so we can swim in it until the end of October. I'd like you to see it."

Peter thought for a moment and agreed to Morgan's invitation. He would take the train to Bethesda and Morgan could pick him up at the Bethesda terminal.

"What's your wife like?"

Morgan smiled and said, "I met Patty in college. She's from Syracuse and was her class valedictorian. She went to Brown on scholarship. Christ, she graduated Phi Beta Kappa and could have gone to any grad school or law school in the country. Instead, she decided to stay home with the kids and does some free lance writing. She's gotten some stuff published in "Life" and "Look." She also does some writing for trade journals like "Architectural Digest." She's smart as hell and to top it all off, a great wife."

"You're a lucky guy, Morgan."

After he got off at the Bethesda terminal and up the steps, he saw Morgan and two little blond girls standing at the entrance. Morgan was wearing plaid Bermuda shorts, white crew socks, and white tennis shoes. His legs looked like toothpicks poking out from under the shorts and every part of his exposed skin was pale white. The little girls were wearing sun dresses and their chubby legs were attached to white sandals. They each had sun glasses with frames shaped like hearts. They must have been eight and six and were exactly how Peter would have predicted for Morgan's kids. They waved at him as soon as they saw him.

The ride to Morgan's house was animated as the kids peppered him with questions about his swimming skills and breath-holding ability. The older one leaned over the front seat about two inches from Peters face and announced as loud as she could, "My name's Joyce, my dad says your name's Pete, right?"

Before Peter could speak, the younger one pulled Joyce back by her hair and pushed her-self in the location her older sister had occupied and screamed loudly, "I'm Christine and you work in the same office as daddy; he told us you help him put all the criminals in jail; that's what my daddy says."

Peter smiled and looked at Morgan, who had a sheepish grin on his face and gave Peter a quick wink.

Peter wryly offered, "Oh, girls, I don't have to give your daddy much help...he puts all the bad guys in jail without help from anyone."

The girls ignored Peter as they lunged and clawed each other without restraint. Morgan was oblivious to the commotion and leaned over to Peter, "Well, Pete, how's the prep going for the trip to Texas? Everything's pretty much in hand, right?"

Peter was distracted by the commotion in the back seat and didn't hear Morgan. He knew Morgan had said something, but Peter's attention was drawn to the rear. The kids were screaming and crying simultaneously and Peter was tempted to pull them apart. Again, Morgan asked Peter about his assignment and finally Peter was able to make out the question.

Looking in the back and answering Morgan at the same time, he responded, "It's going well. Fort Worth looks tough, but I should get the itinerary there before I start fretting. The president is going to be in Chicago about two weeks before Texas and in Miami and Tampa a week before. Nothing is going to happen in any of those places. Those cities are headquarters for two Mafia families. Hey, Morgan, are you going to let these kids kill each other?"

Morgan took a minute to answer and then finally, "Huh?" He finally looked at the melee in the back. "Oh, hey you guys settle down before I tell your mother. I swear to God if you don't knock it off, you're going to live with Pete and never see Ajax again!"

Peter was satisfied Morgan took control, as the kids settled down immediately, but he had to ask, "Morgan, who the hell's Ajax?"

Quietly, as though he was letting him in on a national secret, "Ajax is the Irish-Setter next door who comes over to our house every morning. Patty feeds him and the girls play with him for hours. They have adopted him, but more accurately, he has adopted Patty."

Leaning closer to Peter so the girls wouldn't hear, Morgan whispered, "I swear the son of a bitch gets a hard on every time he looks at my wife. He plays with the kids as an excuse to visit with her, no shit."

After a few minutes, they pulled onto a cement drive. The bottom half of the house was sand stone and the top half was white clapboard siding. In the middle was a large sand stone fireplace chimney. They walked through the garage to the back yard and in the middle of the yard was an in-ground swimming pool. The water was crystal clear and reflected the blue bottom. In the pool, swimming laps was a thin female figure in a dark one piece suit and a white bathing cap. Her strokes were efficient and powerful and when she would get to the wall she would do a flip turn and begin another powerful freestyle. Peter noticed she would occasionally turn her head to catch a breath and all of it seemed effortless. Morgan got her attention and she climbed out of the pool. She pulled off her swim cap and exposed short, light brown hair. Peter had seen her picture on Morgan's desk, but it didn't do Patty justice. She was very attractive. Her chest was still heaving from the exercise and on the inhale showed some cleavage.

She offered her hand, "Pete, it's good to finally meet you. Girls, go in and get your suits on while Daddy and I cook and chat with Daddy's friend. Sorry, I'm a little out of breath, haven't done much swimming since high school; was on the swim team but as you can see, I'm not very fit for the exercise yet."

Peter took her hand. "Patty, it's good to meet you. Morgan talks about you constantly," Peter lied.

She smiled at the comment and as she turned away, "Can I get you a beer or something else to drink? I hope you brought a suit?"

As she turned to walk toward the house, one of her cheeks protruded from her suit and showed how tanned she was. Her cheek was four shades lighter than her legs, arms, and face. Not wanting to be obvious, Peter averted his gaze.

"Yea, I'll take a beer please and no, I didn't want to ruin any appetites with the sight of my body in a bathing suit," Peter said while gently tapping his protruding stomach.

Morgan and Patty laughed a hearty laugh as she went into the house and Morgan poured charcoal briquettes into the bottom of a grill. He soaked the charcoal with lighter fluid, "I'll let the fluid set in before I light it. That's the key to a good charcoal fire, you gotta let the fluid soak into the charcoal so it burns completely and gets white hot—that's when it cooks best."

Peter nodded in agreement even though he didn't have any idea how to cook on a grill or how to manage charcoal. Morgan proudly announced, "This lot is nearly four hundred feet wide by six hundred feet long. It's huge for suburban Bethesda. Someday it will be worth a fortune, mark my words."

Peter took a swig of the beer Patty had just given him and replied, "Wow, this is a big lot and with a swimming pool too; I'll bet you'll do ok if you ever sell."

Peter said what he knew Morgan wanted to hear. Joyce and Christine jumped into the pool and started to splash each other and it again escalated quickly into an all out brawl. This time, both parents were oblivious to the fighting.

Patty sat at a picnic table about ten feet from the grill, crossed her tanned legs sipped on a bottle of beer, and said, "Morgan tells me you are responsible for presidential security. That must be pretty interesting and exciting."

Peter noticed how nicely shaped her dark thighs were but again tried to hide his glances, "Actually, it's pretty boring most of the time. It involves a lot of logistical stuff and coordination with D.C. and the Field Offices. Thank God, nothing ever happens so the president comes home in one piece."

She smiled, nodded and asked, "When are you going to light that grill, Mr. Morgan?"

"Soon my dear, soon," He put his arms around her shoulders. "I don't want to see a tasty little thing like you go hungry."

In mock anger, she padded off to the house again with her fleshy cheek making its appearance. Morgan looked toward the pool as his girls threw each other around like rag dolls.

"You know, I had to make a decision, Pete. I either was going to put in a bomb shelter like the rest of the ass-holes in the neighborhood or a swimming pool. I picked a swimming pool and hope we and the Russians never have a face off. Do you think I made the right decision?"

Peter thought for a moment and said, "If there's an atomic war, being in a bomb shelter is only going to delay the inevitable. Eventually, you will have to come out and to what? A radioactive waste land? You've heard the cliché that in a nuclear war the 'living will envy the dead.' I'm pretty sure that's true."

Morgan nodded in agreement, "Get ready for the best steak you have ever tasted."

Peter looked over at the pool and the churning water and it seemed a school of piranhas had been dropped into it instead of two kids, "I can't wait Morgan, I can't wait."

Morgan called to his wife, "Patty bring out the beef it's time to put it on the grill."

After a thoughtful moment,. Peter proffered, "You're a lucky guy Morgan….I hope you know that." Morgan smiled in response.

Peter took a large swallow of beer and just tried to absorb the scene and enjoy someone else's life for a minute.

CHAPTER EIGHTY

Washington D.C., October 1, 1963

The next day at the office, Peter thanked Morgan for his hospitality and ordered flowers to be delivered to Patty. He called Dallas to prepare for the president's trip in two months. John Zain, the office Agent in Charge, asked Peter to come down to Dallas a little earlier because in Zain's own words, they had so much to do that they couldn't see straight.

Peter realized field offices could be busy and agreed to arrive earlier. He asked Zain to send any information he had on any new suspects. Peter made his usual request for a field agent to drive him around the city. Nothing was more frustrating than trying to find someplace or getting lost.

Zain timidly replied, "Peter, that's another thing, I don't have an agent I can spare, but I think I have a volunteer from the Dallas P.D. to get you around town, is that ok?"

Zain was under a lot of pressure from D.C. to get his case load reconciled before his retirement. He also knew to *get along you have to go along* so he agreed to a Dallas P.D. driver.

"John, please be sure he is a cop, though. I'd feel better with someone who has some local authority just in case, ok?"

Zain agreed, "If they can't spare me a cop, I'll drive you around myself."

It would take a few days before the files on any suspects would arrive via mail. He was amazed the Bureau still used mail to get things around to the offices. They were able to send Tela-a-Types but that was discouraged because of cost. He was getting flak for using the telephone too much to make calls to the field offices, but disregarded the complaints and called whenever he needed to make arrangements.

He called Maggie and asked for her assistance when the files of new suspects arrived. Maggie answered the phone in her usual hurried state and Peter felt both rushed but summoned the courage to ask, "Mag, Rinella here, how you doin?" Without waiting for a response, "Mag, I'm getting a list from the Dallas office on some guys they've provided. I was just wondering if......the files are incomplete. Maybe we have something in the central system that might help....?"

Peter knew Maggie was irritated but she seemed to be softening, "I guess, Peter, but God it's hard to keep up with your requests. How many names do you think it'll be?"

Peter noticed she was using his first name and wasn't as short with him as she had been in the past, "Mag, don't know yet. I have to wait for the mail to get here. Dallas is bogged down with a million things and they asked me to give them a hand. I said I'd help, ok?"

Maggie didn't reply immediately but finally said, "Ok, Peter I'll see what we can do. Let me know when the stuff gets here."

Peter began to realize his increased interest in Maggie made her a lot easier to work with, and besides, he might be able to get a date or two.

"Mag, I know you said you weren't interested the other day but I still would like to have dinner with you, maybe a nice evening with nothing more than conversation, I promise."

There was silence for about a minute and finally she said, "What the hell? Ok, why not? When do you want to do it?"

Peter was shocked but managed, "How about day after tomorrow? That'll be Friday night. Do you like Italian or what?"

Maggie thought for a second, "You know, Peter, I really would like pizza. I don't want any fancy place, because, who knows, if you spend a lot of money there's no telling what you might want in return. Let's just go to some place where we can get pizza and a few beers."

Peter replied, "Mag, I promise, no matter how much I spend, there'll just be conversation and nothing more."

She laughed a little, "Don't worry about that agent Rinella, I'll keep you to your promise."

CHAPTER EIGHTY-ONE

Washington D.C., October 3, 1963

The cab pulled in front of Maggie's building and before Peter could get completely out, she came bounding down the front steps. She jumped in the back seat with Peter and he noticed how athletically she handled the steps and how attractive she actually was. She had her hair pulled back in a bun and her blue eyes were sparkling with mascara, something she never wore at work. Her cheeks had some color to them and as she turned her knees toward his but not touching him, she asked, "Well, Peter, where we goin? I hope it's a decent place after all you should know a good pizza place, right?"

Peter tried to look insulted, "Oh, because my forefathers came from Italy I should be some kind of expert on pizza pies?!" With more mock ire he continued, "Pizza, as we know it, with tomato sauce and cheese is an American invention. Italians in Italy have nothing like it. My father had no idea what American pizza was and, actually never had any. Now, in answer to your question, I do know a good pizza place, Missy, but not cause I am Italian, its cause I love to eat! We are going to Enrico's. It's not very big and is kinda of a neighborhood bar, sorta. I mean, the tables have the stupid checkered table cloths and wine bottles with melted candle shit on it, but it has the most incredible pizza pies you will ever eat!"

Maggie leaned forward and listened as Peter felt the need to explain, "The guy who runs the place, I guess Enrico, looks exactly like a pizza man should look—you know like Chef Boyardee on those cans of terrible pasta. No kidding, he's round, dark, and got this little waxed up mustache under a round nose, just like Chef Boyardee. And, if that isn't enough, Enrico's has *Rolling Rock* Beer on tap."

"What's *Rolling Rock* Beer?"

Peter, proud of himself for stumping Miss Know-It-All about everything, answered, "Rolling Rock, my dear, is a product of the Latrobe Brewing Company, Latrobe, Pennsylvania, and was, without question, the personal favorite of my Aunt Carmella."

"Well if it's good enough for Aunt Carmella, it sure as hell is good enough for me," Maggie laughed.

They arrived in front of Enrico's and hopped out of the cab just as it was beginning to rain. Maggie easily beat Peter to the door. The restaurant was nearly full with couples and two or three families with young children. Peter asked to be seated away from the kids. He ordered for both of them and made sure to order a pitcher of Rolling Rock.

When the beer arrived, he poured their glasses and toasted, "To Mag, and her wonderful work ethic and cute blue eyes."

She toasted in return, "To Peter, and his line of b.s. and eyes as dark as that."

They clinked their glasses together and took a sip of the beer and Maggie commented, "Ya' know Peter; it really is pretty good tasting beer. Old Aunt Carmella knew what she was talking about, huh?"

Peter smiled broadly, "Oh she sure did. Be careful, though, because under the influence of Rolling Rock it was rumored my aunt committed all sorts of unspeakable acts."

They laughed heartily and killed another pitcher of beer before the pizza arrived. Maggie took a piece and gingerly ate around the melted mozzarella. Peter watched contentedly as she ate her pizza.

She noticed he wasn't eating. "How come you're not eating? ....it's not poisoned is it?"

Peter laughed, "Oh I'm waiting for it to cool down a bit. Unlike some folks, I can control my hunger in the face of a scalded mouth."

"To bad for you buddy that means more pizza for me. Pour me another beer...I gotta cool off the burn in my mouth."

Peter ordered another pitcher of beer and he settled back for a Pall Mall and she a Camel. They became reflective and Peter brought up the president's visit to Texas. He started,

"Mag, if anything happens to J.F.K I'm done. I guarantee it. Hoover will need a scape-goat and it will be me and some field agents."

Maggie offered, "Nothing is going to happen to him, between the Secret Service and the Bureau who would have the guts and or the brains to assassinate the President of the United States?"

Peter responded, "Maybe I'm paranoid, but sometimes I see a huge network financing and planning some kind of plot. Other times I can see just one nut plugging the president because he's got nothing better to do. Either way, Mag, they can get away with murder, if we aren't lucky enough to stop them. Yea, it could happen. I lay awake at night thinking about it." After a beat Peter said, "Ok, enough of that. Tell me about you, Mag. How did you get with the Bureau? Where are you goin' from here?"

She had graduated from the University of Minnesota after a terrible life at home with an abusive, dictatorial father and passive mother. She then fell into a failed marriage with an equally mean and abusive husband and later, a job with the Minnesota State Police. After her divorce, she tested into the Bureau.

She had no idea what her future would hold. She asked him about his past and he told almost everything, leaving out Cam's death. Like her, he had no idea where he was going, only where he had been. He noticed her looking at her watch and knew it was time to get her home. On the ride home, they chatted easily about nothing and when they pulled up to her apartment, Peter said, "Mag, I know what I promised and I'll keep my word but...are you sure you don't want me to come upstairs with you?"

She smiled and put the tip of her slightly wavering finger to his chin, "I knew you'd try and am flattered you did. I wouldn't mind that but......I don't think my girl friend would like it too much."

Peter started to laugh. Surprised she asked, "What the hell's so damn funny?"

Peter could barely speak but finally, "Maggie, you have no idea how life repeats itself. I had this same conversation with another woman, once upon a time, and she gave me nearly the same answer. How's that for luck?"

Peter escorted Maggie to her front door, "Maggie, be careful. If folks in the Bureau have an inkling of your relationship it will be bad for you. You know how conservative these people are."

Maggie looked Peter directly in the eyes and said, "Peter, I have some stuff on the highest people in the Bureau. You know the old cliché about 'people in glass houses?' Some of these people are living in a greenhouse, trust me."

Peter opened the door to the building for her and was about to turn away when she took his face in her hands and kissed him....really kissed him. She took his right hand and brought it up to her left breast and he gave her breast a little squeeze.

She pulled away from him and said, "Rinella, thank you for a most enjoyable evening."

Still in shock from their surprise parting, Peter replied, "The pleasure was all mine. Maybe we can do it again sometime, huh?"

Walking through the door and not looking back Maggie replied, "We'll see, we'll see."

CHAPTER EIGHTY-TWO

Washington D.C., October 8, 1963

On Wednesday, the package from John Fain arrived Certified Parcel Post and, after he signed for it, he turned to Morgan, "There's gotta be a better way to get stuff from one office to another than the Post Service?"

Morgan was busy looking at another file and without looking up, said, "Someday they will send this stuff immediately over the wire like a small teletype machine or something, but in the meantime, we'll have live with it."

Peter pulled out what looked like five or six files each with a different name on the tabs. As he pulled the files out, a note from Fain dropped on his desk. It read,

> *Pete, here are some suspects we have added to your list. Could you run these by Information and see if they can add anything to the files? It'd be helpful if they'd track down current addresses. I have an opportunity to take my retirement and am leaving in two or three weeks. I'm really tired of all the baloney and need to get out. I won't have the chance to meet you in person so just call Jim Hosty if you need anything.*

He brought the files up to Maggie and found her hunched over her desk. She had a cigarette in her left hand and was drumming the desk top with her right hand. He startled her a bit with his entrance but she smiled as he gently placed Fain's files on her desk.

"I had a good time Friday. I really enjoyed myself; you're a very interesting woman. Hope you didn't get in trouble with your friend?"

A malicious part of him wanted to get her on the bad side of *her friend*. Maggie looked at him and continued smiling, "Me too, it was fun." She didn't say anything. "Actually, she was asleep when I got home." Without any interruption, she quickly asked, "So what have you got here?"

Peter explained Fain added some suspects not on the original list and needed last known whereabouts for them. Maggie took a drag on her cigarette and looked at the list and began writing down names and social security numbers of the five or six names Dallas had provided.

"I'll call Social Security and if any of these geese have worked, we can locate them pretty quickly. You know it's too bad the Field Offices couldn't do that, huh?"

Peter looked at Maggie's brow wrinkled from the prospect of more work, and said, very meekly, "Then I wouldn't be able to spend this time with you."

Maggie looked directly at Peter and didn't know if that was a clumsy attempt at intimacy or if he was just being a smart ass.

"Rinella, have I ever told you what a goof you are?"

Peter smiled at Maggie, "I don't know how you can insult someone who is so totally devoted to you."

Without looking up, she finished writing down the names, "Have a nice day, Peter. I'll call you as soon as I get the stuff you need."

On the elevator down, he remembered that October 7th was Vinnie's birthday and he had forgotten to call him. Standing at his desk, he picked up the phone and, as he dialed his son's number, he mumbled to Morgan, engrossed in his files, "Do you think somebody will get upset with me making a personal call?"

Morgan barely looked up and said, "How the hell will they know it's a personal call? You make thirty calls a day. If they get pissed about just one call I'll share my wife with you."

Vinnie was pleased to hear his dad's voice and, when Peter invited him to dinner to celebrate his birthday, he quickly agreed.

"I'll be there for some serious man-to-man eatin', drinkin', and talkin'."

Peter impishly asked, "How old are you, by the way…..twenty five or twenty six?"

Vinnie laughed heartily, "Great dad you are. You don't even know how old your beloved son is. I'm twenty two for Christ's sake, dad!"

Peter laughed, "You're lucky I remembered what day you were born let alone what year it was. I barely remember what I ate for lunch."

CHAPTER EIGHTY-THREE

Washington D.C., October 9, 1963

Peter called Mimo for the motorcade plans in Tampa, San Antonio, Fort Worth, Dallas, and Austin. The route themselves would be secured by the Secret Service. He certainly couldn't do any better than they, but if one of the venues had a particularly long motorcade or parade route, then maybe the presence of one of the suspects in one of the five cities might indicate a possible attempt. Of course, he was just grasping at straws and trying to fill time until he got to Florida and Texas.

The phone rang at the White House when an out of breath voice answered, "Hello, El-Youssef, here. How can I help you?"

Peter grinned, "What the hell were you doin', runnin' up and down the steps for exercise. This is agent Rinella. Do you have a few minutes?"

Mimo seemed bothered, "I guess agent Rinella, what's up?"

Peter asked about the motorcades at the venues. After a minute, Mimo replied, "Hmm, as far as I know, the president will be landing directly at McDill, no motorcade there. In Texas, he will be going directly to the Aerospace Medical Health Center speech in San Antonio and directly back to airport. I think that will be at normal travel speeds and no announced parade. He then goes to Fort Worth and there will be a short motorcade to his next speech, I think, but I'm not sure of that."

The young man paused for a minute. Peter heard him shuffle some papers. Peter heard him huffing as he riffled through the papers. He sighed, "Oh yes, here it is. He flies from Fort Worth to Dallas and there will be a longer parade from Love Field to his next speech at the Dallas Mart. The plans of Austin are not firmed up yet. The more I think about it, I'm sure the only extended trip will be at Dallas. The limo will only be at Love Field. If he was going to be in a parade anywhere else, they'd have to get the limo to the other venues and, as far as I can see, it's only going to be in Dallas."

Peter was curious, "Why's the president flying from Fort Worth to Dallas? It's not very far right?"

Mimo thought for a second and said, "I don't have anything to do with those kinds of things but maybe they don't want to waste time driving and can use that time for the appearance in Dallas. It makes for a little less prep not having to take care of the trip from Fort Worth to Dallas. I don't know."

Peter continued with his thought, "Who decides what and how the presidential visits are set up?"

Mimo answered, "As far as Texas goes, the Democratic National Committee, Vice President Johnson, Governor Connelly and the president himself decided where he would go and how big the events would be. Apparently, the president and his advisors are concerned about keeping his numbers up in Texas for his re-election."

Peter could sense the younger man was trying to get off the phone but had to ask, "Who decides if the bubble is used on the Lincoln?"

Quickly without hesitation, Mimo replied, "The president, he wants people to be able to see him. He feels it's important for them because it may be the only time they'll see a president and the bubble gets in the way."

Peter, as an aside almost, "I bet the Secret Service always hopes for bad weather. I know I do."

Mimo grew impatient, "Agent Rinella, I've got a lot of work to do for the president's trip to Florida. I have so much stuff going on....Call the Secret Service if you have any more questions. I've gotta get going."

Peter had no intention of calling the Secret Service in D.C. The Secret Service agents would resent his intrusion and that would only irritate the already bad relations between them and the Bureau. He decided to call their field office in Dallas and speak with agent Biggs. He doubtless had as much information as D.C. and knew better what was going on in his city. Hopefully, he wouldn't be resentful of Peter's interest and questions. After two rings, a pleasant young voice answered the phone.

"Department of Treasury, Secret Service agent Henry Biggs here, what can I do for ya?"

Peter noticed Texans had a particular drawl. It wasn't as pronounced as someone from Mississippi or Georgia but it certainly had a very Southern influence. Speech came from behind their tongue. It was thicker than any other place in America. Henry Biggs, Peter could tell, was a native Texan.

"Agent Biggs, my name's Peter Rinella. I'm a special agent with the F.B.I. out of D.C. assigned to our Internal Security Division (when he used this, the Secret Service didn't feel threatened in its presidential security duties) that sometimes leads me into security matters for the President. I'm calling to tell you that I'll be coming to Dallas before the President's trip and might need your help in some of my investigations."

Biggs was silent for a while and Peter actually asked if he was still on the line when Biggs finally responded, "Yeah, yeah, I'm here but I guess I don't understand what sort of investigations you might be conducting that could be related to the president's trip or his security."

He got that most of the time from Secret Service field agents who really didn't realize how heavily involved the Bureau was in Presidential security.

To ease his fears and be completely honest, Peter explained, "I have been investigating organized crime and its involvement in a possible attempt on the president's life. I've got nothing to base it on, but we all know how the president and his brother have pursued the Mafia and could, maybe, be a target for the mob."

Biggs was silent for the whole of Peter's explanation but was quick to ask once Peter was finished, "Doesn't Washington have the same information you have?"

Peter answered, "We have shared it with them, and actually your folks in D.C. gave me a list of potentials. Our investigation of the mob is far more extensive than anything they have so it's easier for me and the Bureau to follow our investigative trails than to try to convey all that to you guys. It'd be impossible. In fact, it's hard for me to include my own Field Offices in the loop."

Biggs finally seemed to understand what Peter said, "Ok, I guess we're all after the same thing…the president's safety…so if I can help, let me know. I'm sure you'll give me any assistance if I ask for it, right?"

Instantly, Peter responded, "Of course, I'll do whatever you need and give you everything I have. Oh, by the way, John Fain and Jim Hosty told me what a stand up guy you are and to call you to set things up."

Biggs seemed pleased with the act of deference, "Well, thank you for your consideration…I surely appreciate it."

Peter pushed the conversation, "Do you have any names that are different than the ones your folks in D.C. have compiled?"

Again, the younger man was silent for what seemed like minutes when finally, "Agent Rinella, I have no goddamn idea about a list of anything from our D.C. headquarters. What list is it? They haven't sent us anything like what you are talking about?"

174

Now it was time for Peter to be stunned. How was it that a list of potential assassins put together by the Secret Service in D.C. wasn't shared with its field offices? Peter felt compelled to explain, "Er, I'm sure it's just some sorta oversight. I'll get you the list I have but you have to forget where you got it. We have checked all the names that apply to the president's visit and will, if possible, have any and all suspects under visual surveillance. If you guys are spread thin doing what you do for a presidential visit, we'll make contact with your suspects and keep an eye on them too, until the president gets out of town. I promise you that."

Biggs was still angry about the poor communications out of Washington and complained, "How the hell can we do our job out here in Texas when the big deals in D.C. don't share anything with us?"

Peter replied, "I don't know about you guys, but it's impossible for the Bureau to keep up with the huge amount of information and then send it from headquarters to every field office. Jesus Christ, even Air Mail Special Delivery takes one or two days to get from D.C. to any place in the U.S. Some things and, worse yet some bad people, are bound to fall through the cracks."

Biggs, pacified, said, "Well thanks again. Send me that list, although, I'm not sure what I'll do with it, but I'd sure as hell like to have it. Of course, if I need any help I'll get in touch with you and vice versa. Ok?"

Peter thanked Henry Biggs and promised to call him again with any pertinent information and to personally drop off the suspect list.

CHAPTER EIGHTY-FOUR

Washington D.C., October 12, 1963

Peter hadn't seen Vinnie for a few months and realized, again, what a handsome man he had become. He was at least six foot two and had his mother's softer, better looking features. He didn't have Peter's prominent nose or his shit brown eyes, but his mother's more delicate nose and her amber colored eyes. He did, however, have Peter's dark olive skin.

"Well what do you feel like eating, Mr. Birthday Man? Could you go for a steak or a nice dish of pasta or what?"

Vinnie thought for a minute, "Dad, I really would like to have a nice big steak, medium rare with a baked potato. Pasta out always tastes like shit."

The Omaha Steak House was just what both of them wanted, huge steaks and a good selection of beers on tap. Peter and Vinnie both ordered T-Bones with baked potatoes. Together they polished off a full basket of warm bread, and to save space for dessert, completely ignored their salads. Vinnie had an incredible peach cobbler while his father demolished a cheese cake with strawberries. Both of them were completely stuffed but were in the mood to talk over their coffees.

Peter lit up his Pall Mall when Vinnie began, "Dad, I know this is a terrible time to talk about this after we just consumed 2000 calories each, but I'm worried about you. I'd never say anything to hurt your feelings but you have to start getting yourself back in shape. I've noticed you are starting to get a little thick around the middle and the Bureau fitness test is comin' up fast."

Peter knew his son didn't give two shits about the Bureau's fitness test and was only interested in his trying to get his dad's heart in the best condition possible. Peter also knew he was a candidate for a heart attack. He took a deep strong drag on his cigarette and looked at his son.

"I know, I know. In fact, someday I'm going to throw these things away. I gotta tell you my wind is terrible. Christ, I can barely run five hundred feet let alone two miles; I am going to have a helluva a time keepin' my shield next year."

Peter changed the subject, "Well, what have you decided on doin' when you graduate in December? I hope ta hell you don't follow your girlfriend around the country while she goes to med school and you don't do shit about your future."

Vinnie agreed, "You're absolutely right, Dad. No matter where she goes, I'm applying to Pitt and Dickinson. If she happens to get into med school near one of those places, ok. If not, well, our relationship will have to be able to deal with the distance."

Vinnie was certainly far more focused than he was at the same age. Vinnie, at least, had a plan and seemed to be well on the way to its execution. Peter was curious about Vinnie's selection of law school so he asked, "Why the law, Vinnie? You could do so many other things."

Vinnie had given it a lot of thought because he answered before Peter was hardly done with the question, "I've always been able to communicate pretty well and I'm able to reason well enough. I can work something to its logical conclusion. I figure that's what you need to be a successful attorney, so why not?"

He was silent for a minute to study his father's reaction, "In the final analysis, Dad, I think the law will give me a chance to make a real difference in people's lives and in my own at the same time. All of us are trying to make some mark in this world before we leave it, right?"

Peter understood, "Vin, of course, everyone wants to make some kind of difference. Life has a way of just rushing past us and before we know it, it's gone. That's sad huh?"

Vinnie nodded in agreement again, "I had a history professor who said 'history is a whirlpool with most people stuck somewhere in the middle until they are swept down the vortex. Some people, by virtue of talent, luck, or a strange mixture of both can work their way to the outer edges of the water and in those outer currents, they can be seen. In very rare cases, they are able to affect the speed of the water.' What he didn't say, dad, was in the final analysis we all go in the same direction."

Peter looked at his son and said, "Well, all my life I've been stuck in the middle of some pretty big whirlpools, and sure as hell, I've never made it to the outer edges and changed a damn thing. The good part of my job now is looking out for one of the most important men in the world who lives on the outer edge. Am I just clutching at some straw here?"

Vinnie looked at his father and felt a mixture of love and sympathy, "Dad, your job is really important in the entire scheme of things. Jesus Christ, if someone assassinated the president the entire course of history would be changed."

Peter loved Vinnie because he was his son but also because he was a nice guy trying to ease his father's pain. All the talk of the individual and his destiny in history made Peter uncomfortable.

He lit another Pall Mall and asked, "How's your mom and the suck fuck she married doing?"

Vinnie was surprised by the quick change in subject and also amused by his father's description of Ray Ward, "They're doin' ok, I guess. I know you don't want to hear this dad, but Ray isn't a bad guy. I mean, he's no you, but he does exactly what mom wants and would die trying to make her happy. Christ, Dad, he even lent me some money to buy my car. I paid him back pretty quickly, but he never asked me for it."

Peter reacted angrily to Vinnie's revelation and spat out, "Why the fuck did you ask him and not me for the money, for Christ's sake, Vinnie? He stole your mother away from me and he is doin' stuff for my son I should be doin'."

Vinnie was surprised by his father's outburst, "I asked him for the money because I knew if I borrowed it from him I'd pay it back. If you gave me the money, sure as shit, I wouldn't have paid you. No one could ever take your place in my life, Dad, no one. If I am anything it is Peter Rinella's son and nobody can ever change that."

Again, Peter felt the warm rush of love for this young man who invariably said the right thing at the right time. Peter knew Millie was responsible for Vinnie's temperament, probably more than he was.

He smiled at his son, "Happy Birthday, Vin, I am proud to have you for my son, and no disrespect to you, but Ray Ward can go fuck himself."

He put his arm around his son and hugged him as hard as he could, "I have to go to Dallas next month….the president is goin' there at the end of November, but when I get back, let's get together again; I'd like to meet your girlfriend, ok?"

Vinnie kissed his father on the cheek and hugged his shoulders, "By all means, Dad… after you get back from Texas, we will get together, promise."

CHAPTER EIGHTY-FIVE

Washington D.C. October 13, 1963

The next morning, Peter found a note from Morgan,

Call Johanson, she's got some info for you. MM

Peter was going to take the elevator up to Maggie's office but the elevator was stuck somewhere, so he ran up the three flights of stairs to her office and nearly died of exhaustion. He thought to himself just as he went into her office, *Holy Christ, I'm in terrible shape! I could barely make it up the steps. Man, I gotta start doing something."*

When he entered her office, Maggie cheerfully greeted him, "Well, Rinella, I have some information on the guys you gave me. I got their current employers from Social Security; all you have to do is call them and get what you need."

She handed Peter the list he had originally given her with the names listed and their employer.

> *James Parker, Zinc and Metal Processors, Dallas Texas; Charles Parker, Dallas Feed Company, Dallas Texas; Earl Robinson, Blackburn Construction, Irving Texas; Franklin Goodrum, James & Brown Well Services, Dallas Texas*

She seemed pleased with her efforts and looked toward Peter for validation, but he was engrossed in the list and forgot her presence until she asked, "What do you think? I mean is it what you expected?"

It dawned on Peter what Maggie was looking for and he quickly answered, "Yea…yea..Mag this is great, but what about this one name where no current employer is listed?"

Maggie looked at the list and said defensively, "You gave me five names and I gave you back four with current employers and you're still not happy?!! Let's see what that name is… 'Lee H. Oswald, hmm…I… can't remember what I found with this guy….let me find my notes….oh yea...his last employer was the Reily Coffee Company in Dallas, but according to Social Security his Social Security Number didn't appear on the third quarter return for Reily. He either quit or was fired from that job. Social Security doesn't have any returns yet for the fourth quarter so we don't know if he has gotten a job somewhere else. I guess you and the boys in Dallas are going to have to earn your salaries by visiting all these guys.

Peter thanked her for her work, "As usual Mag, you do incredible work. No one will ever know exactly how important you are to the organization."

Maggie smiled at Peter, "You know, Peter, we have information on almost anybody you can ask about. If we don't have it, we know how to get it quickly."

Peter understood, but didn't have a clue where she was going until she pulled out a fairly thick folder that she threw on the table. Peter picked it up and read its tab, "Rinella, Peter, J." He saw all the landmarks in his life, every one. He was surprised that the Bureau maintained a file on one of its agents. He tried to hide his discomfort.

"Oh, I suppose they have one of these on everybody who works for the Bureau, right?"

Maggie nodded in agreement, "Yep, even me, though that file is not here, of course, and I can't access it."

Peter thought for a moment, "Well, we have a file like this on the Parkers, Robinson, Goodrum and Oswald, yes?"

A smile crossed Maggie's face as she pulled out file folders with their names on the tabs and laid them on the desk for Peter to scan.

"Don't suppose I can have these can I? I'd sure like to take them to Dallas with me."

Maggie nodded in the affirmative.

Peter was grateful and honestly meant it. "Mag I owe you the best dinner possible. When I get back from Dallas, I am taking you to the fanciest place we can find."

"Rinella, that sounds great. You better have some money though, because I have a big appetite."

Before he was about to leave, a question crossed his mind, "Mag, in the restaurant when I was telling you about my past, you knew pretty much what I was going to tell you, huh?"

180

Maggie was quiet for a moment, "Yes, I couldn't resist pulling your file. You're a lot more than what's in the folder, though."

Pleased with her answer, Peter said, "I can't wait to get back for that dinner, Mag."

CHAPTER EIGHTY-SIX

Washington D.C., October 26, 1963

For two weeks Peter pored over all the files for all the suspects. He read and re-read every bit of information. He felt confident that the Florida trip was secure and he concentrated on Fort Worth-Dallas-Austin. He called Dallas and told Jim Hosty he would be arriving in Dallas on November, 20th and asked for a ride from the airport.

"John Fain told me you guys have a million things to do with the president's arrival and I thought I might visit with the Parkers, Robinson, Goodrum, and Oswald."

Hosty readily accepted the offer, "You mean you were able to find these guys? Christ, I haven't had any luck."

Peter smiled thinking about Maggie and her associates and actually thought about taking all the credit. But instead he said, "Our Information People are incredible at tracking somebody. We got employer addresses on all of them but Oswald. Apparently, he left his last job in July and we can't find him. "

Hosty replied, "I've got a folder on him that is as thick as the Bible. I'll give it to you when you get here."

Peter wasn't sure if Hosty was joking or not. "I have the bare bones description of times and places for him but my stuff ends with his discharge from the Marines and his defection to Russia."

Hosty said, "Wait 'til you see what he's been up to since. The only good thing about Commies is that they aren't predisposed to violence. They are all about the rhetoric."

Peter agreed heartily, "Yea, it's usually the other side of the coin you have to watch. That's why I'm gonna look up the Parkers, Robinson, and Goodrum first. After I see them, I'll pay a visit on our friend Oswald."

Hosty agreed, "Don't forget to get my file on him when you get to Dallas, it'll give you somewhere to start anyway."

"Will do," Peter said before hanging up the phone and added, "See you on the 20th."

CHAPTER EIGHTY-SEVEN

Washington D.C-Dallas, November 18, 1963

The three hour flight to Dallas was forgettable. The man next to him introduced himself as Richard Malley. "My friends and family call me Chip," he said after they shook hands.

His father and grandfather were Richards and he was Chip to establish a difference among the Malley clan. The Malley's were from Ireland and came to America to escape the Potato Famine.

Not trying to be a smart ass but honesty wondering, Peter asked, "Didn't ALL the Irish come to America to escape the Potato Famine? Christ every Irish guy I knew back home got here because his family couldn't grow potatoes."

Chip seemed a little offended but it didn't stop him from saying, "Oh God, no, some came a lot later to reconnect with their families who were in the first wave of immigrants; and some to avoid the civil strife in Ireland. The ones who came later were the nannies and maids. The earlier immigrants own all the real estate and bars."

He said that with a hearty laugh and Peter didn't know if he was serious or not. Chip asked, "Why are you going to Dallas? Is it business or pleasure? Why on earth anyone would go to Dallas for pleasure is beyond me?"

Peter smiled, "I'm going to Dallas on business, how 'bout you?"

He leaned closer to Peter and whispered, "I'm an interior designer and Mrs. Connelly has hired me to do some changes to the Governor's mansion in Austin. I must be discrete because she doesn't want the citizens of Texas to know she is spending money with an out-of-state talent."

Peter asked, "It's important that nobody knows who decorated the mansion?"

Chip, startled by Peter's question, "I told her to tell everyone that she had all the ideas on her own and that would make her the most popular First Lady in Texas history. Look at Jackie, for God's sake. She had a tour of the White House showing what awful taste she has."

"Mrs.Kennedy did her own decorating?" Peter interrupted.

"If that's what you call it. It was terrible, but everyone was 'ooing and awing.' Jackie sure is beautiful and so sweet, but she should hire a professional decorator. She doesn't make those beautiful gowns for herself, does she? Hell no, she hires the most expensive talent she can for those adorable creations. Every woman in America thinks she can do interior design and Jackie's no different."

Peter started to zone out of the conversation as Chip ran on and on about gowns and decorating but knew if he just nodded in agreement it would save him from any deeper interaction. Chip wasn't through, "Have you noticed Jackie's hair?"

Peter was starting to despair at the conversation. Chip droned, "Every woman in America is trying to look like Jackie. The only problem most women have is that they're paying fifteen dollars to have their hair done and Jackie is spending two hundred dollars. Now what kind of result can you expect for fifteen dollars?"

Peter muttered, "Not much, I'll bet."

"You and I know you get exactly what you pay for and nothing more."

Peter pretended he was asleep for the balance of the flight.

CHAPTER EIGHTY-EIGHT

Dallas, November 18, 1963

When the Eastern flight landed at Love Field, Peter remembered it was the airport the president would be landing at in less than a week. As he walked down the movable steps for disembarking, he reached for a cigarette but decided not to because he had smoked five Pall Malls listening to Chip for the entire five hour flight. When he got into the gate area, he looked around for his escort and caught a glimpse of a man with a badge hanging out of his suit jacket upper pocket. The guy was Peter's height and coloration with the same semi-balding head. He was wearing a gray serge suit, a white shirt, and a dark grey tie. He was holding a white hat in his hands and looking over all the passengers as they entered the building. He knew this had be his escort and he walked up to the man and introduced himself.

"Hi, I'm Special Agent Peter Rinella, F.B.I. D.C. and you?"

The man smiled immediately and stuttered as he introduced himself, "I....I...am.....Dante Augello......Dallas P.D."

Peter wasn't sure what he said, "Your name is Dante Augello?"

Augello smiled, nodded, "Yes, my friends call me......Danny. After...I relax a little......bit I won't stutter as much"

Peter thought to himself, *Is he the best guy they could send over for me?! Jesus Christ, I hope he relaxes or our conversations are gonna take five hours between his stuttering and my repeating everything I think he said. What the hell!*

Peter didn't want to make Danny more nervous knowing it would increase his new partner's stammering, so he smiled a lot. He liked Danny's looks for some unknown reason. He just felt an affinity for the guy that was beyond compassion for Danny's stuttering issue but he couldn't pin it down.

Danny asked, "Where....where do you want to go, the Federal Building or.....your hotel?"

"I don't know what hotel I'm staying in, maybe they will know at the F.B.I. office."

All the men in Dallas were sporting the same white, wide brimmed hat that Danny was wearing and Peter asked, "What's up with the white hats you guys wear here?"

Danny smiled and nearly without a stutter, "I....I don't know. When I....got here from New Orleans about two years ago....all... the men had them...so I got one."

It dawned on him why he liked Danny. *Jesus Christ, we look alike. We could be cousins.* Peter asked Danny more about his back ground.

"You said you came from New Orleans. Were you a cop there? I don't notice a Cajun accent so you aren't native to New Orleans?"

Danny nodded, "Oh..nooo. ...I was born and.....raised in.....New York.....I was a cop there actually for eight.....years....when I got the job in New Orleans and then after two year I came here."

Peter processed the information, "You're full blooded paisano? Where did your people come from in Italy?"

Danny smiled again and was very happy to share, "My....mother.....is from Naples and my...dad was from Sicily. They....met....here...when they...were.....kids and got married. No one in either family spoke to them for..marrying...someone out of....their province."

Peter laughed out loud at this, "My father used to say 'Italians are the craziest people on earth because they place the province above the country and sometimes above the family.' He was right."

Danny nodded in quick agreement. Peter felt good about this guy. Danny leaned over to Peter, "Are....you......looking for some female company tonight?"

Peter thought for a moment, "Danny, it's been awhile for me so, yeah I wouldn't mind a visit if you can arrange something. I like women with curves."

Danny smiled a wide grin, "No...problem...I have the exact one for you and...I'll pick up the cost."

As they pulled in front of the Federal Building, Peter was certain he and Danny were going to be very good friends.

CHAPTER EIGHTY-NINE

Dallas, November 18, 1963

Peter and Danny rode the elevator to the ninth floor and when they got off, Peter was surprised. Inside a room probably thirty by forty feet, were at least fifty desks. The room was a sea of white shirts.

He commented to Danny, "In D.C. we share an office with two, four guys at the most. The phone ringing as much as it does here would drive me nuts."

Danny pointed to the periphery of the room, "I think the offices with the glass partitions are where the supervisors are."

Peter nodded and asked an agent at the first desk where Jim Hosty was. The young agent pointed across the room and said, "Special Agent in Charge now is Gordy Shanklin. Who are you?"

Peter replied quickly, "Oh I'm sorry, I'm Special Agent Peter Rinella and my partner here is…"

The young agent nodded and interrupted Peter with, "Oh, we know Danny. Yea, go over there to see Shanklin first."

Peter and Danny wound their way through the maze of desks. When they got to the office Peter noticed a new sign on the door etched in a dark mahogany wood, "J.Gordon Shanklin, Agent in Charge."

Peter knocked on the door and a voice from inside called out, "Come in and make it fast."

Peter and Danny hurried into the room and were enveloped in a cloud of thick smoke. Shanklin had a cigarette in the ashtray and a pile of papers in front of him and he barely looked up to acknowledge them. His chin was prominent, bounded by a turkey waddle, and his ears popped out from his head, or so it seemed, because of his swept back hair. Peter introduced himself. Shanklin scanned his papers.

"You're Special Agent Rinella? I'm glad you're here, we have a lot of cases pending and the president's visit just adds to the complexity of running one of the largest field divisions in the Bureau."

Peter immediately apologized to Shanklin for taking up his time but added how pleased he was to be able to help the Dallas office with the president's visit. He asked, "Has it been ok'd with the Dallas P.D. for officer Augello to be my guide and escort for my entire stay in Dallas?"

Shanklin scanned his papers again and shuffled from one to another, "I've spoken to Chief Curry.......and...a... he says it's fine if Danny works with you."

Peter was surprised that everyone knew Danny on an apparent personal level. Peter asked if he could visit with Jim Hosty.

"No problem whatsoever. Jim has an office over there, pointing to another enclosure on the other side of the huge room, and he'll give you all the help he's able. He's busy, lost in thought again, I don't know what he'll be able to do for you."

Peter felt obligated to respond, "I understand completely, but I'd just like to introduce myself and see if he has anything new."

The room was so thick with cigarette smoke a clear view of any of the three men was difficult and Peter strained to see Shanklin. "Do you have any objection if officer Augello and I investigate the three or four names Agent Hosty gave me?" he asked.

Shanklin picked up another pile of papers, "Umm, no, no, not at all, knock yourselves out, if you need any help with arrests or warrants or anything like that you can call Chief Curry or me. Now, if you don't mind, good to meet you agent and nice to see you again Danny, but I have lot of shit to do."

Peter and Danny made their way across the room. Hosty stood up immediately when they entered, wrapped his big hands around Peter's and immediately shook Danny's. He motioned for both of them to take a seat and began the conversation.

"Agent Rinella, Peter, it's good to meet you. I appreciate you helping me out with the names I sent over to you. I wish I could give you one of our agents, no offence Danny, but we can't spare a soul. Danny here will do a great job, though."

Danny beamed and Peter nodded, "Oh, that's ok; Danny and I will get around just fine. As I told you in our phone call, I'll pin down the Parkers, Robinson, and Goodrum before I look up Mr. Oswald. Is that ok?"

Hosty thought for a second, "That's your call, but this Oswald is one serious nut case. He's from another planet, I swear. After you get done with the other three, we can discuss Oswald. How long do you think it will take you with the other guys?"

Peter shook his head, "Jim, I have no clue. Your guess is probably better than mine...You know what it takes to track some of these people in Dallas."

"You know Pete, I'd say two or three days for them. You think the others are a bigger threat than Oswald?"

Peter nodded, "The guys in the KKK or the John Birch Society are far more dangerous to the president than a nutty Communist. Communists are in the business of stealing secrets not killing our presidents. It will make me feel better if all the fruits on the right are located and we are sitting on their laps before we locate our friend Oswald."

Hosty shrugged, "Ok, good. If I can help in any way, let me know."

"Yea, Jim, can you tell me what hotel visiting agents use when they're in town? Who accepts a Federal account...or do I have to pay for it...and voucher the expense?"

Hosty quickly replied, "The Brown, yea, the Brown will bill the Bureau and most visiting agents stay there. It's an old place but is clean and nice, really. The television system is pretty good, I'm told."

Peter smiled, got up, motioned for Danny to join him and extended his hand to Hosty,

"It was a pleasure meeting you, Jim. I'll be here in the morning to get started. Hopefully, I have a room there and if anything comes up in the meantime, give me a call"

He pointed to the door and placed his hand on Danny's shoulder, "Let's get going my friend. You know where we're going, right?"

As they walked out the door and into the huge room, Danny stuttered, "I... I... know.....Dallas like the back...of...my...hand."

Peter noticed Danny was looking at his palm with his affirmation and he spat, "I'm lost for sure. You don't know the BACK of your hand from the FRONT of your goddamn hand."

They both laughed until they got on the elevator.

CHAPTER NINETY

Dallas, November 18, 1963

The Brown must have been built around the turn of the century and had to have been the grandest hotel in Dallas at the time. It was fifteen stories and was faced in a cream brick. The lobby was built with dark mahogany and granite. Peter imagined Dallas hotels would be bright and sandy or something similar to an arid motif. The designers of the Brown tried to duplicate fine hotels in New York and Chicago.

Peter and Danny walked up to the desk and a young man on the other side of the dark black onyx counter asked pleasantly, "May I help you gentlemen?"

"My name is Peter Rinella, I'm an FBI agent from Washington. Do you know if I have a reservation for a stay of, let's see, five nights?"

The desk clerk ruffled through a series of folios behind him and fished one out, "Yes, Agent Rinella, you are confirmed to stay until check out time Friday, which is twelve, will that be ok?"

Peter thought for a second and asked, "Hmm, I may have some work to finish on Friday afternoon. Can I extend my stay one additional night?"

The clerk nodded and made a notation on his chart.

Danny escorted Peter to the elevator, "Ok…..I'll get some lovely girl to come up to your room at eight o'clock. Is that ok?

Peter looked at his new acquaintance, "That paisano would be a wonderful thing."

Leaning toward Danny's ear, Peter whispered, "Young is fine but make sure she looks like a woman, please. I like curves, nothing too thin. I can't stand bony women."

Danny nodded in agreement and departed as Peter got on the elevator and told the operator his room number while he was waiting for her to rip his stomach out with the shot upward. Surprisingly, she was easy on the controls and Peter made it to the eighth floor with his insides intact. Appreciatively, he gave her a dollar hoping she would be on duty for his entire stay. He opened his door to his room and quickly looked around and found the bathroom which he promptly used. He splashed some water on his face and looked at the room service menu because his watch read six o'clock. It dawned on him that Dallas was an hour behind D.C. so he adjusted his watch but was still hungry. He decided to wait for awhile before ordering room service knowing how pissed D.C. would be with his extravagance. There was talk that all agents would be given a per diem and anything they spent over that would be their responsibility. Until then, Peter concluded, he would still order room service and hang the Bureau with the additional service charges, *fuck em, they stick me in the most fucked up places. The least they can do is pay a room service bill!*"

He sprawled on the bed with the menu contemplating his meal and dozing for awhile. He woke up at six o'clock (Dallas time) completely famished. He ordered a steak with mashed potatoes and a bottle of Millers. He reclined back on the bed and thoughts of Cam and his father washed through his mind in and out with no particular events attached to them, just their images. He considered how much time had elapsed and how their places in his personal history had been written and ended. He couldn't conceive that they were no longer in his present and would be absent from his future. He was unable to process where time had gone. He thought, *how could those twenty or so years just vanish? What I have done with my life? Jesus Christ, how much time do I have left? What's after this?*

His thoughts settled back to his daughter and father and their deaths. He was instantly overcome with grief, and anxiety as the thoughts gushed in with no control or modulation. Then it began. The demon emerged with full fury. His heart began to race, perspiration poured from his head and nearly every pore of his body. He felt a tremendous urge to rip his clothes off, and to run screaming at the top of his lungs. He consciously restrained himself to keep his position on the bed, his chest heaving, as though he had run ten miles. He knew these feelings well and that they would eventually end, but that was no consolation. He was in the presence of his personal and brutal demonic possession. He could talk himself out of the suffocating and narrow physiological tunnel by relaxing and taking easy, oxygen filled breaths. Slowly, he was able to gain control of his thoughts and pulled gradually away from the thinking which had started the agonizing episode. He forced himself to think about the mundane arrival of his steak dinner and the exciting arrival of Danny's gift. As his body complied, his pounding heart and forced breathing began to descend to normal levels. He was spent as a response to the physical demands of "the demon" and nodded off. He heard a knock on the door and a voice announced the arrival of his dinner. After the waiter left, Peter took the lid off the plate and suddenly realized the demon had taken his appetite. He forced himself to take a few bites, but his taste was absent. He was both depressed and angry with himself for allowing his anxiety to take physical control. What was more frustrating was the knowledge that he was the perpetrator of his own misery. He forced himself to try two more bites and felt the nausea of the meal sitting in his unwilling stomach. He sat on the edge of his bed and turned on the T.V. with the controlling device and watched "Get Smart." The program eventually wormed its way into his consciousness and the bumbling character of Maxwell Smart made him laugh out loud. He thought how he might be considered a real life Maxwell Smart in the seeming incompetence of his actual investigations and that made him laugh even harder.

When his guest arrived, he planned on taking her to the bar for a few drinks. He wouldn't think of putting that on his hotel tab, but he knew a few agents who did by having the bar run the bill through the restaurant and calling it something else.

He heard a light rap at the door and a voice call out, "Mr. Rinella, this is Marlene, our friend Danny arranged a meeting for us."

Peter opened the door to a young woman with brown hair about five feet-five or six. She had a dress on with tan shaded nylons. She was wearing high heels that added three or four inches to her height. She had high cheekbones and full lips. Her eye lids looked like they were half closed and they covered light colored, almost gray eyes. Her skin was tanned and, when she turned to lay her jacket on the chair next to the bed, he noticed she had a small waist but a very ample and round ass. She had nice breasts and he almost could see her nipples through the silky dress.

She began, "Danny said we could have some fun together and I would be in safe hands because you are an F.B.I. agent?"

Peter was pissed with Danny for telling Marlene that he was an F.B.I. agent. The people in D.C. would cast a harsh eye on an agent spending his nights with an escort.

Peter nodded, "Marlene, please call me Peter. Yes, you'll be perfectly safe with me, I promise. I thought maybe we'd go down to the bar for a drink or two, is that ok? I mean, you are old enough to drink, right?"

Marlene laughed at Peter's obvious exaggeration of her age but was pleased anyway and, reacting with mock anger, "Yea, Peter, I'm old enough to drink, and do lots of other things too. Are you sure you want to go down stairs right now?"

"Yea, I think so. I'd like to talk a bit just to get to know each other. Is that ok? Danny made arrangements for you to spend the night?"

"Oh yes, I'll be glad to spend the night if you want me to. Let's have those drinks and get acquainted."

CHAPTER NINETY-ONE

Dallas, November 18, 1963

They took a table in one of the corners. The bar was dark and the only light came from the candles on the tables. Marlene took a sip of her drink and a drag off her cigarette.

"Why are you in Dallas, Peter? Is there some big investigation or case here?"

Peter looked at her as though she was nuts, "Marlene, I, I can't really say why I'm in town. It's kind of official business."

Marlene was surprised and seemed hurt by his response and Peter felt like a shit heel for taking *the holier than thou official business posture* so he volunteered, "You know the president is coming to Texas this Friday and I'm here to sort of make sure he doesn't have any trouble while he is here."

He felt better with the general answer. After he took a sip of his drink, a drag from his cigarette, asked through his exhale, "So, Marlene, what's your story? You're obviously not from Texas, what's your last name?"

She tapped the ash off her cigarette, "Wilson, or that is what I was born with. I'm from Ohio, near Akron. I've been married once and after my divorce, I decided to get rid of everything from that encounter including my married name. So I legally changed my name back to my maiden name. What else do you want to know, Peter?"

Peter thought for a second and remembered not to ask, how does a nice girl like you… but instead, "Is this all you do?"

She smiled, "No. During the day, I work as an accounts receivable clerk for a wholesale food company. I make sure their customers pay their bills. It doesn't pay very well but it's honest work. Also it'll give me a way to earn money when men like you aren't interested in spending time with me. Of course, I do this because it pays great and allows me to do something I enjoy and would do for free."

Peter smiled at her honesty but felt compelled to ask, "Are you tryin to say you enjoy the time you spend with all your customers? Isn't that a big myth *Johns* have, that their *escorts* are really enjoying the experience?"

She was silent for a second while she sipped her drink and smoked the last of her cigarette, "Most of the time it's ok, really. I mean it's not like a permanent relationship or anything like that, but physically, if you're with the right guy, it's enjoyable. If you're not with the right guy it's not nearly as much fun, if you know what I mean?"

Peter sipped his drink, "How'd you meet Danny? Is he one of your customers?"

She shook her head from side to side, "No, though I would spend time with Danny if he asked. We met through mutual friends. We've known each other for a year or so but this is the first time he's used my services."

Looking down at Peter's nearly finished drink, Marlene asked, "Are you interested in going up to your room?"

When they got inside the room Marlene quickly pushed herself against Peter and began kissing him up and down his neck and nibbling at his ears. She pulled off his shirt and unbuttoned his pants, undid his zipper and pulled them off with some force. She ripped off his boxers and pushed him back on the bed. She stepped back from him so he was able to get a good view of her as she stepped out of her dress and he saw she was wearing nothing but a G-String, the things Peter had only seen strippers wear. Her bra matched her flimsy underwear and she removed it, exposing breasts the size of medium lemons. She slipped out of the G-String and exposed a pubic area that was neatly trimmed. Peter had never seen a pubic area so neatly manicured. He liked it. Marlene straddled him and continued kissing up and down his body. Peter liked the feel of her next to him, but images of all the women who had meant anything to him, began to flash through his mind. As quickly as he could, he pushed their faces from his mind and forced himself to think about the sexy woman who was about to make love to him.

CHAPTER NINETY-TWO

Dallas, November 19, 1963

He didn't have a great night with Marlene. After a few minutes he was unable to perform. This was the first time in his life when his mind was very willing but his flesh wasn't. He apologized ten times.

She seemed mildly amused by his situation, "Don't worry about it, Pete. It happens to a lot of guys at some time or another. I have been with a few men your age when it has come up, er, occurred, and really, it's not a big deal, er, an issue, really."

Peter looked at Marlene, and even in his misery, he had to laugh at her unintentional puns. "You know, Marlene. I would appreciate it if you kept this between just you and me? I don't think there's any reason for our friend officer Augello to know."

Marlene smiled, "Of course, I understand completely."

Peter was appreciative, "Marlene I wouldn't say anything if you went home tonight. I know Danny asked you to spend the night, but if you will keep some things to yourself, I definitely will say what a wonderful sleeper you are."

She nodded and seemed truthful, "I really wouldn't mind spending the night."

Peter looked at her half closed eyes and put his hands on her shoulders, "I really need to get some sleep, and I have a lot of stuff to do tomorrow. If you're in bed with me I may not be able to do much damage but I sure as hell will keep tryin and God knows that will keep me up, for sure. No, you better go home honey. I promise Danny will be none the wiser."

She shook her head in agreement and before leaving, "I won't be able to see you at all during the week but Thursday night, if you're willing. I'm sure we can have some fun, and, who knows, it might be what you expected."

Peter smiled at her and gently nudged her toward the door, "Friday is going to be a very important day with the President arriving and I'm going to probably be goin' nuts tryin' to tie up any loose ends. I don't know about Thursday, I'll get in touch with you through Danny, ok?"

She smiled and kissed him gently on the cheek and whispered, "Everything's going to be fine."

By the time Peter got to bed he was exhausted but couldn't sleep. He was mulling over his poor performance in bed, the full schedule ahead of him, and how average his life had been and was doubtless going to be until he died. He thought about his ex-wife and Cam and he couldn't shut his mind off long enough to let him fall asleep. He rolled over a million times until mercifully, in exhaustion, he fell asleep. The phone was ringing incessantly in his sleep and finally woke him. He wanted to grab it and throw it out the window.

He heard Danny on the other end, "Peter... Danny...It's seven-fifteen."

Peter thanked him for the wake-up call when he really wanted to tell him to go to hell, but instead, "I'll be down in twenty minutes. We can go in the restaurant and get a cup of coffee. I need a cup bad, paisano."

Danny had a "Morning News" in his hand and was scanning the inside pages. The front pages read, "Presidential Motorcade Route" and all Peter could do was whistle through his teeth and mutter, Why don't they give anybody trying to whack the president a little more time to figure out where the best place to hit him will be?"

Danny was oblivious to what Peter said and had to look at the front page when it dawned on him why Peter was concerned. Danny read down the page and read out loud the tentative time line for the president's arrival in Fort Worth, his time table in Dallas, and his schedule in Austin.

Peter shook his head, "Not only will everyone know where the president will be but also what time he'll be there. That's great. Let's get a cup of coffee and then get me down to the field office. I need to call Secret Service agent Biggs and make an appointment with him."

Danny nodded at every comment and made mental notes of what he had to do for his charge.

CHAPTER NINETY-THREE

Dallas, November 19, 1963

The large room in the field office looked even larger in the morning light. The only constant was the endless ringing of telephones. Every ten seconds a phone rang. The sound made Peter uncomfortable. He walked over to Shanklin's empty office. His secretary told Peter her boss would be out for the rest of the day and mentioned distractedly, "Oh, I almost forgot, your boss called and asked you to call him as soon as you got here."

Peter knew it must be important for H.Z. to phone him. As quickly as he could, he called H.Z. and heard his distressed voice, "The Miami P.D., through one of its informants, uncovered an assassination attempt on the president. They have tapes of some right wing KKK guy saying 'the president was going to be shot with a high powered rifle riding through Miami.' The Miami P.D. got in touch with the Secret Service and instead of a motorcade; they used a helicopter to get the president in town. My question to you, Pete, is where the fuck were you, goddamn it!!?"

Peter was totally stunned and couldn't form an answer in the face of H.Z.'s wilting anger. After a minute he croaked, "I....I didn't know he was going to Miami, for Christ's sake. The White House itinerary had him only in Tampa at some goddamn Air Force Base. Who'd be able to do anything there? I had no idea, and any way, I thought the West Palm Secret Service detail and our offices in Florida are all over security, so I decided not to make the Florida trip."

H.Z. wasn't mollified by Peter's explanation, "Listen and listen well, my friend, the only fucking job you have is the president. If you give a shit about your career make sure you do your job. Do you understand me? Am I making myself perfectly clear?"

Peter was in shock and answered in a muted "yes." He was astounded by the news of an actual plot to kill Kennedy and also by the incredible anger and malice in H.Z.'s voice. He never expected such venom.

Peter was still shaking his head at the news when he heard Danny ask, "What's up? You….you look like you saw a ghost. You're as white as a sheet of….paper."

Peter quickly told Danny what transpired in Miami. Still in a daze, Peter wandered over to Hosty's office and found it empty. He got back to the desk Miss Dunleavy assigned to him and began making calls to the employers of suspects. Augello followed him around like a lost puppy and it was irritating. After H.Z.'s tirade, Peter couldn't concentrate because he was so shaken. He forced himself to call *Zinc & Metal Processors*, in Dallas, to get James Parker's home address. To call a suspect's work address was difficult, because an innocent person could be painted with the ugly brush of investigation when the F.B.I. called. Peter would say the "Bureau was conducting an investigation on another person the employee knew; or the employee was listed as a reference and the Bureau needed to confirm the information." If he was believable, often the employer would allow Peter to interrogate the suspect at his work place. This assumed, of course, the subject was no physical threat. Because he had Danny as a backup, he might be able to interview some of the subjects at their homes, if he had to.

He reached James Parker and asked to visit him at his house, located outside of Arlington. Peter hit the jackpot when he discovered that Charles Parker was James' brother and he might be around, as well. He next called *Blackburn Construction* in Irving. His conversation with Earl Robinson was terse and to the point.

Robinson asked defensively, "Why y'all callin' me at work? Why does the F.B.I. want ta talk ta me?"

Peter explained it was nothing but routine questions and it would only take a few minutes. He asked when they could meet at Robinson's home. He explained that if Robinson refused, the Irving P.D. would pick him up and deliver him to Peter in Dallas. Robinson said he worked second shift at the construction company doing security work, and ten in the morning was a good time.

The next call was to *James & Brown Well Services* in Dallas. Franklin Goodrum was a well tender and moved from well to well. Peter got Goodrum's home number and surprisingly, Goodrum was home to take the call.

He told Peter, "Yer lucky to reach me…not feelin real good today….have a case of the brown bottle flu…."

With that he laughed and asked why Peter and the F.B.I. would want to speak with him. Peter gave the standard, "It's just a routine investigation and we want to ask you a few questions."

Goodrum surprisingly offered to come down to the F.B.I. office with, "Ya know, I've seen that Federal Building fer years and wanted to see what it was like inside. Can I come by and meet with ya there say about one o'clock today?"

Peter was shocked by his response and didn't reply right away but finally said, "Sure, that's great Mr. Goodrum. Come up to the eighth floor and tell the girl at the information desk you are here to meet with special agent Peter Rinella. That's R..I..N..E..L..L..A.. Got it?"

Goodrum quickly answered yes and the meeting was set. Peter leaned back in his chair and was pleased how he had made all the appointments necessary in the space of less than an hour. The call from H.Z. was starting to fade. He looked at Danny who had hardly uttered a word from the time they got in the building.

"Well Dante Augello, how about your new guinea partner now? Impressed, huh?"

Not knowing exactly how to respond, Danny shook his head, "You... you really are something...yep."

Peter took that as a rousing endorsement and lifted Danny and his wide brimmed white hat from their perch, "Ok buddy, before Goodrum gets here, you gotta get me over to the Secret Service office so I can talk to the agent who runs that office....His name is Henry Biggs... you know him?"

Danny shook his head no, but said he knew how to get to the Secret Service Offices. On the way down, Danny asked, "What...what did you think of Marlene?"

Peter felt guilty for not having acknowledging Danny's *gift*, "Oh Christ Danny, I'm so sorry for not thanking you...she was amazing. I might want another date with her on Thursday, I'll pay of course. I'll let you know for sure so you can arrange it. The only problem is that Friday is going to be a bitch with the president coming. I'll need all the rest I can get on Thursday night."

CHAPTER NINETY-FOUR

Dallas, November 19, 1963

The Secret Service office was in a free standing office building somewhere in Dallas, Peter had no idea where. They drove forever to reach the nondescript building. It was three stories and its directory listed Biggs' office on the third floor. Peter suggested to Danny that they take the steps instead of the elevator.

"I need to get my ass in shape and the stairs are about the only exercise I ever get." he said as he labored up the stairs.

Danny cursed Peter to himself by the time they got to the third floor and discovered the stairway door was locked and they had to return to the lobby and use the elevator. Peter wasn't pleased with his decision either and puffed as much on the trip down as he did on the trip up. Danny looked at Peter's chest heaving from the short walk up the stairs.

"You...You're in worse shape than me."

Between pants, Peter agreed and with irritation, "Just get on the goddamn elevator and don't worry about who's in good shape!"

The elevator doors opened to a fluted cherry color information desk and an attractive young lady sitting behind it. Her name plate read *Joanne Stearns*. Peter was irritated with Danny's editorial comment about his fitness, but he was still able to pleasantly identify himself and Danny. He asked to speak with agent Biggs. Henry Biggs came out to greet Peter and Danny and showed both of them into his office.

Biggs' office was large and had three windows facing the outside and a pleasant view of the Dallas skyline. The walls were paneled in some sort of oak colored paneling and his desk wasn't the usual government issued metal with green padded desk chair. He had a cherry wood desk and a high backed leather chair. The glass desk top was perfectly clean and had a green colored leather bound blotter perfectly positioned in the middle of the desk. Biggs must have been six foot three or four. He had crystal blue eyes and his bronze colored hair was cut in a crew cut with the front and sides of his hair propped up by some kind of hair preparation.

He leaned back in his chair and tapped his fingers together, "Well, it's great to meet you. I'm gonna thank you in advance for any help yer gonna be givin us."

Peter was reminded how Biggs' accent was pure Texan. The younger man began, "Is there any kinda help or info I can share with you or, for Chris sake, you with me?"

"Well Henry, I'm sure you've heard about the fiasco in Miami, huh?"

Biggs looked at Peter with a shrug, "Yea, I got bits and pieces from the D.C. guys who just got here. I'm telling you getting information around the offices is like pulling teeth. Some stuff gets through…Stupid stuff and some stuff doesn't…important things, sometimes. It used to be that D.C. would send an advance team to help prepare. They would arrive three to four weeks in advance….not on this one. Shit, they got here three days ago, but we had to do the best we could with most of the advance security measures."

Peter shook his head in amazement and explained he was meeting with some subjects who might be a danger to the president. He assured Biggs he would pass on any useful information. Peter made a passing reference to the president's itinerary.

Biggs laughed, "How bout the *Morning News* or the *Times Herald*, you can get a complete schedule in either paper. Everyone knows he'll be landing in Fort Worth at nine and press the flesh with the crowd before he leaves for the Chamber of Commerce."

Peter interrupted, "Does that makes any sense…I mean shaking hands and getting close to who knows-what in some crowd? Based on what we know about Florida."

Biggs thought for a second, "It's really not a big problem at the airport because we can control the crowd on the tarmac. Clint Hill's men will be all around him and we'll have guys in the crowd. The motorcades to and from the speaking events are my big concern. Every building is an opportunity to pop him. To make matters worse, the motorcade routes in Dallas and Austin are convoluted and it's going to be a real bitch maintaining the forty-four mile an hour speed of the motorcade. That'll make any shot a lot easier. How can you control those situations? Think about that …every one of our office buildings…."

Peter asked Biggs to take him through the motorcade routes, even though they were in the papers. Biggs detailed for them the arrival in Fort Worth, the meet at the airport and the trip to the Chamber of Commerce breakfast meeting. He explained the motorcade route to the

Fort Worth Airport and the arrival at Dallas' Love Field at eleven forty and another crowd handshaking opportunity.

He continued, "The motorcade route to the Dallas Trade Mart and his luncheon should take about an hour or so and will travel through Dallas down Main Street on Elm Street through Dealey Plaza and the Triple Underpass. The president will be in the limo with Governor Connelly and his wife and the Vice President and Mrs. Johnson will be in a limo behind the president. After his speech, the president and Mrs. Kennedy will retrace their steps and fly to Austin where he will make a short speech, and spend the night in the governor's mansion. The next morning he's back to Washington."

Peter and Danny were silent while Biggs described Kennedy's visit. Peter made mental notes of the itinerary and heard Biggs finish, "I wish ta hell he would just get in at the airport and drive in a closed car at about eighty miles an hour to and from every place he is going….but that aint happenin."

Peter nodded in agreement and told Biggs he had to get back to interview Franklin Goodrum. He asked the younger man if he knew of Goodrum, Charles and James Parker, Earl Robinson, and Lee Oswald.

Biggs thought for a second, "Nope. Haven't heard of any of em. Nothin."

Peter thanked him for his time and pulled Danny up and, as they made their goodbyes, assured him he would keep in touch.

CHAPTER NINETY-FIVE

Dallas, November 19, 1963

Peter greeted Franklin Goodrum pleasantly and showed him to an interrogation room Miss Dunleavy had arranged for them. Goodrum combed his thick salt and pepper back around his ears and wore a short sleeved white shirt and a thin black tie. He had black horned rim glasses and looked around the offices and the interrogation room as though they were downtown Paris.

"This is an amazing place…I mean, I never knew there were this many agents in Dallas."

Peter had to develop some sort of conversational relationship, "Yep, Franklin, this is a really large field office. I'm not sure but the Special Agent in Charge here tells me it's the largest field office in the country. That's hard to believe, isn't it?"

Goodrum looked at Peter somewhat surprised by the question, "Well, you surely would know, wouldn't you, comin' from Washington and F.B.I. headquarters?"

Peter was pleased that Goodrum reacted to his question, "I work in the Internal Security Department of the Bureau, and while I have a lot to do with field offices, I really don't know the particulars about the number of agents and stuff like that. I thought New York and L.A. had larger offices than Dallas but a lot of that has to do with how the geography is divided up. Dallas has nearly all the southwest United States while the other cities' offices are responsible for their city."

Goodrum seemed satisfied with Peter's answer and nodded and waited for Peter to ask a question. Peter laid a file folder on the table so Goodrum could see the file and his name on the tab. Peter was silent and leaned back in his chair. After thirty seconds, he opened the file and looked at Goodrum while he read and asked, "You're a member of the John Birch Society, eh Franklin?"

Goodrum looked directly at Peter, "Yes, I am, and as far as I know, that's no crime, is it?"

At first, Peter didn't say anything, then shook his head, "Of course not, our concern, and my job, is for the individuals who misunderstand what their group says and act in ways which are dangerous to others, specifically, in this case, the President of the United States."

Goodrum looked around the room oblivious to what Peter had said and was silent for a minute and suddenly, with a razor focus, looked directly at Peter and said, "I have never done anything which would lead you or anyone else to think I would harm the president. I think he is a spineless traitor and should be impeached for what he is doing to our Constitution, but I am perfectly willing for our system to take care of him. I think he and his little brother Bobby represent what is evil about American politics. I believe, in time, everyone will agree with me agent Rinella."

"Franklin," Peter said as he reached again into the file folder and pulled out a poster, "did you have anything to do with this?"

The poster had two grainy pictures of Kennedy and was boldly titled, *"Wanted for Treason...THIS MAN is wanted for treasonous activities against the United States."*

Under the pictures and headline were seven enumerated statements detailing the president's betrayal of America and the Constitution. Peter laid the poster in front of Goodrum. Goodrum looked down at the poster without touching it, and said, "I may have had something to do with it but it doesn't say anything about hurting Kennedy, does it?"

Peter agreed but replied, "Franklin, you aren't trying to incite anyone into doing something before the system catches up with the president, are you?"

Goodrum smiled, "No agent, I'm not. Words don't hurt people, do they? Jefferson said, 'If you are comfortable with the truth, lies will never bother you.' I think you and the people in Washington aren't comfortable with the truth. I think Kennedy has lied so much to the American people he doesn't have an idea what the truth is. All the rest of you are doing your damn best to assist him in setting up a police state and harassing people like me who see what is going on here."

Peter looked directly into Goodrum's jet black eyes and saw belief in them. It was frightening and distracting, "Franklin, as you know the President is coming to Dallas on Friday. I will do everything I can to make sure he has a forgettable visit. Don't be surprised if you have someone accompanying you on your travels while the president is in town."

Goodrum was silent for a minute, "Well thank you for the chance to see the office, agent Rinella, I would like to leave now."

Peter nodded and showed him to the elevator and said, "Remember, Franklin, we're watching you."

As Peter walked away from the elevator, Danny came down the hall and asked, "How... how'd it go? You get anything?"

Peter shook his head, "Not a thing...only that maybe he was responsible for the *Kennedy Traitor* poster that has been on telephone poles around Dallas. We have to be at the Parkers' house at three this afternoon, can we make it ok?"

Danny nodded, "Yea...yea. No problem...Remember I know my way around here pretty well." Peter laughed to himself knowing how well *Danny knew his way around* and smiled as he said, "Let's get some lunch, I'm famished."

After lunch, they left for Arlington and Danny told him they were forty-five minutes away from the Parkers house. He added, "I...might have to call the Arlington P.D. after we get there."

Both men were silent and Peter had time to think about how quickly his life had flown by. He felt like some character who had taken a nap and on his awakening somebody announced, "forty years of your life have gone by and you have missed everything but the tragedies." The trip to Arlington was through prairie land, exactly what he imagined Texas to be: arid, sandy, white and windblown.

Peter turned to Danny, "When the sand blows over the roads, it looks like the roads during a snow storm back home, huh, Danny?"

Danny stared straight ahead and nodded in the affirmative. Peter's mind bounced from image to image and person to person. Despuerto, Perkins, Millie, Mae, Vinny, Kathryn flowed in and out of his brain like rivers through a landscape. His mind fixated on the face of his daughter. Her voice and smile flashed again and again through his consciousness and lingered while the others fluttered quickly out of his brain.

Suddenly, his mind was walking down another sand blown road. This time he was with Cam; it was eight years earlier and they were at the outer banks of Virginia. He arranged a family vacation there and after a day at the beach the two decided to walk to a store down the road about a half mile from their cottage. They were chatting about nothing when Cam asked Peter if he knew of Sarte or Camus. Peter replied honestly that he had never heard of them.

Cam patiently discussed both and attempted futilely to explain Existentialism. Peter then realized how smart she had become or sadly, how stupid he was. In either case, he had an appreciation for her not only because she was his daughter but also because she was talented.

"Dad, you know Camus said, 'don't wait for the Last Judgment, it takes place every day.' He was right. Every day we have an opportunity to do what is right and good, or not. If we operate from a position of love, we can't help but do what is right—it's impossible not to."

While he didn't understand Camus, the remembrance of the moment pulled his heart and ripped at his throat with sadness and despair. Her absence left him half a person.

CHAPTER NINETY-SIX

Dallas, November 19, 1963

His painful reverie was interrupted by Danny's halting voice, "We…are almost there… maybe…maybe another mile or two to go…not much farther for sure."

Peter nodded as Danny steered the car through a dirt lane that ran for a quarter of a mile.

He turned to Danny, "How'd you know this was the right drive to pull into, for Christ's sake?"

Danny smiled at Peter as though he finally got one up on him, "There was a name on the pole back there. It……it said Parker."

They pulled in front of a one story white frame house with a screen door slightly ajar and a gray front door behind it. The house looked like it hadn't been painted in twenty years and seemed as exhausted as the fifty six Ford Fairlane parked in front of it. The floor boards of the porch creaked under their weight and Peter felt as though they were about to fall through them.

Peter tapped on the front door and looked at his watch and said to Danny, "Nice job paisano, we're only ten minutes late. Hopefully the Parkers didn't have a previous engagement."

The door opened and on the other side, was a man with a two day old growth of black and gray beard and beads of sweat on his forehead. His hair was greased back and he wore a white t-shirt with tobacco stains on the front of it. He had a wad of chew in his right cheek and he looked directly at Peter.

"You'd be the F.B.I. agent, right? I mean who else would a come dressed this way ta visit me, huh?"

Peter tried to be non-confrontational, "I'm special agent Rinella with the F.B.I. and my partner here is Danny Augello with the Dallas P.D. If we can have a few minutes to talk with you and your brother, I'd be most appreciative."

Parker stepped around them and leaned over the railing, and spit out some tobacco juice, "I guess I have a few minutes, my brother had to work over and couldn't make it."

Peter noticed a line of tobacco tinged spittle down the front of Parkers lip that extended down to his chin. Peter replied, "That's ok, we'll make arrangements to see him tomorrow or the day after, which Parker are you?"

Peter knew which Parker he was talking to because he had a mug shot provided by the Texas Correctional System from when James Parker had been jailed for the attempted murder of a black minister in Amarillo. Parker escorted the men to a dark, cluttered sitting room with furniture surrounded by piles of papers and magazines. Everything sat on an area rug with huge holes showing the brown floor underneath. Parker sat in a chair and motioned for Peter and Danny to sit on the couch facing his chair. The couch was stained so Peter and Danny sat on the edge to avoid any possible contamination.

Parker looked away from the men and answered Peter's question, "I'm Jim Parker and you goddamn well know who I am. Are ya tryin to tell me ya don't have my picture in that there file yer carryin?"

Peter was surprised by the aggressiveness of his answer and tried to parry the attack, "Of course, you're right, but sometimes a picture can be misplaced in a file or the picture is so old the subject er, person has changed so I always try to ask just to be sure."

Parker wasn't convinced, "Bullshit. Do ya think I was born yesterday? So why the fuck are ya here?"

Peter noticed on a wall in an adjoining room was a huge soiled Confederate flag. Peter didn't answer immediately.

Parker repeated, "So agin I'm askin why you here? Sure as hell ya aren't here on a social call are ya?"

"We're here because, as you know, President Kennedy is coming to Texas on Friday, and, how can I put it? You and your brother have been quite outspoken critics of the President. We've heard that at your Ku Klux Klan meetings some folks talked about killing him. In fact, Jim, you have a very violent history. We want to make sure you keep that violence in check while the president is in Texas."

Parker wasn't surprised by Peter's statement and deliberately picked up an empty brown *Lone Star* beer bottle and spit into it, "If yer referin to the murder of that nigger minister in Amarillo I was freed by a jury. Now, don't get me wrong, I'd like to see somebody kill that nigger lover and his nigger lovin' brother too, but I aint gonna tell anybody ta do it and I sure as hell aint gonna pull the trigger either."

Peter really didn't expect any more out of Parker but knew he had to press on, "Well, Jim, you won't have a problem with somebody from the Dallas P.D. or Texas Rangers spending some time with on Friday with you?"

Parker was angered by the suggestion and said, "Listen you greasy dago, I want you to hear me and hear me good, you and your nigger lovin' cops better stay far away from me and my brother if you know what's good fer you... get it!?"

Peter looked at Danny, who was totally unfazed, and he looked back at Parker as he motioned for Danny to get up. Peter moved toward Parker, within inches of his face and whispered in a controlled tone, "Now it's time for you to listen, and, listen well. We are going to be watching you whether you want us to or not. If you do anything out of the ordinary, we will arrest your ugly ass and throw it in a cell with a *mullanjan*".

Parker was stunned by Peter's response and looked at him open mouth disbelief.

"Parker, do you know what a *mullanjan* is? It is an egg plant which is shiny, black; it's what we greasy dagos call big black Negroes. So, my friend, don't abuse me or any of the guys who will be your companions in the next week because if you do, you will be sharing a cell with a *mullanjan*. I promise you he will gladly tell your fortune. Do you understand me... you sonofabitch?"

Parker just nodded. Tobacco spittle trickled out from the side of his mouth.

Peter moved away and took Danny's arm and led him to the door and said, "Jim, I'm so glad we have had this discussion and agreed on some things. Tell your brother to call me at the F.B.I. number in the book to set up an appointment tomorrow sometime, ok? Oh, if he doesn't, I will have him arrested for anything I can think of...maybe jackin'-off in a public place and my partner here will testify to the act. By the way wipe the fuckin' tobacco shit off your chin."

As soon as they got in the car, Danny started to howl with nervous excitement, "Do...Do you think he's a threat?"

Peter waited for Danny to back the car out of the drive way, "Danny, guys like that are violent, and they are gonna attack somebody who is defenseless. Whacking a Negro minister and taking a shot at the President of the United States are two entirely different things. Of course, I might be totally wrong and end up the biggest goat in history, so I want to make sure somebody is sitting on the Parkers, just to be sure."

Both men grew silent. Peter felt uncomfortable with the silence and decided to make small talk to break it. He lit up a Pall Mall with the lighter in the car and blew a line of smoke away from Danny and out the window. As if on cue, Danny reached into his pocket and took out a Kent and lit it as well. Peter noticed a change in Danny's smoking choice and this gave him an opportunity to end the painful silence.

He leaned toward Danny to get a better look at Danny's smoke, "Hey, that's a different cigarette, isn't it? You usually smoke Camel's or Lucky Strikes right?"

Danny didn't blink and replied, "Camels, usually, these are Kent's."

Peter didn't give a shit what Danny was smoking but decided to press on simply to fill the time on the way back, "So, tell me why you are smoking Kent's instead of Camels. What's the big deal about Kent's?"

Danny took a hit on his Kent and said, "Kent has a *micronite* filter. *Micronite* cleans out all of the impurities in cigarette smoke."

Peter didn't want to embarrass his new found friend, but he couldn't suppress his laughter and, through his laughter, "You gotta' be kiddin' me?!! You're smoking Kent cigarettes because they're healthier for you than Camels? Give me a fuckin' break. They're both gonna kill ya!"

Danny grew silent and again Peter felt compelled to break the silence with some more chit chat, "How 'bout we go to dinner tonight? You have to know some good place to go, right? That is, of course, unless you have to go home to your family or something."

Danny smiled at Peter and said, "Why…why don't you come to my house tonight? My wife and kids would love to meet a big shot from Washington."

Peter thought for a moment, "Sure, why not, as long as you're sure your wife won't mind. Jesus Christ, maybe she won't want somebody just dropping in on her with no notice."

Danny quickly replied, "She's…she's Italian too, so you know she won't mind another for dinner even though…He's as ugly as you."

Peter laughed at Danny's attempt at humor to make his partner feel better. Peter had Danny pull over so he could call Hosty from a pay phone to tell him what had transpired with Parker and let him know that he was going to Danny's. After a fifteen minute drive, they pulled into a cemented drive of a modest ranch style house.

The sun had set and Peter could see the lights in the house on and the image of what looked like two boys watching a black and white television. When they entered the house, Peter could smell the wonderful aroma of some kind of beef cooking and the warmness of the house enveloped him. It was like the days in Frederick before Millie and the kids left. The whole environment of a cooking meal and the kids contentedly occupied reminded Peter of a past long gone. Danny pulled Peter into the kitchen to meet his wife,

"Grace...Grace, this is Peter Rinella. He's...he's a special F.B.I. agent from Washington D.C."

Peter noticed Grace's surprise. In fact, Peter was sure if Grace had a hammer in her hand instead of a pot holder, she would have hit Danny on the head for bringing an unannounced guest.

She quickly got over her surprise, "Agent Rinella" She gave Danny a sharp glance. "It's a pleasure meeting you and thank you for coming to our home for dinner. She glared at Danny again. "We're only having meat loaf and mashed potatoes with some string beans....I hope that's ok?"

Peter knew Grace was uncomfortable and quickly said, "Please call me Peter or Pete, Grace, and I love meat loaf. It's one of my favorite meals. I'm so thankful for sharing dinner with you."

Danny was smiling all the while and told Peter, "Come...Come and meet the other Augellos. This...this is Carlo and this one is Thomaso.'

The boys were probably nine and six or close to that and shook his hand with energy and warmth. Danny gave Peter a beer and they sipped on their beers until Grace put the meat loaf on the table. Peter enjoyed the meal. He wasn't sure if it was the food or the whole wonderful family atmosphere. He was glad Danny had brought him home to meet his family and he would remember the evening for the rest of his life.

CHAPTER NINETY-SEVEN

Dallas, November 19, 1963

When Peter got back to the hotel, he listened to the radio and pulled up station KLIF and some disc jockey named Chuck Dunaway. Dunaway played something called the *Top Forty*. He figured out Dunaway played the forty most popular songs in the Dallas and Fort Worth area and of course, they were all rock and roll songs. There was a rumor that the Bureau was conducting an investigation in the playing of music on radio stations. Some record companies were paying disc jockeys money to play their records in an attempt to boost sales. Peter scoffed at this waste of resources, *is that all Hoover has to do, for Christ's sake, is investigating whose songs get played on the radio?!!*

Peter got up and turned the radio off and noted to himself how not one song Dunaway played was worth listening to and he thought, *J.Edgar, you couldn't pay me to play that shit!*

He laughed like a mad man at his own humor, turned on the T.V. with the controller gadget, crawled into bed, and prayed he would quickly fall asleep. His prayers were answered and sleep came quickly and gently. He got up at seven, showered, shaved, and flipped on the radio.

Promptly at eight, a deep sonorous voice announced, "All the news from around the world and right back home in the greatest area in the world, this is Dan Rather on loan from our T.V. Station Four."

As Peter expected, the Kennedy visit was the lead story. Even though it was Tuesday, the locals started to pick out their spots on the motorcade routes in Fort Worth and Dallas. Because Kennedy would be arriving in downtown Dallas around twelve-fifteen or twelve-thirty, Rather reported, many Dallas citizens were going to spend their lunch hours up and down Main St, on the steps of the Old Court House and all over Dealey Plaza. Rather played interviews with average Dallas citizens who excitedly told the interviewer where they would be standing for the visit. He interviewed another, whose name Peter didn't hear, who said he was purposely avoiding the president's visit because Kennedy was a traitor to America and was *far too friendly to Russia, Yugoslavia, and Poland*. He knew this was a big story for a city like Dallas which seldom was visited by a sitting president. He knew Americans had the right to some access to their president, but in terms of the president's security, such access was a pain in the ass. He made his way to the ever present Augello in the lobby.

Peter quickly extended his hand, "Well, paisano, I have been here two days and you got me laid and fed. I haven't got that kind of treatment from guys I have known for forty years. Shit, if I'd a known you were such a good host, I'd have come to Dallas two weeks earlier."

Danny just nodded and smiled and thanked Peter in his halting way. He was proud of himself and invited his new friend to a strip club called *The Carousel Club*. Danny added, "It's a nice place. Some...Some Jew from Chicago owns it."

Peter appreciated the invitation, but reminded his partner a lot depended on the meeting with Charles Parker. "Yea, maybe we can go there tonight, but we have to finish the Parker meeting this afternoon. And, don't forget Danny, we have to be at Robinson's house in Irving by ten."

Peter gave Earl Robinson's address to Danny, and his partner quickly assured Peter, "I know...know exactly how to get there."

Danny was trying to impress him with his knowledge of the Dallas area and Peter had to admit his partner had not made too many mistakes. Danny told Peter Irving was only twenty or thirty minutes away from downtown Dallas. Before they left, they stopped at a diner called the *New Yorker* and it offered a Texas version of what a New York diner would serve. Peter ate too much and complained to Danny how he needed to get in shape for his Bureau fitness test.

Danny was sympathetic to Peter, "I...I have to lose twenty pounds myself."

Peter looked down at Danny's stomach and was sure he had to lose more than twenty pounds to get in shape but didn't have the heart to say anything. The trip to Irving took a little more than twenty minutes so Danny was not off by much. He complained that the traffic fooled him and was responsible for the delay. They drove for another ten or fifteen minutes until they found the address Robinson had given Peter.

The house was neat. After a minute of knocking, the door was opened by an older woman Peter guessed to be in her seventies. He asked for Earl Robinson, showed his badge to the woman, who never lost a beat as she hollered over her shoulder for Robinson to come to the door. The old lady didn't invite them in and Robinson met them at the door. He edged past the men, closed the door behind him and faced them on the porch. He looked from Peter to Danny repeatedly and, though he didn't stutter as badly as Danny, he spoke haltingly as though he had to contemplate every word. Peter identified them and asked Robinson why he thought they were visiting him.

Robinson thought for a second and said, "I, a, have no idea of why you are....here...Why?"

His right hand had a tremor and Robinson had to hold it with his left hand to control the shaking.

Peter replied to the question as directly as he could, "I'm an agent from Washington here in preparation for the president's visit on Friday. We know you're in *Texas Free Citizens,* which has publicly called for the assassination of the President. How many members are there in Dallas Fort-Worth?"

Robinson seemed surprised by the question and took his usual time answering but finally replied, "I'm not going to do anything to the traitor. I can speak for our members, too, and can tell you they will do nothing to your president. Our membership is large, but I can't really tell you how many active members we have because I honestly don't know."

Peter wasn't satisfied with the answer but had no way of knowing what the truth was. He pressed Robinson for more information, "Who're the officers of the *Texas Free Citizens* and how come you can't tell me how many belong to your group?"

Again, Robinson took his time answering, "I am just a regular member who does P.R. work for the group and talks to the papers and stuff. Our executive committee comes from different parts of Texas. Clyde Johnson, our President, and Jeremy Peters, our vice President, are from Houston. We don't have a treasurer....don't have any need for a treasury. We just pass the hat to raise money for our copies and stuff like that. I have been passing out bulletins in Dallas to alert folks here about how Kennedy has lied to the American people. He was even married before and got divorced and kept the whole filthy thing secret."

Peter knew the Dallas P.D. got Robinson's name because of his public activity and traced the bulletin back to him. Peter asked, "Well Earl, how do we know you folks aren't going to act on your statements?"

Robinson thought for a moment and grasped at his hand as the tremor increased and said, "This isn't the time for action. We feel the American people will do our job for us. There will be no way in hell he is going to be re-elected. Why should we waste a bullet on the lying traitor? He's not going to be here after 1964."

Peter was strangely convinced by Robinson's explanation, not because he believed Kennedy would not be re-elected, but because he felt Robinson really believed Kennedy wouldn't be re-elected.

"You wouldn't be upset if we had somebody watch you while the President is in town and maybe some of your friends in the group?"

For once, Robinson quickly responded, "Not at all. In fact, they will have a pleasant trip to Houston where I will be meeting with our group at Clyde's house."

Peter was pleased with that response, "Nothing will make me happier, Earl, nothing."

CHAPTER NINETY-EIGHT

Dallas, November 20, 1963

When they got back to the office on the eighth floor, Peter asked the receptionist if he had gotten any calls.

"Yes," she replied, "Your son called and asked you to call him when you had a moment, nothing urgent."

Peter was surprised Vinnie called and was glad there was *nothing urgent*, but was hoping for a call from Charles Parker. He decided to talk to Hosty about coordinating the surveillance units for the Parkers, Goodrum, and Robinson. He and Danny, if warranted, would watch Oswald, and, if not, could help other agents with other subjects. He was a little worried that Charles Parker hadn't called and was sure he would visit Parker at the Dallas Feed Company if he didn't call by two or three o'clock.

Peter dialed Vinnie's number, grateful the long distance charges would be assessed to the Dallas office. Almost sure his son wouldn't be there to answer the call. Unbelievably, he heard Vinnie's voice on the other end. Peter was surprised and was almost at a loss for words but finally got out, "Vin what the hell are you doin home? How come you aren't at class or out tryin to find a job?"

Vinnie laughed at his father's surprise and said, "My class was cancelled today because the prof. got sick and, luckily, I was able to come home to get the news."

Peter asked immediately, "What news?"

His son responded, "Well, Ray Ward had a heart attack and is in the hospital. I know he wasn't high on your list but Mom is taking it pretty bad and I thought you should know."

Peter was instantly relieved it wasn't anything bad about someone he cared about and said, "Phew, I'm glad it wasn't you or your mom. That's too bad, I guess. Is he going to live or what?"

Vinnie heard the obvious relief in his dad's voice, "They don't know yet. The doctor told mom it looks ok because the pain has subsided but he isn't certain if any heart damage was done. The next few days will tell the tale."

Peter really wasn't very interested but tried to pretend he cared. He felt compelled to change the subject to something he really cared about, "How are you doing, ok? What about your mom?"

Vinnie was amused by Peter's attitude, "Well, dad, I got a job at a title insurance company starting in January. The guy who runs the office said I can work searching titles and stuff like that until I go to school in September. You know I'm going to Dickinson, right?"

Peter honestly couldn't remember if he knew Vinnie told him where he was going, and lied, "Yea, I knew that. Remember, you told me the last time we spoke….and your mom?"

Vinnie remembered he hadn't told his father where he was going to law school but didn't feel like arguing and simply said, "Other than Ray, she was doing great. She is doing well at work and has been walking every morning to stay in shape. Now she's a basket case, of course.

Peter was angered by the thought of Millie fretting over the health of her second husband, "Christ Vin, I'm in the Dallas office and the Bureau is giving these guys balls about their phone charges. I gotta get off. Let me know what happens."

As he hung up Danny found him and asked, "What…what was that all about?"

Peter, still peeved about Millie and her feelings for Ray Ward, spat out, "Just some bullshit back in my old home town."

Danny was satisfied and handed Peter a note from the receptionist that notified him of a call from Charles Parker saying he could meet him on Thursday at three o'clock at the feed mill. He looked down at Charles Parker's file folder and noticed he was involved in the same crime as his brother, yet the state didn't choose to prosecute. Charles was the Grand Wizard of the local K.K.K. chapter. He was probably more influential in the Klan than his brother and surely knew what was going to happen to the minister, if he didn't plan the attack himself. Nevertheless, he avoided charges and prosecution.

Peter leaned over to Danny and asked him, "I don't suppose you know anything about Charles Parker, do you?"

Danny looked at Peter and seemed to think awhile, "No…No…I don't. Why do you ask?"

Peter was thinking out loud and said, "Well, the Amarillo cops got enough evidence on James Parker to arrest him and the D.A. got enough evidence to prosecute, yet nobody thought to go after Charles who probably masterminded the whole deal. What the fuck? Are you kiddin me?"

Danny was amazed as well, "That…that does sound funny, doesn't it?"

Peter, now conscious of his partner said, "You're goddamn right that sounds funny. Maybe we can ask him how that happened."

Peter knew he had some time to fill and looked at the next folder and subject, "L.H. Oswald." The file folder was thicker than all the rest by two or three times and the size of it alone was intimidating. There were twenty pages of biography on Oswald, not to mention all the background material, verifying all the biography.

Throwing the file on the desk at Danny's direction, Peter said, "Now, paisano, this guy is going to be a lot of work. Jesus Christ, some books aren't as thick as this folder."

Danny nodded at Peter and started to open the file when Peter said, "Danny, let's go get a drink. We can look at this thing when we get back. I guess I'm gettin' lazy, but I'll deal with it later."

CHAPTER NINETY-NINE

Dallas, November 20, 1963

Danny pulled Peter into the Carousel Club; the one Danny said was *owned by a Jew from Chicago.* The bar and stage were backlit but all the tables and seats in the club were in virtual darkness. The amount of smoke in the room was thick enough to hide an elephant. Danny motioned to the stools at the end of the bar and Peter followed his direction. Five guys sat the bar which could have accommodated thirty five people. Peter looked toward the stage and saw a bleached blonde with bird like fans covering the interesting parts of her body. The stripper dropped one of the fans from her breast, and, almost instantaneously, raised the other to cover it so the audience was deprived of the sight of her body. She was skillful in the way she could coordinate the movement of the fans in time with the music. The guys at the tables were getting increasingly frustrated with her fans and began to holler for her to drop them and show them her naked body. She changed the pace of the fan movements so the audience would get longer views of her body. From his vantage point, Peter saw she was naked except for two little pasties on her nipples and a small diamond patch over her vagina. Peter noticed she had shaved her genitalia.

The bar maid came over to get their drink order and asked, "What's up Danny...who's your friend? What'll you have, pal?"

Peter ordered a scotch and water over ice and was surprised when his order came with a bottle of beer that Danny hadn't ordered. He was even more astounded when the bar maid announced, "It's on the house Danny, enjoy yourself."

Peter asked his partner, "Come here often Danny? How come the free drinks?"

Danny smiled, "I...I come here once in a while. I...I know the guy who owns the place. A lot of guys from the department come here."

Peter nodded. A lot of the local cops had deals with club and bar owners for free drinks in exchange for information about when vice might be investigating their establishments. After the bleached blonde was through, a few of the patrons threw some money on the stage. She came down the steps, put her arm around Danny, kissed him on the cheek and looked over at Peter, expecting Danny to introduce them.

Danny finally got the message and said, "Sylvia...this is Peter Rinella...he's an F.B.I. agent from Washington."

Her breasts were clearly visible through the nearly transparent cover. Peter looked down at her vagina to see if she looked any different a few feet away. She was wearing a flesh colored g-string converging on the triangle between her legs. Peter saw Danny take a ten dollar bill and put it on the side of her g-string. She reached down to take it out and gave Danny another kiss on the opposite cheek and quickly rubbed off her lipstick from his face. She tried to make small talk with Peter about Washington when a thin dark man approached Danny, shook his hand, and said something Peter couldn't hear.

Realizing Peter was not interested in chit-chat, Sylvia winked at him and departed to the backstage dressing room. Peter asked Danny, "So, how much goddamn time do you spend with these girls? I mean from Sylvia.....Marlene...Christ you must be getting laid all the time. They all know you for God's sake."

Danny laughed out loud, "No...Not me no way...Jesus Christ Grace would kill me...and it aint right when you're married. Plus....who knows where these whores have been...I don't want to bring anything home."

Peter looked at Danny seriously and asked, "You mean you sent Marlene over to me and she might have clap or something. Jesus Christ, Danny, if you're afraid of getting' anything why the fuck would you send it my way??!!"

Danny seriously answered, "I...I thought you would use rubbers. You didn't go down town, did you?"

Peter replied quickly with, "No goddamn it, but you should have warned me."

Danny just nodded and finished his beer and waited patiently for his partner to finish his drink. Peter was still pissed at Danny and wasn't in the mood for another drink, whether it was free or not, and asked, "Who was the guy you spoke to while I was chatting up Sylvia?"

Danny thought for a moment and replied, "Oh...oh, he's one of my snitches. I...stay on his good side and sometimes he takes care of me when I need a hand with...with a case. Do you want another drink?"

Growing impatient with Danny, Peter replied, "Let's get back to the office....we have to look at the Oswald file."

Danny felt guilty for not giving a warning about Marlene, "Are you sure you don't want another?"

Peter shook his head, "No, I told you, let's get back. That file folder is as thick as your mother's ass and we have to get started sooner rather than later. Friday will be coming up before we know it."

CHAPTER ONE HUNDRED

Dallas, November 20, 1963

Peter pulled out the Oswald file and started to read his bio. Most subjects would have an occasional reference to their birth and youth, and if the guy had a run in with the law or something really out of the ordinary, an entry or mention of it would be there. L.H. Oswald's file was complete from his birth on 10/18/39 in New Orleans to his boyhood home on Alvar Street. Peter thought *who the hell has a file so complete and comprehensive? Jesus Christ, my file aint this thick!*

He looked over and saw Danny with his elbows on the desk and his head resting in his hands looking intently at Peter and the file. It reminded Peter of when Vinnie was a little boy watching his mother preparing food at the table. Peter felt bad for keeping Danny from his family since it was five thirty.

"Paisano, go home to your family. There's nothing you can do here."

Danny looked at Peter earnestly, "This...this is really interesting stuff. I...I would like to stay and watch you work."

Peter smiled because Danny wanting to stay also reminded him of his son, Vinnie, who would beg to spend time with his parents while Cam would always prefer being alone with her books.

"Ok, Danny, but if Grace gets pissed, you tell her your new found buddy tried to get you to go home but you insisted on staying."

Danny nodded in agreement and added,

"Maybe...maybe this guy was being watched by a bunch of different people. "Peter asked him for clarification and before Danny could begin, it dawned on Peter what his partner was trying to say, *the reason Oswald's file was so complete was because so many different agencies were looking into his life.*

Peter looked through the file to see if Danny's premise could be verified. Oswald enlisted in the Marine Corps on October 24th, 1956, and on his aptitude tests, scored slightly below average. He scored a 212 and was rated *Sharpshooter* in the Marine Corp. shooting test—just one level below marksman. He attained the rank of Private First Class on May 1, 1957 and two days later given access to *Confidential* security documents.

Peter read this out loud and turned to Danny, "That's why we have all the bull shit bio stuff and the detailed narrative here…because of the security checks to get the *Confidential* clearance."

Danny was pleased with his assessment and gave Peter a broad grin of satisfaction. Peter continued reading the file: In June of 1957, Oswald was given training in radar and aviation electronics. That same month, he was shipped to Japan, and there, he accidentally shot himself in the arm. On April 11[th,] 1958, Oswald was court-martialed for possession of an illegal firearm. On June 27th, of the same year, he was court-martialed again for assaulting a superior and jailed. He spent a month in the brig and was sent to Taiwan where he had a nervous breakdown and had to be sent back to Japan. He was stationed there until he was transferred back to the U.S. on November 15th, 1958 and was granted a thirty day leave. On September 11[th,] 1959 he was granted a dependency discharge because of an injury to his mother and her need for his assistance. Despite the *family need*, Oswald left the U.S. nine days later for the Soviet Union.

Peter again turned to Danny and said, "Yep, right here, the State Department and maybe even the C.I.A. would have been nosing around his background and digging up as much shit as they could. Damn this is amazing!"

He continued reading. On October 16[th,] Oswald arrived in Moscow. Four days later, he was interviewed by the KGB. "That sure as hell would have attracted the operatives in the C.I.A. They must have been shitting themselves trying to figure out what an American was doing being interviewed by the KGB."

On October 21st, the Russians refused to grant him a visa and Oswald tried to kill himself and was put in a psychiatric ward. Seven days later, he was released and applied for Soviet citizenship but his request was delayed. On October 31[st,] Oswald notified the American embassy that he wanted to renounce his U.S. citizenship. His request for Russian citizenship was unresolved for an entire year and he fell in love with a girl who refused to marry him. Finally, on January 4th, 1961, he was offered Soviet citizenship and inexplicably refused to accept it. On February 13th, 1961, he told the American embassy that he wanted to return to the U.S. and was notified at the end of February to come to the embassy to discuss his case. He refused the trip to Moscow and met Marina Prusakova and proposed marriage on April 20th, and married her on April 30th.

Peter murmured, "Holy shit the C.I.A. must have gone on their honeymoon. They probably had the bed wired the way they were following this guy. Hey, Danny, think they helped him slip the rubber on?"

Danny laughed and excitedly said, "Peter…read more. This is interesting."

On July 8th, 1961, Oswald travelled to Moscow from Minsk to discuss his efforts to return to the U.S. and Marina joined him the next day. On August 20th, the Oswald's sent the necessary papers to the U.S. embassy but their exit visas were delayed by the U.S. State Department and he had to get an extension for his Russian visa. His daughter, June, was born in Russia on February 15th, 1962. Finally, on March 15th, 1962, Marina's exit visa was approved and on June 14th they left for the United States and arrived in Fort Worth. On June 26th, Oswald was interviewed by an F.B .I. agent in Fort Worth and again on August 16th.

It was time to send Danny home and complete the file in the hotel room. He was bothered by the fact that there were no records of the F.B.I. interview of Oswald in Fort Worth. He looked everywhere for any mention of an agent or the results of the meetings and none were filed.

Peter mentioned to Danny, "I can't find a thing that documents any interview with Oswald other than the timeline we have here. You know the interrogation took place because there is no reason to mention it otherwise. What agent does an interview and doesn't keep a record of it, or at least a rough description of the event?"

Danny just shook his head as though he was amazed by the occurrence, though he had no idea of Bureau policies and procedures, and was becoming too tired to care. Peter shook his head, put the papers together, and turned to Danny, "How 'bout dropping me off at the hotel and you go home? You look tired and no reason both of us should be miserable going through this shit."

Danny started to protest but saw the resolve in Peter's face and agreed to drop his charge off at the Brown. Danny was silent until he said goodbye to Peter at the hotel. Peter hopped out of the car with his arm clutched around the file folder and said to Danny, "Pick me up by nine, if you can. If I'm not down in the lobby just buzz my room. Thanks for the ride."

Back in his room, Peter continued reading the Oswald dossier. On October 9th, 1962, Oswald visited the Texas Employment Commission in Dallas and scored well on various aptitude tests. On October 11th, he was hired by Jaggars-Chiles-Stovall Co. and was joined by his wife on November 4th. On January 25th, 1963, Oswald made the last two payments to the State Department for money he borrowed while in Russia. On March 2nd, 1963, Oswald and his wife and daughter moved to 214 West Neely Street in Dallas. On April 1st, Oswald was fired by Jaggars-Chiles-Stovall and moved to New Orleans, without his wife, on April 26th, when he visited the unemployment office in New Orleans. Here he found a job at the Reilly Coffee Company on May 9th and started to circulate handbills for the Fair Play for Cuba Committee on May 29th. After May 29th, two other entries appeared, the first was Oswald's dismissal from the Reilly Coffee Co. on July 19th, and an appearance on radio station WDSU on August 21st to debate Ed Butler, a right wing organizer and an anti-Communist. Peter was growing weary of the mind numbing dates and erratic behavior of Oswald. His head began aching like he was being hit by a hammer. It was time to stop and regroup tomorrow. He would interview Parker and make arrangements to meet with Jim Hosty about the Oswald file. He ordered room service, ate it, drank a beer and mercifully, quickly fell asleep.

CHAPTER ONE HUNDRED-ONE

Dallas, November 21, 1963

Peter was waiting in the lobby and exactly at nine Danny walked in the lobby. He had never noticed before, but Danny walked on his heels or at least the heels struck first and his toes were pointed out. He walked like a penguin with a gray flannel suit and a wide brimmed white hat. He had to restrain this thought or he wouldn't be able to look at Danny in any serious way. When they got to the field office, Peter and Danny went to Hosty's office.

Peter tapped on the door and waited for Jim to invite him in, "Jim, I have some questions about Oswald and I'm you can help me. I figure when he defected to Russia everybody in the world was watching him, right?"

Hosty nodded in agreement. Peter continued, "So, when he gets back here, we interview him apparently to make sure he's not some kind of Russian agent, right?"

Hosty again nodded in agreement and said, "You can imagine a guy with all kinds of security clearances comes back from Russia, we have to determine exactly what he told the Russians, as well as what he is doing back."

"Ok, I understand all of that but my question is how come there is no record of the Oswald interviews and who was the agent who did the interview?"

Hosty thought for a moment and asked, "There's no record of our interrogations? Huh, maybe they didn't uncover anything of substance to report. Christ, Oswald bounced around so much from New Orleans to Dallas and everywhere in between it's amazing we have been able to keep a complete file on him. He has been assigned and reassigned to this office at least three or four times. Every time that happens, files get mailed and who knows what got lost. I talked to an agent from New Orleans named John Quigley, and he said Oswald requested an interview. He told Quigley that he was concerned he was being followed by the

Bureau and wanted to know what our interest was in him. Quigley said he seemed a little goofy but Oswald was certainly no Russian operative."

Peter just shook his head and Danny seemed totally oblivious to the whole discussion. Peter offered, "So, as far as we know, Oswald is some nut case who is dedicated to Fidel Castro but wants to support him from Dallas or New Orleans, yes?"

Hosty shook his head, "Oh, that's not all of it. I didn't even give you all the stuff I have on this guy. I actually found out where his wife is but I haven't been able to locate him. You're not going to believe this--the C.I.A., of all people, tipped me off that Oswald was in Mexico and went to the Cuban embassy. He tried to get a visa to go to Cuba. Well, the Cubans refused and threw him out of the embassy. He wasn't happy with that so he went to the Russian embassy and tried to get another visa to visit Russia for Christ's sake. They stonewalled him because they figured he was a complete nut and he had no choice, but to come back to the U.S. So he came back to New Orleans. Now, he's out of my office but his wife moved to Irving and she is pregnant with their second kid."

Peter was surprised the C.I.A. actually passed some information to the Bureau. They closely monitored the Russian and Cuban embassies, and probably every other Communist embassy in the world. Peter also understood how someone could easily get lost in the Bureau's surveillance system assuming they just appeared nuts and not dangerous or criminal. Apparently, the Oswald interviews that got lost indicated Oswald was not deemed a threat to the security of the United States.

Hosty lit up a cigarette and continued, "I did stop out at the house where Oswald's wife was living. She is staying with a family called Paine...Ruth and Michael. Actually they are separated. I didn't meet the husband but I did talk a minute with Ruth. She seemed to be a nice enough lady and the neighbors say they're pretty normal folks."

Peter interjected, "You weren't able to see Oswald's wife?"

Hosty replied, "The first time I stopped to see her she was out or asleep or something, but I stopped again, let me see my notes....yea, on November 1st and met with Mrs. Paine and Marina Oswald. Marina doesn't speak English worth a shit and I had to have Mrs. Paine interpret for us. Oswald's wife was really upset. I mean, she must have thought she was back in Russia and I was the KGB. She was as red as hell and was distressed to say the least. I didn't want to upset her so I told her I was just trying to find Lee to ask him a few questions about what he was doing and stuff like that. She and Mrs. Paine didn't know where he was living but thought he was going to get a job in Dallas somewhere. I went back again on November 5th and Marina wanted the plate number off my car and my card. She didn't know where I could get in touch with Lee so I asked her to give him my card and tell him to call me so we could meet. Jesus Christ, Pete, a fuckin week later on November 12th, when I get into the office, there was a note from Oswald tellin me to 'leave his wife and family alone or he was going to blow up the F.B.I. office.' Now, if I wasn't so busy, I would have arrested the sonofabitch for threatening a federal agent, but I have so much on my plate I couldn't fit another thing if I had to. Plus, I have no idea where the bastard is. If you want, why don't you go out to Irving and let him be pissed at you, and who knows, take a piece out of your ass."

Peter agreed, but told Hosty he was meeting with Charles Parker at three o'clock and would have to drive out to Irving on Friday morning. Peter added, "I know the president will be here around twelve or twelve thirty so if I get out there early enough and find Oswald, Danny and I will track him down before the president gets to Dallas. Are you ok with that Danny?"

Danny shook his head, "It...it will only take a little time to get there."

Peter asked Hosty to set up surveillance units for the Parkers, Robinson, and Goodrum. Hosty took their addresses and made the necessary calls to set up the arrangements for the tails.

Peter put his arm around Danny's shoulder and said, "Let's go my friend, we have to see Charles Parker at three and Jim probably wants to get back to work."

CHAPTER ONE HUNDRED-TWO

Dallas, November 21, 1963

Peter and Danny were parked at the front gate of the Dallas Feed Mill promptly at three o'clock and watched the employees file out. None of them looked like the pictures they had in the file folder. The pictures weren't the clear mug shot photos but grainy newspaper pictures of Charles in his KKK robe in front of a burning cross and on the steps of the Old Courthouse on Main Street. Peter thought he may have missed Parker when a man probably six foot and one hundred eighty pounds walked up to their car. The man was wearing a dark suit and carrying the prerequisite white hat. Instead of a tie, he had a string thing around his neck with a metal fixture at the top of the crossed strings. Texans were fond of these string ties.

The man sauntered up to the car and asked Danny, "Are you agent Rinella?"

Danny nodded his head toward Peter. The man walked over to the passenger side, "Agent Rinella, I'm Charles Parker. What can I do for you?"

Peter gave Danny a look of amazement and opened the door of the car to join Parker. The wind picked up and Parker's dark brown hair was starting to swirl in the wind. The surprise must have shown on Peter's face as Parker asked, "You were shocked to see me in a suit, agent Rinella? You thought maybe I would have a job in the feed mill as a laborer?"

Peter was put off balance by the question and had to think how to answer and finally said, "Well, I suppose I expected you to be more like your brother. I wasn't expecting you to come out in a suit, yeah--I guess, you having a job as a manager surprises me."

A smirk creased Charles Parker's face, "Not all of us are the rednecks you expect us to be. Just because we have definite opinions about the well being of the white race and Christianity doesn't necessarily mean we are brainless clods. In fact, agent Rinella, we are far smarter than the niggers who are constantly trying to pollute our race and this country with their inferior genes."

Peter had heard it all before and wasn't interested in arguing race relations with him. He fully understood that people like Parker classified Catholics and Italians only slightly above Negroes in their world view. He knew Parker, despite his appearance, was not much different than his brother.

Peter asked Charles, "Did you happen to talk to your brother? Do you know why we are visiting you?"

Charles nodded, "Yes, and he also mentioned how short you were with him. He said you were here regarding the president's visit on Friday. What else…oh, he said you were going to have someone watching him until the president was gone. Is that a pretty accurate recap, agent Rinella?"

Parker's light brown eyes were set in a thin, creamy face and his complexion was grainy with pock marks, maybe the result of some teenage skin condition or chicken pox.

"You got it exactly. We will also have somebody looking after you. I do have a question for you Charles, if you don't mind. I've looked at your files and talked to both of you and I can't imagine your brother planned and attempted a murder on a minister in Amarillo without your help, and at the very least, your knowledge of what was going to happen. I've had a hard time believing that you had nothing to do with it."

Parker brushed his windblown hair off his face, "My brother was found innocent of murdering that nigger. Let's get that straight. If he did do it, which he didn't my brother acts on his thoughts and beliefs and I act on mine. We are independent people. We are at ground zero in the race war about to explode in this country and not you or the nigger loving administration is in any position to stop it. If someone doesn't stop the niggers and the communists, America will be gone and we'll end up working the plantation for them. As far as I'm concerned, you and the liberals you protect, aren't much different than the niggers and the communists."

Peter was growing increasingly tired of Parker. He got into the car and just before he closed the door, he looked directly into Parker's eyes and said, "Look over your shoulder starting tomorrow. You will see one of my associates there. Like I told your brother, don't fuck with them and mind your business. After the president is gone, you and the assholes you play with can say whatever you want and dress in your sheets and burn your crosses….I don't care. I just want the president out of Dallas healthy and in one piece. Got it?"

Peter slammed the door and Parker nodded and tipped his hat toward them as they pulled away.

CHAPTER ONE HUNDRED-THREE

Dallas, November 21, 1963

When Peter and Danny got up to the office the receptionist had a note for Peter. It simply said,

See me, G. Shanklin

Peter showed Danny the note, "What's this all about? I wonder what he wants."

When they walked into Shanklin's office, Shanklin motioned for Danny to leave the room. Peter sat down, lit a Pall Mall and waited for Shanklin to begin the conversation. "I guess you met with Charles Parker, agent Rinella?"

Peter was amazed Shanklin knew about the meeting with Parker. Peter shook his head yes and was about to ask how Shanklin found out so quickly about the meeting with Charles Parker when Shanklin continued, "You know, agent, we have a mandate from D.C. and Justice to keep a very close eye on some groups who are judged to be dangerous. In order for us to monitor the groups, we place operatives within them at the highest possible levels."

Everything suddenly became clear to Peter. Charles Parker was an F.B.I. informant. He may have been totally complicit in the minister's murder, but wasn't charged because he was on the Bureau's payroll and was sending in information about the Klan. Because of his leading position in the local chapter he was privy to a lot of information about the Klan in Dallas as well as nationally. Parker probably called Shanklin and told him to call Peter off. Peter understood all of the complexities of dealing with Charles Parker, but didn't much care. He also knew to openly disregard Shanklin's advice would be career suicide.

He pushed Shanklin, "So, you don't think it is necessary to put a tail on Charles Parker?"

Shanklin, looking over Peter's shoulder at something behind him replied, "Yes, that's what I am saying. Mr. Parker knows he must cooperate with us or his future will be in question. He definitely is no threat to the president and if you delve too deeply you might compromise his position with us. Do you understand me, Rinella?"

Peter nodded in agreement but decided not to tell Hosty to pull off surveillance of Charles, and if Shanklin said something, he would say he forgot to notify Hosty. Peter thanked Shanklin for his "guidance" and said his goodbyes.

He quickly left the office and grabbed Danny by the arm and said, "Well, paisano, we have to look up our friend Oswald this afternoon, if possible, and tomorrow morning for sure. If we go tomorrow, I want to get out to Irving long before the president gets into Dallas."

Danny nodded and replied, "Let's...Let's go tomorrow. If...If we can find out where he is we can put an eye on him before the president gets here."

Peter agreed and realized that he wouldn't be able to accomplish much at four thirty anyway, and by the time they got out to the Paine's house it would be five fifteen or later. He was tired and asked Danny to drop him off at the hotel where he decided to have dinner. Peter dutifully asked Danny to join him, hoping he wouldn't because conversation with Danny was taxing. Danny declined saying he had something to do at home. After dinner, Peter got to his room wishing it was the same time Friday and that everything was over and the president was on the "safe leg" of the trip to Austin.

He flipped on the T.V. A special news broadcast came on detailing the president's arrival, and, for the tenth time, a list of his itinerary and time schedule. Peter just shook his head in disgust. He knew he had much to accomplish on Friday and needed to get some sleep.

He was about to turn the T.V. off when he heard a light knock at the door and a voice say, "Pete, it's me, Marlene. I was just hoping you could use some company because I sure could."

Peter smiled to himself knowing how hookers play to the ego of their customers. Peter opened the door and looked at Marlene's sleepy eyes and firm breasts.

"Marlene, tomorrow is going to be a bitch of a day and I need my rest. I ......oh, come on in. I gotta tell you I hoped you'd come over; I missed you."

Peter realized how juvenile he sounded talking to some prostitute like she was his prom date, but he really meant everything he said. She walked in and kissed him full on the lips. He met her tongue with his and eased away and looked into her face, "Marlene what is your....fee...for spending some time with me?"

She didn't bat an eye and said, "To spend the night is usually two-fifty but I will discount my services for you."

Peter laughed to himself and thought, *the ground rules are established. It's good to get a reality check. The good thing is that she sorta wants to be here enough to give me a discount."*

Peter ran his hands under her skirt and felt between her legs and noticed she was wearing another g-string. He brought his hands behind her head and caught a slight waft of her pleasant feminine aroma on his fingers. Peter pushed her to the bed, unzipped, unbuttoned, and pulled off her clothes so he could see her in her nakedness. The sight of her was exciting and he tore at his own clothes to join her. He completely forgot about using some sort of protection. At that point, he didn't give a damn.

The sex was better this time. He didn't fizzle out in four seconds and she seemed to honestly respond to him. They laid next to each other in complete silence. He jumped up to go to the bathroom and she didn't move a muscle and looked like she was sleeping.

"How long you gonna keep doin this? I know it pays well but it has to be a shitty way to make a buck?"

She smirked a little and replied, "Pete, don't be offended, but would you want me to quit just after I've fucked you two or three more times. How would I make this kinda money? Let's not be hypocrites, if I didn't do this, you would have never have 'gotten to know me' right?"

Peter had to agree with her logic. He wanted some company and asked, "You'll stay the night? I'd like you to, if you could."

She smiled and kissed him lightly on the lips, "Of course, I said I would and I'd really like to. Do you snore?"

Peter thought for a second and replied, "Shit, I don't think so...nobody's complained about it yet, how bout you?"

She shook her head no and slid over so Peter could get in bed beside her. She turned so her back would face him and he put his arm around her waist. In two minutes, she was asleep and he began a sleepless night. Everything that needed to be done the next day and all that could go wrong, kept running through his brain. Fortunately, the feel of Marlene's body and the hope of another sexual encounter kept the "demon" at bay. He didn't have the heart to wake Marlene. He decided to let her sleep for a few hours before he'd try to rouse her for some more fun.

He must have tossed and turned a million times and couldn't find a position in bed that was comfortable. He couldn't shut off his mind and the night dragged on cruelly until finally he fell asleep at four o'clock. Danny's phone call jarred them awake. Marlene jumped up before him and ran into the bathroom. Peter looked at the clock next to the bed and noticed it was eight thirty. *I thought I told him to get me up at seven?*

As soon as Marlene got out of the bathroom, Peter reached into his wallet and Marlene quickly offered, "How bout a hundred? I'm embarrassed to charge anything but I need the money."

Peter smiled and said, "Bullshit, take the money….I appreciate you spending time with me."

He laid two hundred into her hands, kissed her on the cheek and squeezed one cheek of her ass. "If I get back to Dallas," he said, "I want to see you again. Here's my number in D.C. if you're ever around there."

She kissed him on the lips and rushed out the door. Peter looked at his watch and realized he was running an hour late. He didn't have to shower just shave and get dressed. Since they were really running behind, there was no need to stop for breakfast and just grab a cup of coffee and a donut. He got down to the lobby at nine and Danny was there pacing.

Peter said, "Did you see Marlene? Jesus Christ, I thought I told you to get me up at seven. Man are we behind."

Danny just nodded and looked to Peter for some direction. Peter responded, "Let's grab a cup of coffee here and get down to the office. I have to check to make sure everything went ok in Fort Worth. I'm certain I'd have gotten a call by now if it hadn't."

CHAPTER ONE HUNDRED-FOUR

Dallas, November 22, 1963

They arrived at the field office and it was nearly deserted. Peter knocked on Gordon Shanklin's door and popped his head just inside and asked, "Did it go ok in Fort Worth?"

Shanklin motioned for Peter and Danny to step in further and replied, "Just great. The president got to the Chamber breakfast and gave one of his 'Jackie accompanied me' speeches. He is still shaking hands with all the people Connally and Johnson arranged for him to meet. His timetable is on schedule. He will arrive here just before noon and hit downtown about twelve fifteen or twelve thirty. The route has been sealed off and all the roads leading to the city will be shut down until the president is well on his way. What are you guys doin?"

Peter didn't know how much Shanklin knew so he replied, "We are goin out to Irving to interview another subject."

Shanklin nodded as he took a hit on his cigarette and looked down at some papers on his desk. Peter took this as a signal to end their meeting. He looked at his watch and noticed it was nine forty-five.

He asked Danny, "How long does it take to get to Irving from here?"

Danny responded quickly, "About...about fifteen, maybe twenty minutes, I think. The traffic will be comin into town not out."

Peter did the math in his head, "That gets us there at .....What.....ten fifteen or so....huh?"

Danny felt a sense of urgency, "I...I know a short-cut and can get us there sooner."

The trip to Irving took longer than Danny said it would. Peter leaned over to Danny when they were still in the car at ten twenty- five and asked, "What the fuck? I thought you were takin a short cut...this has turned into an expedition."

Danny looked embarrassed,"I...I think I got lost, but I'm ok now. We'll be there in five minutes."

Peter's patience was strained, "Why didn't you get on the radio and ask the Irving P.D. how to get to the address we need?"

Danny could barely respond, "The car radio aint working. I...I don't know what's wrong with it."

Peter felt a tremendous urge to put a foot in Danny's ass for taking the "short cut" and not checking the radio. At ten thirty, they finally pulled up in front of 2515 West 15th Street. It was a modest one level house, bordered by cement driveways on both sides, neat, and unremarkable. Peter heard a television broadcast in the house with details of the President's trip.

The door opened and a tall, thin faced, auburn haired woman in her forties or fifties smiled and said, "Yes....how can I help you?"

Peter showed his badge and ID, introduced Danny, and asked if she might have a few minutes to talk. She smiled again and showed them to the dining room table where they took seats around it. The aroma of baking pumpkin and apple pies filled the house and covered them in a delicious blanket.

Mrs. Paine saw Peter inhaling and savoring the aromas and volunteered, "Marina loved our Thanksgiving pies so I'm teaching her how to bake them."

Peter nodded in understanding as Ruth quickly added, "We met with an F.B.I. agent a couple of weeks ago. He asked about Lee. I'm assuming that's why you're here?"

"Yes, Mrs. Paine. We are trying to find Lee and were hoping you or Mrs. Oswald might be able to help us."

Marina Oswald entered the room. She was an attractive brunette whose crystal blue eyes glistened across the room. She carried a baby in her arms and had a three or four year old girl in a yellow jumper timidly hanging onto her skirt. When Marina saw Peter and Danny, her face blanched immediately and she took a step or two backward and nearly tripped over her little girl. Ruth Paine quickly spoke to her in Russian and Marina stopped her retreat.

Ruth said, "Marina doesn't speak much English so I'll have to interpret for you. Russians don't trust authorities like police so she tends to be a little nervous when they're around."

Peter liked Ruth Paine instantly and asked, "Do either of you know where Lee is living. I'm told he doesn't stay here."

Ruth interpreted the question for Marina but answered for both of them, "No, he doesn't stay during the week. Some weekends he will spend the night. He did come over last night unannounced and he stayed over. He and Marina had an argument over something and he left early this morning."

Peter thought, *goddamn it, I should've come over last night.* The little girl reminded Peter of his Cam. Peter smiled at her and she smiled back. The more Ruth spoke the more upset Marina became. She started to cry and said something to Ruth.

Ruth translated, "Marina is upset because Lee has been acting very strangely. He has been very agitated and nervous, more than usual. She's afraid he's going to do something to get her in trouble with the authorities."

Peter looked at Marina and asked Ruth, "Why does she think he's going to do something bad?"

The little girl mustered some courage, left her mother's side and ran into another room. Before they responded he asked, "Are you sure she doesn't know where Lee lives?"

Ruth asked the question and Marina shook her head no. She got up and went into the room the where the little girl had gone. A minute later the child came running out with a picture frame in her hand and ran to Mrs. Paine's side.

Peter asked, "Is that a picture of her or her mother?"

Ruth Paine shook her head no. "It's a picture of Lee."

Peter looked at the picture and a tremendous ominous fear swallowed him. It was a picture of a slight, balding man in his mid twenties holding a scoped rifle and a revolver tucked in his pocket.

Peter asked Marina, who had just re-entered the room, "When was this taken?"

Ruth passed the question on to Marina, who replied through Ruth, "In March or April of this year."

Peter was getting more nervous by the moment. The bio on Oswald, he remembered, indicated he was a marksman and the rifle in his hands was certainly capable of making a sniper's shot. The tapes from the Miami informant mentioned a shooter with a high powered rifle. Marina held up a porcelain cup and inside the cup was a gold wedding band.

Peter looked toward Ruth, who interpreted Marina saying, "This is Lee's wedding ring. He also left one hundred and seventy dollars and told her he loved her and the children very much. It's unusual for Lee not to wear his ring and to leave any money with her."

Peter felt beads of perspiration running down his back as anxiety tore at his stomach. He smelled adrenalin in his nose and asked plaintively, "Please, can you remember where he lives?"

Ruth translated and both shook their heads no. As if a thought just struck her, Ruth said suddenly, "Why don't you go down to where he works?"

Peter felt relief with this assistance and immediately screamed "Where does he work, for God's sake?"

Ruth surprised at his reaction said, "Well, he works at the Texas Book Depository."

Peter asked, "Where is that, in Irving?"

Surprised that Peter didn't know where the Book Depository Mrs. Paine answered, "I don't know the street address but it's in Dallas in Dealey Plaza. You know the building with the big Hertz sign on the roof."

Bile ran up his throat…the presidential motorcade was going through Dealey Plaza. He quickly turned to Danny and pulled him close and whispered, "Call your office and tell them to get some people to the Texas Book place. There is a possible assassin there. Use the phone I saw in the next room."

Danny nodded excitedly and said, "Ok…Ok will do."

It took all his control not to scream again and he said, "Just make the fuckin' call now!"

Peter heard Danny dialing the number and his stammering instructions and wished he had made the call himself.

He turned to Mrs. Paine and asked, "Did you see Lee this morning?"

She replied after a moment and said, "Oh yes, he got a ride with one of our neighbors and was carrying a brown wrapped pole or something. In fact, I hollered at him and asked what he was carrying and he said it was a curtain rod for somebody at work."

Peter was in a full sweat because he knew Oswald was not carrying a curtain rod. He looked toward Danny and asked, "Did you get through? Are they going to send some people over there?"

Danny was gasping and could only nod yes. Peter thanked Ruth and Marina, grabbed Danny and pulled him through the door. Danny was shocked at Peter's urgency and asked, "What's …What's your hurry? We have it taken care of."

Peter was running to the car and looked at his watch. It was eleven thirty. He spat at Danny, "Do you think after all the bullshit work I've done that I'm not going to be there when they collar him? This is history and I have uncovered the whole thing. Do you think, you dumb bastard, I'm not going to get something other than a pat on the head from the fuckin' Dallas P.D. for this? Get me down to the Texas Book Depository, NOW!"

CHAPTER ONEHUNDRED-FIVE

Dallas, November 22, 1963

The traffic into Dallas was as thick as any he had seen in any major city. Peter turned to Danny and screamed, "Can't you make any better time? Jesus Christ, turn on your siren. You have a goddamn siren in this piece of shit don't you?!!"

Danny sheepishly nodded and turned the siren on but it was a futile attempt to break out of the traffic jam. He looked toward Peter and explained defensively, "We…we've blocked all the roads leading into Dallas."

Peter screamed at Danny, "Drive on the fuckin' berm or the fields over there but get us into downtown Dallas. The president will be by the Book Depository between twelve fifteen and twelve thirty, but sure as hell your Dallas P.D. buddies will have everything done. You better get us there before they lead Oswald's ass off to the station. I gotta be there!!!"

Danny wound his way onto the side of the road with his siren blaring. He was able to make it around the traffic with a clear path ahead of them. They finally got to the outskirts of the city and to the Stemmons Freeway. They turned onto Industrial Boulevard and were going to take it down to Commerce Street which bisected the motorcade route, but traffic was backed up at a road block set up at Commerce. Danny reversed and attempted to cut across to Center Spring Road, but it also was blocked off and traffic jammed.

Peter screamed to Danny as he looked at his watch, "It's twelve ten, let me out. Jesus Christ, I can make better time on foot."

He looked to his right and saw the building with the "Hertz Rental" sign and knew it was the one Mrs. Paine mentioned. He ran toward the building not knowing if he would be coming to the front or rear. His breath was labored and his throat and lungs started to burn. He felt his heart pound in his throat and his legs felt like they had lead in them. He cursed Pall Malls. After what felt like a marathon, he approached the rear of the building and a sign, "Texas Book Depository

Receiving Dept." A solitary white delivery van was parked at the loading dock. Peter ran up the stairs and through a man door and into the building. He was surprised that no security line had been set up around the building. *Where's the Dallas P.D?*

He felt uneasy about the situation but realized the president would be past the building in five or ten minutes. He looked frantically around the first floor for anybody who could tell him what happened to Oswald and the Dallas P.D. The building was empty. Everyone was along the parade route waiting for the president. *Where the hell is everybody? Christ, don't tell me they grabbed him already.*

He walked past the elevator and looked up the shaft; he could see it was at the top floor. He found a narrow stairway and began to make his way up the stairs as fast as his leaden, fatigued legs would take him. The front of his legs burned like a hot poker had been inserted in them and the back felt like someone had attached a vise.

When he got to the fifth floor, he heard a door slam below and Danny's voice holler, "Pete.......Pete.......Pete" With every mention of "Pete," Danny raised his voice a little louder.

Peter knew he couldn't wait for Danny and finally made his way up to the top floor—the seventh. He drew his gun and hoped he could settle down enough to make a shot if he had to. He looked feverishly through the room and saw no one. He looked down the elevator shaft and saw the car was on the next floor down and thought *goddamn it, it's on the sixth floor.*

The descent was more painful than the ascent and his left leg began to cramp. When he got to the door, he slowly opened the door and looking around the room, he saw a wall of books lined up around a window in the corner of the building. At the top of books, he saw the tip of Oswald's head. He was looking down with the rifle Peter remembered from the picture Ruthie Oswald had shown him. Pete heard the roar of the crowd erupting from the other side of the building and knew the motorcade was seconds away from the sniper's vantage point.

Peter took a deep breath and tried to steady his hand and his brain. In that fraction of a second, he knew he was on the very edge of history and redemption. He raised his gun and prayed the difficult shot would stop Oswald and save John F.Kennedy. Suddenly and inexplicably, he heard an echo reverberate in his head. It rolled in waves and he was on the hard cement floor with a heavy leather shoe on his chest. He forced his glance up and was looking down the barrel of a revolver.

The foot and the revolver belonged to….. Danny, who said, "Don't….don't move. If you do I'll have to kill you."

The demon clutched at Peter's throat as he heard the crowd noise grow as the motorcade passed below. He felt totally helpless as he heard Oswald draw the bolt back and a bang sounded. He heard Oswald swear, "Goddamn it… missed."

He heard the bolt again and another bang and Oswald mutter, "Got im."

Again, the bolt slid back, a crack, and Oswald said, "Even better."

Peter's stomach was about to lose it contents, when Danny yanked him up to his feet. Danny screamed at Oswald to leave the rifle and help him with Peter. A minute later a smallish dark-haired man with dark glasses emerged through the door to the sixth floor. Peter recognized the thin, dark man as the one Danny had met at the Carousel Club.

"Agent Rinella, we need you to co-operate for your health as well as your son's. We have someone outside of 1419 Houserville Road, in State College. Unless my man hears from me by ten tonight, your Vincent will not make his first year in law school. Heroics on your part will only result in your death and the death of your son. Do you understand?"

Peter nodded in agreement. He knew Vinnie's life was nothing to someone who had just assassinated the President of the United States. They made their way down the elevator and to the back of the white van parked at the loading dock. The small dark man sat in the driver's seat and turned around to say, "Agent Rinella, we are taking you back to the hotel and will sit there with you for a few hours to see how this works out. Let me repeat; don't try to be a hero now. You will get yourself killed and your son in a coffin. I guarantee it."

Peter sat quietly in the van and knew he had missed his only chance at separating himself from the crowd in history. He also knew he had put his son in jeopardy and that brought the demon tearing at his chest again.

CHAPTER ONE HUNDRED-SIX

Dallas, November 22, 1963

Peter walked slowly up to the hotel elevator with his two captors on either side. He didn't utter a word. When they got to the room he turned to the dark man and asked, "What happened to Oswald?"

Turning on the radio, the dark man responded "After he helped us with you, he made his way out the front of the building and back to his apartment. Hopefully, the F.B.I. or the Dallas police will be arresting him very soon. I have to go out, Danny, I'll be back soon."

Peter knew there was nothing he could do so he just looked at Danny who was staring at him and felt compelled to ask, "Why ...Why did you do this to me?"

Danny looked genuinely sad when he said, "I...I had to, or my family...."

Peter knew Dante was presented with the same Gordian knot he was given and had no options, but to do what he was told.

Shortly after they arrived, the T.V. was full of bulletins detailing the shooting of the president and his trip to the Parkland Memorial Hospital. After five minutes, the dark man returned and Peter was finally was able to place his accent. It sounded very similar to Kathryn's but a little thicker. He was French. It was consistent with his theory that the mob would use a foreign hit man. The Frenchman must have planned the entire operation and must have been in Dallas for months in advance of the president's arrival. Peter had to know who was behind the assassination.

He asked his two captors, "So, who was responsible for this? I mean, who paid for the whole scheme? How the hell did you get that nut Oswald?

The two men looked at each other and the French man shrugged and said, "Well, I guess it doesn't matter now because you aren't going to be telling anyone. The hit was ordered by Carlos Marcella in New Orleans. Bobby Kennedy had him deported in chains. Mr. Marcella is a proud man and this indignity sealed the president's fate. He knows to kill a dog you cut off the head and not the tail. If you cut off the tail, the dog still lives and can deliver a painful bite. He found Oswald in New Orleans and convinced him that he was a Castro sympathizer and that the Cuban revolution could only be preserved by the elimination of Kennedy. I took care of the logistics here in Dallas."

Peter knew getting Oswald was a stroke of genius and no one would suspect a Commie with an off the wall past to be a shooter for the mob. Had he not known better, Peter would have bet his life that somebody like Oswald would have been operating alone. Peter knew all the loose ends would be tied up fairly quickly. He was sure he was one of those ends.

He made one last attempt, "What makes you think they aren't going to erase you two guys?"

The Frenchman replied, "I don't know about him," he nodded towards Danny, "but I have made special arrangements to insure my survival beyond today. My employers know that my unexpected absence will, as you say, blow the whole thing wide open."

CHAPTER ONE HUNDRED-SEVEN

Dallas, November 22, 1963

At one-o'clock, the voice of Walter Cronkite announced the death of Kennedy. The Frenchman and Danny nodded toward each other and shared some sort of information Peter couldn't hear.

Peter heard the Frenchman say to Danny, "Oswald said he knew he missed the first but hit him with the second and the third took the top of his head off. There was no possibility he would survive the last shot, none. We did our job Dante. Let me go down to the lobby and make a phone call and I'll be back shortly."

Peter grabbed at straws and asked, "Paisano let me get out of here so I can call someone to get to my son's place. I promise no one will know your role in this rat's nest."

Danny felt honest compassion for Peter, "Pete...I can't... my family is at stake here too. Plus...He personally has to call off the hit on your son. He'll...be back soon. If you aren't here, your boy is as good as dead."

Peter knew what the answer would be. Peter looked earnestly at Danny, "I don't give a shit about what happens to me, Danny. Promise me you will make sure he calls off the hit on Vinnie. You don't owe me shit, but I have to know my kid is going to be ok."

Danny didn't respond but nodded yes to Peter's frantic plea. After five minutes, the Frenchman returned to the room with a small black leather bag about the size of Aunt Carmella's change purse. He motioned for Danny to come close to him and whispered something to him. Danny shook his head. Frenchy opened the bag and pulled out a syringe that was full of some nearly opaque liquid.

He quietly said to Peter as he approached, "Agent, this is Potassium Chloride. I'm going to inject about 30 or 35 ccs into the hairy area of your underarm. This thin needle will make the puncture impossible to see. Because the needle is so thin, I'll have to inject it slowly so as not to cause a swelling in your arm pit. It will take a little longer than normal to get it all in, but I assure you it'll be a relatively painless way to die. You may notice your heart beat wildly, but that'll be the only sensation you'll have because I've mixed a sedative in the cocktail. It'll seem you suffered a fatal heart attack in your room which technically, will be true. I hate to do this, but Danny did everything he could to keep you from getting to the Depository... but you wouldn't allow that would you? You left us no choice."

Peter was becoming absolutely panicky as the demon began to grab his throat, chest, and stomach. He was about to pass out in fear from the situation that would mark his death. He broke out in a cold sweat and his breathing became completely erratic. He knew he was about to die and suddenly, when it was apparent nothing could be changed, a strange calm and acceptance washed over him. Inexplicably, the whole scene seemed to slow down as though minutes became hours and time itself warped into non-movement. He looked at Danny standing by the door and saw remorse. He looked at the Frenchman and saw neither remorse nor pleasure, but professional detachment.

He put his hand up to the assasin, "After you do this, please, please call off the hit on my son. He doesn't have anything to do with this. Killing him would be pointless."

The Frenchman looked directly into Peter's eyes and both could see almost into the souls of the other, and he answered, "As soon as you are gone, your son will be safe."

Peter nodded and said, "Now do what you have to do and get this shit over."

The Frenchman said, "Lie on your side and raise your arm over your head. It'll take a few minutes to empty the syringe."

Peter felt a pin prick in his arm pit and burning as the fluid entered his arm.

After he had completed the injection, the Frenchman said, "Why don't you lie down? It shouldn't be long now."

Peter laid his head on the pillow and began to feel his heart beat out of rhythm, taking on a life of its own. He had never felt this increased activity without some exertion or demonic appearance.

He smiled when he thought about how he wasn't consumed by fear at this, the most frightening time of his life. For once, he knew the final outcome of events and he felt acceptance. His body began to feel flushed as his heart began to beat more crazily, he started to get dizzy and his chest ached. He was overcome by a tremendous fatigue and exhaustion. He felt a shiver go up each vertebrae of his back into the base of his neck and finally into his jaw. A moment later, the cold shiver was replaced by enveloping warmth. He closed his eyes and absorbed the peace and tranquility. He felt a sudden coolness again among the warmth and shivered once more in reaction to it. He tried to open his eyes but wasn't able. With all the will left in his body, he lifted his torso and whispered something to the Frenchman. He collapsed on the pillow and drifted away.

The Frenchman put his fingers on Peter's throat and checked for a pulse. Feeling none, he turned to Danny still frozen at the door and said quietly,

"It's over. He's gone...Ok, I'll leave first and you wait about ten minutes to go. Come back in a couple of hours to discover our friend... Understand?"

Danny nodded and asked, "Lavalle, what did he say to you before he...died?"

Walking through the door without hesitation, Lavalle replied quietly, "He said, 'sorry...oh God I'm sorry'"

EPILOGUE

The November morning in Meadville was exceptionally cold and clear. The cold singed the inside of his nose. He was making his way up Willow Street hill and the sun was coming up over the incline. The sun's rays seemed to explode through the bare trees at the very top of the hill. His legs were heavy and sorely fatigued but he ignored them to make his way up. Halfway there, he noticed two figures at the top with the brilliant, explosive sunlight as a backdrop. He knew the figures instantly--although he was blinded by the light and was unable to make out their faces. He sensed the presence of his father and his daughter and felt complete and total serenity. Peter had finally found the peace he had spent his entire life searching for. This place and this time was exactly where he belonged.

Author's Biography

Gary DeSantis is a 1970 graduate of Allegheny College, Meadville Pa. with a BA in History. He has read and written extensively on twentieth century American history. He is a contributing writer to the *Erie Times* and *The Meadville Tribune.* He has retired from a family business where he worked for the past forty years and spends his retirement in his lifelong home of Meadville, Pa.